Good Intentions

— A Novel —

Bob Zeidman

Swiss Creek Publications

Cupertino, CA

Copyright © 2012 by Bob Zeidman

All rights reserved. No part of this book may be reproduced in any form or by any electronic or mechanical means, including information storage and retrieval systems, without permission in writing from the publisher, except by a reviewer who may quote brief passages in a review.

Second Swiss Creek paperback edition 2012

The characters and events in this book are fictitious. Any similarity to real persons, living or dead, is coincidental and not intended by the author.

ISBN 978-0970227621

10 9 8 7 6 5 4

Book design by Carrie Zeidman

Printed in the United States of America

A Walk in the Park

"We the people of the United States..." He paused. It was a cold winter day in Philly, the gusty frigid wind gushing then subsiding, gushing then subsiding, almost regular like a slow heartbeat. A few people walked by, clutching their faux fur collars around their throats, eyes to the ground. Miles Monroe stood upon an overturned trash can, yet still only eye-to-forehead with most of the people walking by. Above him, the statue of William Penn atop City Hall looked over the city, but Penn's head appeared tilted in Miles's direction, perhaps the only one interested to hear what Miles had to say.

"We the people of the United States. We the people! Not the king. Not the president! Not the elites!" A few people took notice. Most walked on by. Miles adjusted his black, thick-rimmed glasses, ran his hand backward over his face and through his loose crop of thin, black hair. A small pile of recycled papers and degradable plastic bottles swirled around his "podium."

"In order to form a more perfect union... Do we have a perfect union? I would say not! Establish justice... Do we have justice? No! Insure domestic tranquility? Provide for the common defense? Promote the general welfare? Now there's something the government does very well. It promotes the general welfare. It promotes welfare for all. It gives jobs to everyone who wants them and money to those who don't want jobs. The inadvertently-unskilled live off our wages. The disenfranchised live off our wages. The minority groups, the minority-majority groups, the plurality-but-previously-disenfranchised-minority groups. The currently-majority-but-historically-underrepresented groups live off our wages. The documented citizens-in-waiting and the non-documented citizens-in-waiting. The alternately-abled and the abled-but-alternately-skilled. The under-educated and the over-educated. The conscientious-work-objector lives off our wages."

A few people had started to gather. They held their coat collars tight around their necks, wrapped their coats tight around their waists. They too became the centers, vortexes, of little turbulent hurricanes of debris swept by the gusting wind. Most listened for a few seconds or minutes before moving on. In all, more people were stopping than leaving – only a few more – making a very small and very slowly growing crowd. Maybe a dozen people stood around listening. One of those people – tall, thin, jet black trench coat, black fedora stylishly tilted, a single lock of wavy black hair showing above a deep-set dark left eye – surreptitiously slipped out his PDA and tapped the screen.

"Where does it end?" continued Miles Monroe. "We're now the minority. We're the work-hard-to-support-our-families-and-be-productive-members-of-society minority. Who protects our rights?"

Winston Jones walked briskly toward Miles Monroe with a small cardboard sign in one hand and his own PDA in the other. Unlike the other passers-by who milled about, meandering slowly, singly or in small groups, Jones had a self-assured stride, his long legs taking confident steps, his head bowed toward the PDA that gave off a soft glow. The others seemed rumpled, wrinkled, slouched. Jones was tall and thin in a pressed, light grey overcoat, nicely fitting his tall, lean frame. He stopped a few meters away from Miles, stared at his PDA, then looked up at Miles.

"And yes we are slaves," Miles was saying. "Modern day slaves. Because even if you love your work. Even if you're producing something useful to society like computers or automobile engines or foods or life-saving medicines. Even if you're keeping records or cleaning floors or collecting trash and recyclables. Even if you're designing energy conserving pencils or taking orders for organically grown, low fat, hypercolloidal foods. No matter what you're doing or how useful it is or how much you love it, you're a slave to our society. A slave to all those hyphenated people who live off your taxes and produce nothing in return."

Jones looked back down at his PDA and punched a few keywords into it. He read the screen, then looked around for a clean, level spot in the park. No less than 3 meters away, no more than 6. He saw a clearing just over 2 meters away but thought twice. No one really measures these things,

2

but still he's from the government and rules are to be obeyed as much as they can be. Anyway, he hates to get into a shouting match. That's not what this is about. If only these eccentrics would get that. This is all about free speech. They have the right to say what they want, but people need to know all sides of an issue. That's fairness. That's what government is about. Fairness.

Jones spotted another area about 4 meters away that looked good, surrounded by tall maple trees in the back and on the sides, but open to the walkway. He moved briskly to the spot. The ground was mostly dirt with a bit of grass, and was hard from this long Philly winter. The trees broke the wind, so no little vortexes surrounded him like they did Miles. It was a bit warmer there too, without the blasting cold breeze. Much more comfortable.

He took the sign from under his arm and propped it next to him on the ground. In large letters it read "Alternate Opinion" and in only slightly smaller letters under that it read "Courtesy of the U.S. Government."

Miles took notice of Jones, trying not to skip a beat, but he got distracted by Jones. Not frightened, but uncomfortable nonetheless, like a child in the playground, chest puffed, putting down the teacher to the other kids but who notices, a bit too late, that the teacher is standing next to him. "Who looks out for us?" he continued. "Us, the small groups of people that pry themselves from their technotainment, from their video hookups, from their blingers and gribbers. People who rise early each morning and commit themselves to being productive and useful. People who slave away at work every day. You and me, folks! Why are we not allowed to keep the loots of our favor?" A young girl giggled. Few noticed the slip as the wind has begun eating every other word. And now there was a new show down the walkway. A few people wandered over to Jones, still reading his PDA, knowing that he was about to begin. These government speakers sometimes have free give-aways and coupons.

Jones finished typing a few more keywords into his PDA as a small crowd gathered. He cleared his throat and looked them in the face. Always meet their eyes, he reminded himself. And point and smile. They like that. Point and smile. "We the People of the United States..." He paused for effect and looked at the eyes of the people in the crowd. He spoke softly with a slow confident cadence. Reassuring. Smooth. "… in order to form a more perfect union…" Another pause, looking into their eyes. A few more people stop by, some siphoned off from those around Miles, others veering off the walkway. "…establish justice, insure domestic tranquility, provide for the common defense, promote the general welfare, and secure the blessings of liberty." Another pause. Voice raised, "The blessings of liberty!" Jones glanced at his PDA, then back to the crowd. He pointed at a young man in the crowd who smiled self-consciously, enjoying the attention. "Not only for ourselves," continued Jones, "but for our posterity!" Another pause. Another smile and point. "Our posterity! Our children!" A few more self-conscious smiles from the crowd.

Jones glanced at his PDA again, then looked up. "Are we so selfish that we would keep these freedoms only for ourselves?" A few heads shook. "Would we deny these freedoms to our own children?" A few mouths made silent 'no's. "And what if your child couldn't work? Would you deny that liberty and freedom and pursuit of happiness to your own child? Of course not. And what if your child had a disability? Who would deny these rights to their own child because of an unfortunate circumstance of birth? Or an accident in a playground due to the shoddy construction practices of a greedy corporation? Or a drunk driver?"

The crowd became a little more enthusiastic. A few more heads nodded, some vigorously. Some of the 'no's were now whispered, not silent. Miles looked across at Jones, his small audience being sucked into the vortex created by Jones's eloquent speech.

"What if your children were learning-disinclined?" continued Jones. He squinted at the PDA – the sun had dipped behind a cloud and the screen took a few seconds to adjust. The pause worked in his favor as the crowd anticipated his words. "Would you deny them their rights because of a genetic disposition toward nonintellectual activities? What if your children were members of an underrepresented minority? Would you ostracize your own child because he or she was different than you? Was a member of a group that has historically been oppressed,

4

disenfranchised, bullied, or ignored? Your own child. And if your child came to this great country without papers – simple, thin recyclable slices of wood with organically decomposing inks? Would these pieces of paper be all that was needed to turn you against your own child?"

By then the crowd was lively. They stood straighter. There were occasional shouts of agreement, 'hip-hip's and 'hurray's (no 'hallelujah's of course). Miles's crowd had vanished except for the mysterious man in the dark black trench coat who tapped his PDA screen a few more times before looking up to notice the crowd gone, the speaker silent. Miles and the man stood alone, then both turned to hear Jones' words.

"Then that is why you work. You work for the good of all. For posterity, for your children. You work to provide for those who cannot provide for themselves. You work to uphold the enlightened virtues expounded by our foreparents in the great Constitution of the United States and all the great constitutions of all the great nations of the world. You are not only the people of the United States, you are the people of the world seeking justice and liberty for all!"

The crowd erupted in applause. The mysterious man walked slowly toward Jones.

Jones smiled, pointed, and nodded. He shook a few eager hands. The crowd walked away, more briskly, more confidently than when they arrived. Some were smiling. Some were talking. Some were whistling. As the last person left, Jones made a few notes in his PDA and put it in his overcoat pocket. He folded his placard under his arm and walked away. Briskly. Confidently. Jones felt good. He liked this feeling. At times like these, after a particularly successful repudiation, he liked being a Repudiator.

Miles struggled to right the trash can, the wind seeming to whip him off balance. Jones walked by, straight and tall, taking no notice of Miles. Miles stopped for a moment, his eyes on Jones walking away, then continued his struggle with the can and the wind and with himself.

A Walk in the Park

Rom Automatic, the man in the black trench coat, watched Jones walk away. A few quick taps on his PDA and a smile appeared on his lips. Well, not recognizable as a smile unless you knew the man. A slight upward movement of the right corner of his mouth – it's all about conserving energy after all.

Dangerous Activities

It was a while ago in Winston Jones' life. So long ago, that he had forgotten it completely.

"Rommy. Rommy," called Imelda from the open front door of the towering gothic house in East Chicago. "Rommy, time for dinner." She walked back into the house. The limos would be arriving soon.

Next to the great house was a fenced-in lot where little Rom Automatic and his "friends" played. The lot had once been the location of the famous Club Lucky. During Prohibition in the 1920s, it was home to blues music and "secretly" served alcohol. It was one of Chicago's poorest kept secrets and was one of those establishments in the city where race and class mattered little. Everyone could enjoy a drink and the slow, sultry jazz of such artists as Doo Lukeberry, Winston Harcourt Brace, Ezmerelda "Big Easy" Bigalo, Lonny St. Gerard, and Gretchen "Smooth" Smuley. The atmosphere was darkly lit and smoke-filled as you would expect. It was noisy with the sounds of murmured confessions, cheesy pick-up lines, clinking glasses, loud arguments, and not-so-occasional profanities. But when the music started, all sound stopped to listen. The haunting magic of that music soothed the savage and refined breasts.

The police never raided Club Lucky. There was no need. They knew the place and often spent hours there after duty, before duty, and on duty. A few of them had some musical talent and formed a group called Chicago's Finest that played more frequently than a group of their mediocre talent would otherwise play at one of Chicago's best jazz bars. They performed in their uniforms, guns holstered at their sides, instruments held roughly just like they played—roughly. Mediocre music but always a crowd pleaser.

After Prohibition the place had its ups and downs. It retained just enough patronage to keep going. In the early twenty first century when tobacco was outlawed, Club Lucky prospered once again as the place for all races, creeds, religions, and classes to relax with some fine alcohol, music, and a good cigar. The jazz revival had taken place and so jazz bands once again played there though the police generally stayed away. The smoke and noise and the smooth, sensuous jazz could almost be from either era, the Roaring Twenties or the Boring Twenty-Twenties.

But it didn't last. Eventually the place was shut down for good as a public health risk. For several years it remained closed, then was bought by a woman in New York. That woman sold it to a corporation in Los Angeles. That corporation was owned by a conglomerate in Mexico with connections to an Iraqi company with headquarters in the Bahamas. The chain of ownership could probably be traced a bit further, but no one had traced it even that far.

In place of Club Lucky opened a simple burger joint. Permits were obtained—the government required all kinds of permits for every kind of business—and the neighborhood came back to life a bit. Not like the old days, but some strip malls, some outlet stores. And the burgers were good. The fries were outstanding. It seemed to do a little more traffic than a burger restaurant should, but no one was concerned much as the neighborhood recovered a little more each year. Then there were rumors. Whispers, gossip, innuendo. The federal government began investigations, and they discovered the secret of the burger joint, whose secret, this time, really was a secret. The burgers and fries contained unsaturated fat with trans-isomer fatty acids. Partially hydrogenated oils. Yummy, scrumptious, deadly trans fats. In fact, not everyone who came there came there to eat the deliciously greasy burgers or crispy crunchy fries. There was a trans fat trade going on in back rooms. Vats of the stuff loaded onto vans being shipped across the country in a complex and difficult-to-track circulatory system of trucking lines, burger joints, warehouses, and fat, happy customers. A veritable poison factory clogging arteries throughout the U.S. and beyond.

The entire system was never fully traced. Other than a few low-level truck drivers, waitresses, and burger cooks, the masterminds of the operation were never discovered or punished. The burger joint was closed down and, as a precaution, the building was demolished leaving an open lot of rubble and dirt. The strip malls and outlet stores closed. The neighborhood fell into disrepair worse than ever before. Prostitutes and drug dealers roamed the streets. It was a strange place for Wesley Automatic to build his luxurious mansion, but the city needed some kind of urban renewal and subsidized the building. As agreed, he used some of the taxpayer money to build the rubberized playground for the neighborhood children. Amidst the dirt and rubble, the empty soda cans and broken bricks, next to the Automatic mansion stood the Automatic playing field. It was a white, sanitary, rubberized field about half the size of a football field. It was enclosed by rubber chain link fence surrounded by large, thick shrubs that did their best to hide the squalor beyond it.

Little Rommy Automatic and seven of his "friends" huddled in a group. Eight little rubber snowmen. Eight white, plastic marshmallow men on a rubbery grey surface surrounded by a rubber chain link fence. Hanging from posts over the fence, watchful electronic eyes kept track of the boys.

"Do it!" said Rommy to one of the other boys. "Dare you!" The other boy was Winston Jones. Though you couldn't tell from the white bubble protective suits that each of the boys wore, Winston was the "African American" one in the group. That meant that his skin was black, though his family could hardly trace their roots back to Africa any more than all humankind can trace their roots back to the first primeval specimens of Homo habilis in Africa. But "African American" was the government approved label for people with black or dark brown skin, and Wesley Automatic wanted to cover as many continents as possible with his son Rom's group of friends.

Winston poked his head out of the huddle to look around at the electronic guardians. Below each was a sign:

Caution: Electronic Equipment

```
Cutting wires may result in electronic
shock that can be fatal or extremely
uncomfortable. Breaking glass can
create sharp shards that can cut and
```

cause bleeding. Loss of blood can
cause death or discomfort.

Below that sign was another:

Caution: Rubber Fence

Pushing objects into rubber fence may
cause them to rebound into you causing
serious injury, possibly leading to
death or discomfort. Do not push or
throw or otherwise direct objects at
any great or small speed deliberately
or accidentally into rubber fence.

Below that was yet another sign with an arrow pointing downward:

Caution: Ground

Ground has been rubberized to minimize
injury. Note that objects should
nonetheless not be thrown, launched,
pushed, prodded, thrust, or otherwise
directed toward the ground or caused
to be off-balance such that it might
fall to the ground under the influence
of gravity as death or discomfort may
occur.

Next to those signs was yet another sign:

Beware of Signs

Do not remove these signs under
penalty of law. Signs are placed here
to warn you of the dangers of this
area for your own safety. Removing a
sign could cause you or another person
to perform dangerous activities
without the knowledge of the dangers
involved, thereby causing death or
discomfort. Also, signs sometimes have

```
sharp edges that can cut you and cause
death or discomfort.
```

Winston put his head back into the huddle. Rommy and his friends were supposed to be playing friendball, a civilized outgrowth of the game of football. Football was outlawed for children in the twenty first century for its brutality. In friendball, two groups of kids (not "teams") each got a ball and threw it to someone else. If that person caught the ball, both groups got a point. If someone missed the ball, both groups got a point. In the end, all points were added up and the group with the most points won.

But Rommy and his friends weren't really playing friendball. Rommy was already 9 years old, and by the age of 5 or 6 most kids understood the pointlessness of it. But the parents insisted. In fact, he could hardly call these kids friends. Each had been carefully chosen by his father to ensure that he socialized with those from various races, ethnicities, religions, and economic backgrounds. Someday Rom would be a great man of influence, holding high office in the land, and he would need to know and experience, and appeal to, all kinds of lesser people. Not many of those kinds of people came into the everyday life of aristocrats like the Automatics, but these kinds of people and their families were always lacking something and Wesley Automatic had the resources to make things happen. In return, these families brought their children to play with Rom who otherwise had no friends. But Rom was destined for greatness and great men often had few peers and fewer friends. So Wesley worked his magic and poof, Rom had friends. In fact, each time Rommy went out to play, his friends were new kids he'd probably never met. Probably, this is, because they all looked alike in their head-to-toe white rubber suits required for children engaging in outdoor activities.

"Dare you, dare you!" The other kids joined in the chanting, but quietly so that the electronic ears wouldn't pick it up well enough to decipher its meaning and put a halt to this raucousness that could possibly lead to vigorous activity that could in turn lead to injury or discomfort.

Winston looked down at the ground, his ears starting to hum with the soft chanting. Winston was a little taller and a little thinner than the other boys, which made him stand out and was probably why the other boys had turned to challenge him with this dangerous activity. He had a nervous habit of tapping his forehead when considering a problem, and he was tapping now as he measured the consequences of this action. In his mind he saw problems as a physical three-dimensional shape with the various solutions being the black edges and colored surfaces of the shape. He literally rotated this representation of the problem in his mind, examining all sides, edges, and vertices until he found one he liked, one that made sense to him. He liked challenges and had a little rebel streak in him. "OK," he said. "Cover me."

Slowly Winston's head dipped down while the other kids closed the gap in the huddle. They surrounded him. Winston felt the sweat begin to puddle on his forehead, too great for the absorbing antibacterial headband to absorb. He struggled and the kids kept up a low mumbling. These kids were smart. They knew that the electronic ears would detect silence and sound an alarm. They knew the precise decibel level that would keep the ears distracted.

Winston struggled a bit more. His arms ached. His left leg cramped for a moment, but he massaged it gently and it relaxed. He wriggled as the other children watched. Rom's eyes widened, both amazed at Winston's daring but also disgusted by his disobedience. A few of the boys gasped. The human igloo remained solid, covering Winston's activity. A few more gasps emanated from the huddle. There was a zipping sound. Then another. The sound of rubber on rubber then rubber on flesh. Then more zipping.

A really loud gasp was followed by a few shouts. The electronic ears electronically perked up. The electronic eyes began swiveling. The electronic guardians knew something was amiss. The human igloo broke wide open and Winston Jones emerged, completely naked, black unprotected skin in the direct rays of the sun.

"Wahoo!" screamed Winston as he broke from the huddle and ran toward the fence. Electronic eyes were pivoting wildly. Red lights atop the fence began flashing crazily.

"Wahoo!" screamed Winston again. The other kids stared in awe. An alarm went off. Sirens rang loudly. Winston was running right toward the fence. The mouths of the children behind their antibacterial masks dropped open in wonder and amazement.

A voice came across the loudspeaker, calm but insistent, "Please stop. Your actions may cause injury to yourself or others." The message repeated as Winston leaped toward the fence and hit it, naked chest first, and bounced back several feet, landing on the rubbery ground. Laughing.

"Emergency" declared the voice from the electronic guardians. "Emergency. An injury may have occurred."

Imelda flung open the door from the great house next to the lot to see a naked Winston writhing in pain. At least that's what she thought as she cried "Ay dios mio" and fainted. Actually Winston was dancing and pounding his fists in the air and laughing. The other kids watched, smiling behind their masks and clapping their padded gloves in a low muffled, rhythmic thudding. Except for little Rommy Automatic who gnashed his teeth and clenched his fists.

Dangerous Activities

Growing Up Automatic

Rom Automatic walked into the great gothic Automatic mansion, the sunset through the stained glass windows of the double doors throwing sharp, colored polygons onto the off-white marble floor and the dark mahogany trim. Rom roughly tore off the pieces of his protective suit, one by one, and tossed them onto the floor. His headgear bounced then slid along the floor into the red velvet curtain at the far end of the hallway. His right glove tumbled and slid into the great marble and brass fireplace. His left glove he slammed down and watched it bounce toward the ceiling then drop and glide toward the spiral staircase in front of him.

"Your friend seems unharmed, thankfully" said Imelda Ramos to Rom's indifference. "Your father has stated very strongly that he would prefer not to pay any more than he must to the families of these children, particularly if they take part in unapproved activities." Rom shrugged. Imelda closed the double doors, one strong, weathered hand on each door. Outside, the ambulance crew examined Winston Jones a few more times for injuries, to his obvious annoyance, before suiting him up once again. The black limousines parked single file along the curb began leaving one-by-one, taking each child back to his family, each with an envelope containing the usual payment plus a bonus to "encourage" them and their families to avoid mention of the dangerous activities that took place in the lot.

Rom walked into the entrance to the large dining room. The dining room was dark like the rest of the house, made of dark wooden floors, dark draperies, and dark mahogany trim. A fire in the large fireplace rather than throwing light around the room seemed to actually throw shadows everywhere that periodically danced and then retreated into the corners. The large twisted metal chandelier held compact fluorescent bulbs in the shape of flames that dripped a sickly yellow light on the large table below.

At the table sat his little sister Cecilia. She played with her ponytails, twisting them around and around in her fingers, staring at Rom, mouthing insults at him but not daring to speak them. Across from Cecilia sat Rom's mother Amelia Automatic. She looked forlorn, as she often did. Her eyes glanced down at the table, then up at Rom, then down, then up, in a pattern like Morse code. It seemed that she was giving Rom a message. Rom didn't know what that message was in its particulars, but he didn't need to interpret any code to know that she was warning him about his father who sat squarely at the head of the large table. At least that was Rom's assumption because all he could see was a newspaper spread out wide, hiding its reader. But Rom didn't need to see his father to know it was him behind that paper. First, no one else in the Automatic household would dare take the seat, or allow anyone else to take the seat at the head of the table. Second, Rom could see the huge furry bear hands, each hand sporting a large, gold, jeweled ring on a single finger, crushing the edges of the papers.

His father was often in a bad mood and often angry at Rom and his mother usually tried to protect Rom from his father's wrath. Rom didn't need the protection, though. Rom could hold his own and was proud of it. Rom, at the young age of 9, already recognized that his father had special goals for his son, was grooming him for a position of power. Rom was, in his father's mind, an extension of himself.

Wesley Automatic was already a powerful man, but Rom would have power beyond even him if Wesley got his way (which he usually did). Wesley had wealth and ran one of the largest corporations in the world. But Rom would have even more power—political power—and that power would have its roots, and lend its influence to Wesley himself.

The lure of this power for Wesley Automatic, this addiction, actually gave Rom himself more control over his father than anyone realized. Once Rom recognized his father's obsession, and that Rom himself was the key to fulfilling this obsession, then Rom had the power. Rom was the dealer, his father was the addict. To the outside world, Rom's father was the master of many things. Rom knew differently.

Rom started a run toward the dining room table, then straightened his legs and locked his knees and surfed on the slippery floor toward his seat at the end of the table opposite his father or, as he thought of it, the head of the table. Rom grabbed the chair back, spun around it, and plopped into the seat, straddling it. His sister and mother looked at him with surprise. They didn't understand.

The bear claw hands lowered the paper slowly. Wesley Automatic's wide, round face was flushed, his caterpillar brows knotted, his thick red lips locked in a grimace. Wesley Automatic's stone gray eyes were canons pointed at little Rom.

"Romulus. I understand that one of your friends broke the rules today."

"Not true."

"Not true? Are you telling me that one of your friends did not break the rules today?"

"Yes, that's what I'm telling you."

Cecilia giggled. Amelia stared at Rom hoping she could telepathically signal that he should just be quiet and listen. Wesley Automatic's face grew more flushed. "So people lied to me? The lawyers lied to me? Imelda lied to me?"

Rom slid his index finger along the edge of the dining room table, a thin film of grease adhering to it.

"I don't know what they said to you, but none of my friends broke any rules today." Rom did not look up. Wesley slowly drew his lower lip over his upper one. There was a pause before Rom continued. "I'm only trying to be accurate here. You taught me to be accurate. In fact, no friends of mine were here today. If you're referring to the group of kids you pay to play with me, one of those kids did break one of the rules today."

Cecilia giggled again. Amelia's eyes widened more, her telepathic message, repeated over and over, was "please stop." It didn't seem to be reaching Rom.

Rom swirled the grease on the table into a small blob with his fingers. Everything in this house had a thin film of grease—the tables, the chairs, the floor—despite daily cleanings by teams of butlers and maids and all kinds of servants. It puzzled him.

"Then I stand corrected. One of the children with whom you were playing in the lot broke the rules. correct?" Wesley swallowed each word with distaste.

"Correct."

"You know, Romulus, that rules are there to protect you. They are in place to keep you safe. They are there to make sure that you live a long, healthy life." Something that Wesley was growing eager to curtail at this moment.

Rom simply swirled the grease and thought.

"And the rules are in place," continued Wesley Automatic," to keep me from being sued out of house and home by some kid that has nothing, wants everything, and blames you and me for his own misfortune. You may not see it. You are smart and educated and come from a good background. You have a good home and a good family. But these other kids have less. Much less. They have been trampled upon by society, and it is our job to help them out of their poverty and their misery. Society does not like them, but we like them. And we teach them. And we invite them to play with you. But they may not understand that we are the good guys looking out for them. They may see our big house and our big cars and your big toys and decide that they can take them away from us because they were stupid enough to break the rules that are there to protect them."

"It's ok dad. No need to worry."

"No need to worry?" Wesley Automatic roared. "No need to worry? Do you want all this taken away from you? Do you want to live like them?"

Rom Automatic looked up from the patterns he was drawing in the table grease. He looked into his furious father's face. "We made new rules."

His father's brow crinkled. "The rules are to protect us. So I made a new rule. Out loud. I told him that if he breaks any rules he could no longer play here. Ever. I said it in front of the cameras and the recorders. He shook my hand. It's binding."

Wesley Automatic was taken aback for a moment. His voice lowered to near normal. "One of the kids said you encouraged…"

"The cameras filmed the handshake. The recorders heard agreement. I made sure."

"A non-binding agreement among minors," said Wesley, much softer still.

"Yes. And how reliable is the statement of a nine-year old that I encouraged that kid to break the rules?"

Wesley Automatic's brow unknit. His face unflushed. Anger was turning to something else. Pride? He wasn't completely sure.

"We make the rules to protect ourselves," said Rom. "You taught me that. I understand it. Is dinner ready soon?" Rom looked back down at the greasy patterns in the table. In the Automatic Mansion, everything slid; everything was a little greasy.

"I'll see what Imelda's prepared," said Amelia Automatic, suddenly very relieved. "I'll check the grillers."

Wesley Automatic had made his fortune selling the Automatic Griller, a compact, computer controlled barbecue grill for cooking tofu and vegetables and all the good things that the government recommended for a healthy diet. It was the best-selling grilling machine in the world. Very few people ever thought to wonder how a company that sold grilling machines could become the largest corporation in the world. Sure the grilling machine was popular, but the idea of a grilling machine company being so large was as ridiculous as, say, a company selling flavored drinks being one of the biggest in the world. Had anyone questioned this fact or investigated the circumstances, assuming they were not bought off or sent on a long, unexpected vacation, they would have found that the trucks that left the back of the Automatic Mansion on the hour every hour were not carrying only grills and grilling accessories. In fact, they were usually loaded with trans fats. The trans fats business had never died and neither had the American taste for it. The black market for trans fats flourished. Wesley Automatic manufactured and sold trans fats from his home and shipped them worldwide. Wesley Automatic was the trans fats king and when little Rom finally figured that out, some years later, he cemented his own power and eventual position in the Automatic dynasty and, more importantly, in American politics.

Oh Canada

Winston Jones felt confident and proud as he walked back home after repudiating the speech of Miles Monroe in the park. Jones' job was useful, fulfilling. He liked countering controversial speech with opposing opinions. Only if people got both sides of each issue could they make informed decisions. His eyelid twitched a little and he rubbed it. There is no truth, he thought to himself, only perspectives on the truth. Albert Einstein had declared this in his theory of relativity. And who would dare argue with Einstein? Although shouldn't there be an alternative to even that perspective, he thought. His eyelid twitched again, several times in succession. He hated that twitch. One time his eyelid twitched about once a second for an entire month.

He needed to clear his head and unwind. Even though his work was good and useful, sometimes it caused stress. It could be an occasional headache. Or the twitch of an eyelid. Or maybe it was unrelated. But he found that clearing his head and thinking pleasant thoughts usually helped. He started racking his brain, searching for pleasant thoughts. None came to him immediately so he pulled his collar up around his neck and decided to just observe his surroundings. No arguments, no philosophies, no politics, just observations.

Jones looked at the sidewalk and observed the dark, snaking cracks in the gray concrete. Broken patches filled in with concrete or asphalt, dog droppings, debris and garbage, and occasional pools of vomit formed a jigsaw puzzle of mismatched pieces. His eyelid twitched. People had developed an ability to maneuver around these things without consciously thinking about them. Jones decided that observing the ground wasn't a good choice for relaxation.

Jones looked at the gray concrete walls and broken brick facades and boarded windows of the houses as he passed. Fire escapes with missing rungs and rusted sides hung partway down the buildings. Music came from the open windows, rap and jazz and rock and pop that mixed with the car horns and curses and arguments to form a cacophony. Poets wrote about this "sound of the streets" as if it were a beautiful noise that represented life and some kind of honest heartbeat of the people. To Jones it felt like irritating noise and he'd forgotten how he, like most others, had learned to filter it out. He felt guilty, because this was a true heartbeat of the common people. His eyelid twitched.

Jones turned his attention to the people passing him, observing their faces, their clothes, and their demeanor. He tried smiling at one or two, but no one made eye contact. Except for the beggars. He had out his roll of "friendship funds" that nearly everyone carried at their side. As a beggar approached, he would roll a bill off the top and give it to him or her. Some people attached the roll to their belts above which was a yellow smiley face with dollar sign eyes. It was considered very fashionable. Beggars would simply walk by and take their own bills off the roll. Jones felt that was somehow impolite, though it was very convenient. There but for the grace of God go I, he thought, as a rather well-dressed woman took a bill from him and moved on. There were rumors that you could make a very good living as a beggar. And that was ok. No position in life was any better than any other. It just concerned him that beggars didn't pay taxes. There should be some solution to that, he thought, and his eyelid twitched.

The houses and shops got a little nicer, a little cleaner, as Jones approached his own house. He lived in one of the "better neighborhoods" though that was really an unofficial designation. He and some other government employees had bought an entire block together, somewhat difficult to arrange, and had all pledged to keep their places clean and neat. So far it had worked well, though it was always a struggle.

As he got closer he saw a police car parked outside his building, its lights flashing though the siren was silent. His neighbor Gertrude Meyerson was outside arguing with the police officer. Gertrude was in her 60s or 70s and was the matriarch of her small family that consisted of her daughter Sarah, Sarah's baby Myra, Sarah's baby daddy Edward, Sarah's other baby Jimmy, Gertrude's son Manny, Manny's wife Jillian, and their three small children Brittany, Matthew, and Britnee.

As Jones approached them, he could hear their conversation.

Officer: "…for a better life. You can't blame them. Things up north are pretty bad."

Gertrude: "Of course I feel for them. I feel terrible for them. But this is my house."

Officer: "Not much I can do ma'am. I can't just barge in there and arrest them."

Gertrude: "Why not? It's my house."

Officer: "Well they haven't done anything wrong."

Gertrude: "They're in my house. That's something wrong!"

Officer: "I mean other than that. Have they committed any crimes while in your house?"

Gertrude: "They're in my house. They're trespassing. That's a crime, isn't it?"

Officer: "I mean a real crime. Have they stolen anything? Have they assaulted anyone? Have they killed anyone?"

Gertrude: "They're very polite. They haven't done any of those things. They say 'please' and 'thank you.' But they're in my house!"

Officer: "Well it sounds like there's no problem. Ask them to help out with the chores. They can do the work you don't want to do. You'll see it's actually a good thing." The officer looked at the building that had some graffiti and a couple broken windows. "They can paint and fix the windows. I've found that they can be very handy."

Jones turned to go into the building. The officer and Gertrude Meyerson hadn't seemed to notice him so far and that was good. He walked quietly, but not quietly enough. Gertrude turned to him. "Winston. Talk to this police officer. You're a big shot in government. You're smart. Talk to him."

Winston turned reluctantly. "What's the problem?" he asked pretending not to have overheard anything.

"There are illegal Canadians in my house!"

The officer's eyes widened. Gertrude quickly corrected herself. "There are undocumented Canadians in my house. They just walked in last night and went to sleep on the floor. I woke up to find them cooking in my kitchen. Three of them. A man, a woman, and a teenager."

The officer explained patiently. "She knows about the situation in Canada. How the government went broke subsidizing prescription drugs for Americans. People are out of work up there. It's terrible. We can't let our friends to the north starve. We owe them."

"But why must they live in my house? This is my house!" Gertrude looked pleadingly at Jones.

Jones stared back for a moment, sympathetically. "But, you know, we have to treat everyone with kindness, especially those less fortunate than us. And Canadians are less fortunate than us. We have things that they don't and they just want a better life for their kids. You want a better life for your kids, don't you Gertrude?"

"Yes," said Gertrude sounding defeated. "But a better life for my kids doesn't include three Canadians living in my house."

Jones looked Gertrude in the eyes. "I'm sure it'll work out ok. Eventually they'll move out. Or you'll get to like them. Ask them to do chores around the house like the officer suggested. I'll bet they'll be glad to. Canadians are very friendly people and they are very good at household chores." Gertrude stared at him blankly, her eyes moist and sad. Jones' voice was smooth and reassuring. "Canadians are very nice when you get to know them. In a little while you'll be glad they moved in."

Gertrude looked down at the ground. The officer looked at Jones with admiration. "You're very good with words," he said.

"Thanks," said Jones. He continued walking toward his house. His eyelid twitched.

Oh Canada

Yesterday When I Was Young

In his apartment, Winston Jones thought about Gertrude Meyerson and her kids. He wondered what happened to their father whom Jones had never seen. Most families did not have a father, so that was normal. "One is as Good as Two" was the official government slogan. Two people have conflicts. One person does not. Scientific studies had shown that trying to get two parents to effectively raise children was virtually impossible. It was at least very disturbing to the children who were always put in a position of choosing between them. Parents, being human, would often have differences of opinion. They often have different temperaments, different social values, different ethnic cultures, different likes and dislikes. In some cases they had different religions, different skin colors, even different politics. Sometimes they had different sexual orientations or preferences. Two people in a closed ecosystem had disagreements, conflicts, fights—it was unavoidable. Children should not have to choose between their parents. Having two parents had been shown scientifically to cause psychological distress. And parenthood often restricted personal freedom, and society, and the government, recognized that personal freedom was a right above all else. So it was more convenient to allow, or actually promote, single parent families. And then it was almost always the woman who remained with the children though the government had been doing its best to encourage men to take on that chore. The government often paid ersatz fathers or "e-fathers" to raise the children while the biological parents remained free to choose their own paths in life. That was "Freedom of Choice," another successful government slogan. The government had found many great slogans to promote healthy lifestyles.

Jones thought about his own family. He had grown up without a father and it was less accepted in those days. Actually he had a father for the first 12 years of his life. Morrie Jones had worked pretty hard and had little time for his son. "Hard Work Will Kill You"—another government slogan. That slogan seemed particularly true to Winston Jones. Hard work had killed his dad. Well, his dad had killed himself, but it was from

27

the stress of all that hard work. Winston Jones resented his father for that and decided he was better off without him. Well, it was more complicated than that, but Winston preferred not to think too deeply about it because then it started to hurt.

His parents did conflict, Jones remembered that. His mom was more about following the rules than his dad. "Rules were made to be broken" was probably his dad's favorite saying. "First you need to understand the rules," he'd say. "Then you need to understand your limits. Then make sure no one will get hurt. Then go do what you want to do." His mom obviously didn't approve of this attitude, but she never contradicted his dad. At least not in front of Winston. But Winston heard the arguments. No one should have to listen to people argue; certainly not young children. Winston cringed at the memory. Fortunately the government had figured this out, but too late for Winston.

His mom really had a hard time after his dad died. She had relied on her husband for a lot of things. And she had loved him and entered a deep depression after his death. She came out of it eventually, but was not really the same. She was all about following the rules. About not taking risks. And she made sure Winston did the same, which was ok with him. Winston saw what risk taking led to. He always resented that his dad's work had taken precedent over him. And it had killed him and taken him away too soon.

Winston Jones' eyes got watery—he knew it was the resentment he felt for his father abandoning him, abandoning his mom. From somewhere a song started going through his head, filtering through the swirling emotions into his brain. He couldn't remember the words, just the tune. It was a memory. It made him cry, but he was not sure why that was. After a while he remembered it was a song his dad used to hum. What was that song?

The Kids Are Alright?

The weather was nice this day. The sun was shining and while not hot, there was no wind and so it felt much warmer outdoors. The sunshine cheered Winston up somewhat and he was looking forward, or at least not so reluctant, to presenting his opposing opinion. He knew he was doing a good thing, bringing a Fair and Balanced™[1] argument to the people so that they have a full understanding of both sides of any issue in order to make an informed choice. He felt good for performing such an important public service. Yes, he felt very good. Just a little hungry, though. Kind of an empty feeling in his stomach. He should have stopped for lunch before coming out here. His extensive training taught him to always have a good, healthy meal before speaking. But many times he's just not hungry. It's hard to explain. He usually has this empty feeling in his stomach, but food just doesn't appeal. He should make another appointment with the doctor about this. The doctor says there's nothing wrong, and any case he takes his required vitamin supplements and nutrient pills, so he's covered. He just doesn't like to eat food.

Food nowadays was made to physically fill the stomach to avoid these kinds of hunger pangs. Fortunately spices that can do serious damage have been outlawed. Salt raises blood pressure—outlawed. Monosodium glutamate causes migraines and heart palpitations—outlawed. Anyway MSG doesn't really taste good it just tricks your brain into thinking it tastes good (Winston used to wonder about the difference between your mind "knowing" something tastes good and being "tricked into thinking" something tastes good, but since MSG was outlawed, the question was a hypothetical philosophy problem best left to academics). Hot spices cause severe nerve activation and open blood vessels, dangerously lowering blood pressure—outlawed. Red meats contain cholesterol—outlawed. Other animal meats were rationed due to objections from

---

[1] Government trademark serial number 75280027, appropriated under the Government Fair and Balanced Act

animal rights groups. Fruits are good but can contain insects, many of
which are endangered, and so fruits are rationed (insecticides are out
because even in the rare case when they're not carcinogens they
indiscriminately murder millions of living creatures). Nuts would be
good if it weren't for the fact that some nonzero percentage of the
population is allergic, and so they're outlawed.

Fortunately there's tofu. There were rumors, though, that the world
supply was running short and that giant soybean farms were springing up
in Asia, competing with indigenous plants for land, water, and nutrients.
The experimental "soylbean" showed promise as a way to embed amino
acids and vitamins into an oil-based digestible food-type product that can
be molded into non-offensive shapes. This would provide all required
nutrients, no harmful chemicals or spices, no fruits or nuts, no
slaughtered animal parts, no cholesterol or trans fats, and would be
filling. The laxative properties needed to be reduced somehow—the one
remaining issue scientists were working to overcome. Also soylbeans
and soylbean products were green products that caused no environmental
damage. These soylbeans would also create a new market for petroleum,
which is a good thing, because a larger market would allow the oil
producing countries to reduce oil prices while still maintaining their
current profits, which would allow the U.S. government to make more
progress in the negotiations asking them to reduce prices and to sell less
oil to auto manufacturers that are simply destroying the environment and
enabling our addiction to gasoline. Surely the Arab, Russian, and South
American countries would finally see this logic and work with us on this
global problem.

Winston shook his head to clear it. He had this habit of going down long
trees of thought, uncovering entwined roots that go deep but just don't
lead anywhere useful. He decided to focus on his immediate task. Once
again, in this park, a speaker was reported giving a one-sided speech.
Winston looked around the park. The nice weather had brought out the
city's youth to enjoy recreation and music in the sunshine. The empty
space in his stomach filled in a bit. The youth are our hope, the
government reminds us.

Good Intentions

Winston spotted the speaker off in a far corner of the park. He could hear some of the words, but with the music playing from the youths' playboxes it was hard to hear everything. There were a few posters around the speaker, but there were people standing around blocking the view. As he approached, he saw one word on a placard that caused him to freeze and that emptiness is his stomach returned full force. The word was "eradicate." That was one of the words that he had been taught to recognize. This speaker was probably breaking the hate speech laws and could be dangerous. Winston pulled out his PDA and began entering some of the words and phrases he heard: *eliminate… destroy… parasites of society… lower life forms… disease.* As he entered the words into his PDA, the speech-o-meter bar moved from pure green on the left to bright red on the right. This one was dangerous and had to be countered. Winston's heart pounded. He started reading his anti-speech coming from the PDA while he was still running to find a spot no less than 3 meters and no more than 6 meters from the hate monger.

Winston stopped at about the 6 meter mark, pressed the 911 button on his PDA; the police would be here soon. The PDA had absorbed the words he put in and had quickly integrated arguments into a repudiation to counter the foul hatred being spewed by the racist-bigoted individual at the innocent passers-by. "All peoples have a right to life!" Winston shouted into his portable megaphone. "All people are equal. Hatred is wrong! Hatred is evil! Genocide is wrong! Love your neighbor as you love yourself! All you need is love! Do unto others as you would have them do unto you! Make love not war. He's not heavy he's your brother. And your sister. Love one another right now." Winston was shouting and sobbing. The speaker hesitated, then paused to look at Winston. The crowd in front of the speaker also slowly turned to watch Winston. As they did, the crowd opened up enough that the signs became clearer. The word "smallpox" appeared in his view. "Eradicate smallpox" was the message of the sign. The man was talking about real diseases, not people. The man was a Vaccinationist a group devoted to eliminating deadly diseases, not eliminating people.

Winston heaved a sigh of relief. He drew his palm against his damp forehead and flicked off the sweat. As trained to do, Winston began slow deep breaths. He punched a few more words and phrases into his PDA, most notably the word "smallpox" and the speech-o-meter slid back down to orange. The police had to investigate at this point—there was no calling them back—but at least there was no appreciable threat. Vaccinationist were extremists, but generally not dangerous. And they were entitled to their speech, at least until any laws were passed otherwise. Now Winston could begin a measured, rational counter argument without fear.

He cleared his throat to delineate the break between his previous, frantic words and this new, calm, rational, argument. "Friends," he started. "Is any one person better than any other person? Of course not. We know that all people are created equal, perform equal, and live equal. We cannot judge people because we know already that all people are equal and thus judging them would be pointless." Winston pointed at a few people in the crowd. "You are no worse than me. You are no better than me. You are my equal." He got caught up in the words, the attention, a feeling of inspiration. This, he reminded himself, is why he loved his job. The flow of words. The PDA gives him the outline provided by the Bureau of Counter Arguments, but he makes it his own.

"We cannot judge any other person. Hurting another person is a form of judgment. It is an extreme form of judgment. Killing someone is the most extreme form of judgment. That is why in a civil society like ours, death is wrong; it is a crime for any reason. Except accidentally or due to insanity or temporary insanity or out of passion or for some other exception. Or for an unborn child that will be a burden to others. But almost all the time it is morally wrong." The crowd was listening to him. Even the Vaccinationist was listening. He felt good. Maybe he was changing minds, influencing people to do good.

"And who are we to judge any living creatures of earth? Who are we to judge any of God's creatures?" Where did God come from? He was ad-libbing and it just came out. He knew better. Mention of God could be offensive to some in the crowd. It would water down his otherwise excellent argument. He knew he would hear about this back at the office. "All living creatures have rights. Would you exterminate your dog or your cat?" The crowd let out a soft hush of 'no's. He knew he was reaching them, and it felt good.

"How about the birds in the trees?" He waved his hands at the trees around him in the park. "Or the caterpillars on the branches?" People in the crowd looked around and shook their heads and murmured more 'no's. "The man over there is small; the woman over there is ugly. Would you kill them?" Oops, another slip. It seemed good before it came out. He'll hear about that at the office too. "Of course not. We don't judge people or animals or insects by their shape or size or cuteness. And so if we take the smallest, strangest, ugliest form of life—the virus— does not the virus have a right to life too? You know that the Endangered Species List was created to protect and preserve forms of life. And so those of us who must prevent Jews from being exterminated and gays from being murdered and spotted owls from experiencing a Holocaust must prevent the genocide of the smallpox virus too. As with all creatures we must learn to live in harmony with it instead of giving in to baseless prejudice and macrobiologism. We must respect all life with only a few exceptions!"

The crowd started to break up. Winston noted some smiles and nodding heads as they walked away. More importantly, they had heard his counter-argument and had left before the Vaccinationist could draw them back in. The Vaccinationist had fancy diagrams of molecules and human cells and statistics— charts and graphs. People don't want that. They want passion. The kind of passion that Winston just gave them.

The Vaccinationist went on with his speech, but more softly and to a much smaller crowd. Winston watched, but only for reference in case he should come up against him again. The Vaccinationist's diagrams were pretty interesting in some sense. Winston learned how a virus moved into a living cell and took it over to produce more viruses. That viruses were not originally thought to be living creatures because they could not reproduce without hijacking a human cell and destroying it. The graphs showed the statistics of the number of people who died from viral infections and how that number had decreased significantly by the end of the twentieth century and how the number of deaths were increasing again. But of course, respecting other cultures, even viral and bacterial cultures, meant that there would be a period of readjustment and equalization. Equalization was always good. Winston had learned that important lesson in school. Over and over and over again.

Winston collected his thoughts as the crowd dispersed, leaving only a few ardent supporters listening to the Vaccinationist. Winston felt good about this and surveyed the area as he strolled slowly to the trolley that would take him back to the office. He watched the youth enjoying their time in the sunshine. The playbox belted out a popular rap song. Though social stratification, and signs used to identify a person's social standing, had been outlawed many years ago, the kids found their own unique ways around this. Well, kids will be kids. The height of a boy's pants waist was inversely proportional to the boy's "coolness" or "hipness" or whatever it was that kids called it these days. One boy had his pants around his ankles, sporting green and gold stripped briefs—certainly at the top of the totem pole if such a thing were allowed. For girls, it was the height of her skirt and/or the height or shortness of her top. One girl wore a couple strips of duct tape around her butt. Probably she was the cool boy's girltoy or baby momma or f-thing, or whatever the term of endearment was nowadays. Well, kids will be kids.

In one corner, a couple of the teens smoked their medicinal marijuana or "med shit" as they affectionately referred to it. At least it wasn't tobacco—that toxin had been outlawed years ago. Some kids seemed to have needles, and that really wasn't technically legal, but at least the needles came from the park dispenser and had been sterilized before use. Winston made a note of it in his PDA. The government would send someone from the Department of Kids Will Be Kids to set up a demonstration of the proper means of heroin injection and then leave them with a DVD of a lecture on the dangers of drug use.

Toward the other end of the park, Winston noticed a privacy blanket, clearly marked with smiley face and "Please Do Not Disturb" written in bold green letters. Next to the blanket was the mandatory condom dispenser, obviously used. Winston made another note in his PDA that someone from the department needed to come clean up the wrappers and used condoms. That should be part of the Sex Ed training, really, he thought. Underneath the privacy blanket, a young couple squirmed around a little too violently such that their legs poked out from underneath with an occasional flash of naked buttocks. A few of the adults nearby turned their heads. It really was a bit unseemly, this public display of affection. The kids were getting a little carried away, but kids will be kids after all.

The kids by the music were dancing, or rather swaying violently, to the rap coming from the playbox. There was a strong beat and not much else, but the kids were having fun, Winston guessed. A young man came walking slowly toward the other kids, obviously some sort of outcast, though Winston cringed a bit at his own inappropriate judgment. Still the young man was dressed nicely in pressed gray pants and pressed white shirt and polished black shoes. He walked hesitantly toward the other kids, several of whom glanced at him but most ignored him.

A rap song came on that seemed to be popular and some of the kids started singing along. They swayed to the beat while shouting out the words: "hey fuck this and hey fuck that" and "mother fucking ho come give me a blow" and "I'll stab my knife into your gut and chop off your head and give it to my mutt" and one that had become a popular catch phrase among kids "I'll cut your cock off and serve it in a stew." Kids will be kids.

The young man walking toward them smiled nervously. He saw the other kids singing along, so he joined them, softly at first. The other kids saw him and gave him a thumbs-up. Some moved toward him and something approaching a smile showed on their faces. They were fascinated by this young man in his strange clothes. As they came closer, the young man sang louder and bounced nervously with the beat. The other kids started grooving or meshing or whatever they called it. They all bounced to the beat and spit out the rap song words. Until the line came up, "hey nigger, hey nigger, hey, hey nigger." At that line all the kids went silent except the young man, smiling and bouncing, who shouted those words at the top of his lungs. The other kids were shocked and moved away. The young man kept singing and bouncing for a few seconds before he noticed that he was alone except for the rapper from the playbox. He stopped and looked confused. Some people in the park pointed at him. The other kids had horrified looks on their faces as they backed away from this evil, hating person that they had almost accepted into their ranks. The boy with his pants around his ankles waddled over and spit on the young man before turning his back and waddling away.

At this point Winston noticed two policemen running toward the young man. The police had come in response to his 911 call about the Vaccinationist. They had been in the park when this young man had pronounced the most vile word in the English language. The police rushed over and tackled the bewildered young man. "You're under arrest" shouted one of the policemen while holding down the boy. The other policeman handcuffed him. "You have violated all decency standards and all decency laws by uttering the most disgusting, demeaning word in the English language."

The police turned the young man over, his white shirt now spotted with grass and mud stains. He looked up at the police officers with a frightened look. Without understanding. "What?" uttered the young man in an unrecognizable foreign accent. The policeman leaned in close so as not to be heard and whispered, "The n-word."

A Day in Court

"Have you chosen your preferred method of swearing in Mr. Jones?"

"Yes I have your honor."

"Well? *New Testament*? *Old Testament*? *Koran*? One of the *Vedas*? *Book of Mormon*? Voldemort's notebook? T*he Book of the Machines*? *An Inconvenient Truth*? Come now Mr. Jones, we have an entire selection but we have to know which one."

"Pinky swear," said Jones. Like most people he didn't subscribe to any particular formal religion and didn't like ceremony anyway.

"Good, that's easy," said the judge from the judge's bench overlooking the courtroom. "Will the court reporter please swear in Mr. Jones?"

The court reporter, a heavy woman with an abundance of makeup waddled up to Mr. Jones, an almost visible wake of perfume trailing behind her and leaving a path of watering eyes and a few violent sneezes. This particular courtroom was one of the few left that was not scent-restricted.

"Promise to tell truth?" asked the court reporter, slightly swallowing the words with her chewing gum.

"I do," responded Winston Jones.

The court reporter held up her pinky and Jones wrapped his own around hers. "Got it your honor," she said, looking up at Judge Mike.

The courtroom was the last remaining one in the court building not yet refurbished in a modern, pleasant décor. Psychological studies had shown that criminals responded best to whites and bright colors and so most courtrooms were made of white Formica and plastic with random splotches of yellows and blues—colors shown to put people in the most pleasing frames of mind. This room, however, was still the old fashioned, heavy, mahogany benches and desks. Dark plush carpeting covered the floor wall-to-wall rather than the more comfortable and energy efficient gray tile. Judge Mike sat high above the others in the dark wooden seat of authority that made him a little uncomfortable because he knew that he was supposed to be a helper, a colleague, an equal, not an overlord. The room would be refurbished when the government found the funds. Until then Judge Mike stooped over to lower his position, his chin nearly resting on his desk. And he dressed in the casual beige corduroy pants and beige polo shirt that represented his position and correctly expressed the perfect demeanor for helping resolve legal differences in a court of law.

Khan Singh, the young boy who had uttered the despicable word sat behind a desk facing the judge, nervously twiddling his thumbs. He had a look of permanent perplexion throughout the proceedings, still not completely comprehending his crime. Next to him sat his court appointed attorney, a disheveled older man obviously nearing the end of his career. At the desk to the judge's left was a crack team of well-dressed government attorneys for the prosecution. One young man in a black fitted suit rose. "Mr. Jones, tell us what you saw on the day in question." The prosecutor lingered on the phrase "day in question." His legal education had not been for naught, he thought. He liked the phrase "for naught" too.

Jones looked at the young man sitting nervously at the desk. "Well. Mr. Singh walked up to a crowd of youth who were enjoying their time at the park. Some were dancing and singing. Mr. Singh joined in."

"To the best of your recollection, what song was the youth singing at that time?"

"A modern song. A rap song."

"At the time of the incident were you familiar with this particular song?"

"I had heard it before, yes."

"And as you sit here today, do you recall the name of the song?"

"Yes, sir."

Good Intentions

"And the name of that song is?"

Jones fidgeted uncomfortably. "It's about certain women in certain professions and certain services they provide to special types of clientele." Jones breathed in hard and swallowed sharply. His eye twitched.

"Yes, and the name of the song?"

Jones looked up at Judge Mike, who had been leaning closer to hear Jones' words. "Your honor, I fear I may be in violation of a statute by repeating the name of the song."

"Well you're Afro-American and if it's about African-Americans then you have immunity from such statutes."

"Sir, I'm an American of Afro-European descent, not technically African American."

"As one of African descent you're still granted immunity. And this being a courtroom, you're probably ok."

"The song title may also be found demeaning to other groups. To women."

"I hereby grant you immunity to say the title," boomed Judge Mike, now curious about the title.

Jones looked at the courtroom audience, most of whom had been busy with their computer pads but were now focused solely on him. He swallowed hard again. "Your honor, I'm not comfortable…"

"Mr. Jones, this is a court of law and you're holding up the proceedings. I don't want to hold you in contempt of court, but I will."

Jones took a deep breath, looked down at the desk, and said the title of the song. The crowd stared at him for a moment. A couple of teenage girls in the back giggled. A few young men smiled and nodded. The others went back to their computer pads, having lost interest. An elderly lady threw up and was escorted out of the court.

A Day in Court

Judge Mike slumped back in his chair. The defense attorney rose to speak. It was not really his turn, but everyone knew that Judge Mike was pretty easy going when it came to rules.

"Mr. Jones, did you actually witness my client uttering the word that he is alleged to have uttered."

"I'm sorry, sir. To which word specifically are you referring?" Winston Jones was a government worker and as such knew the importance of being precise. He knew there could be consequences for not being precise—after all a young man's future was on the line. And he needed to make sure that everything on the record was clear. The entire court proceedings were video recorded.

"You know which word, Mr. Jones. The bad word."

Jones looked at him without speaking.

"You know," repeated the defense attorney. "The… you know… derogatory word." The defense attorney looked pleadingly at Judge Mike. "Your honor, I… you know…" The defense attorney pointed at Jones and started to say something that came out as a kind of gurgle. He couldn't even refer to the word in front of Winston Jones, a black man, without feeling shame.

At the gurgle, the court reporter interrupted. She, too, looked to Judge Mike for help. "I don't know how to spell that. What kind of word is that?" She had stopped her frantic typing, which did not really matter anyway because she typed onto a disconnected keyboard. That was a money saving measure when the video recording devices were finally installed in the courtroom.

"Just type six letter g's followed by a letter h a letter I and two letter k's. That should suffice." Then turning to the defense attorney, Judge Mike said "N-word. Let's just say 'N-word.'" Then turning to Jones, "That won't be offensive will it? N-word?" Jones shook his head. Judge Mike felt good every time he could help in a situation like this one. Then a thought struck him. "So you are an African American, Mr. Jones…"

"Well, sir," interrupted Jones. "I'm proud of my multiethnic background. I'm registered as 'Afro-European' with minor Hispanic and Tuvaluan, although I believe there may be some undocumented Irish a few generations back."

At the mention of Tuvaluan, a few people in the observation stands were heard to gasp. Jones heard it and added, "I assure you I am solidly in the middle class. My Tuvaluan heritage was not enough to gain me any significant part of the Tuvaluan income. It buys me a nice meal every month, though." At that there were a couple scattered snickers.

Tuvalu is a small Polynesian island located halfway between Hawaii and Australia. At one point in its great history it claimed a population of almost 11,000 people though after the great Internet Domain Rush, most moved elsewhere. The population dwindled to exactly 337 people who run the Tuvalu Historical Museum. In the early days of the Internet, Tuvalu was assigned the domain suffix .tv by the Internet Corporation for Assigned Names and Numbers (ICANN), and companies wanting to put television on the Internet clamored for these domain names. Tuvaluans, who for years had mostly subsisted on foreign aid and government subsidies, became sudden entrepreneurs and overnight millionaires. While many Americans secretly admired them, they were considered greedy rich folk who had traded their honest jobs of government work for the not-so-honorable jobs of taking money from people in return for providing them with something they needed.

"So Mr. Jones, did you hear my client utter the N-word?" asked the defense attorney once again.

"Yes sir, I did hear him say that word. He shouted it…"

"And those are the words of the song, isn't that true? My client was merely singing along with the song."

"But they are extremely offensive, denigratory words, your honor," piped in the prosecutor.

"They're the words of the song," repeated the defense attorney.

"But they're very, very, very bad words." agreed Judge Mike.

"Your honor," asked the defense attorney, "are we not still protected by the First Amendment? Do we not still have free speech here in America?" This was not entirely a rhetorical question. The laws changed quickly these days and the defense attorney was not really sure.

"Yes we do," replied Judge Mike making a mental note to check for certain later.

"Your honor," interrupted the prosecutor, "as Justice Oliver Wendell Holmes, Jr. once stated, 'The most stringent protection of free speech would not protect a man shouting fire in a theater and causing a panic.' The question is whether the words used are used in such circumstances and are of such a nature as to create a clear and present danger that they will bring about substantive evil."

"Holmes said that?" responded Judge Mike. "A great judge and a great detective. Who knew?"

"The words uttered by this man," said the prosecutor theatrically, pointing at the slightly cowering Mr. Singh, "created a clear and present danger!"

"He has a point," said Judge Mike to the defense attorney. Then he leaned over and squinted at Khan Singh. "His skin is dark. He's not African American is he?"

"No your honor, he's Indian," replied the defense attorney. Judge Mike perked up a bit. "From the continent of India" stated the defense attorney for clarification.

Judge Mike slumped back a bit, thinking. "Is he here illegally?" asked Judge Mike, then correcting himself, "I mean without documentation? He'd have protected status."

"No your honor. He came on a student visa; he's studying engineering. His documentation is all there."

"Oh." Judge Mike slumped back again, disappointed. "Sexual orientation? Member of the LGBTSR community?"

The defense attorney looked at Singh who appeared puzzled. The attorney leaned in and whispered in Singh's ear. Singh's eyes widened, his eyebrows raised, and he shook his head rapidly. "I guess not your honor," said the attorney.

"Perhaps he doesn't understand English. You know that ignorance of the law is always a good defense. I'm also quoting Holmes I believe," said Judge Mike.

"Speaks it, reads it, writes it. Perfectly fluent."

"I'm trying to help here, you know."

"Your honor, I object," said the prosecutor. His team at the prosecution's table had been furiously passing him notes. "The people needing help here are those who were denied, defamed, and disenfranchised at that park." He smiled at his clever alliteration. "The people who were so bluntly reminded of a past so abhorrent, so abject, so apprehensive, so… obtuse. A past for which we in this courtroom should remain perpetually guilty." His eyes came to rest on Winston Jones in the witness chair who stared back blankly.

At that moment a man burst into the door at the back of the courtroom and rushed to hand the defense attorney a note.

"What is the meaning of this disruption?" shouted Judge Mike. At times like this he wished he was still allowed to have a gavel to bang.

The defense attorney opened the note and immediately spoke up. "Your honor, we just received the results of our blood test and it shows that Mr. Singh does have a bit of American Indian, or rather indigenous American in his past. It seems that his great grandfather on his mother's side…"

"How much?"

A Day in Court

"A drop, but… the psychological tests also show a slight latent homosexual tendency…" Khan Singh looked up suddenly at his attorney, a bit shocked. His attorney nudged him a bit.

"How" said Khan Singh raising his right hand, open palm, and adding a slight lilt at the end.

"Well, then. He can go. The case is dismissed."

"But your honor..." pleaded the prosecutor.

"This man is a victim of our society," said Judge Mike. "He deserves our pity not our so-called justice." Turning to Khan Singh, "You may go, young man. I apologize on behalf of our whole civilization. I also apologize for past repressions, future discrimination, and this entire trial that would not have been brought in the first place if the prosecution had done its job." He looked at the prosecution table using his "stern" face that he had practiced in the mirror so many times. He turned back to Khan Singh. "You are required, though, to perform community service and take advanced sensitivity training just to be on the safe side. You may collect your grievance fee at the office on the third floor. We hope that this fee will make up for this grievous inconvenience and persuade you not to sue the government for bringing false charges. You are all now dismissed." He waved his hand.

The defense attorney hugged Mr. Khan who still looked bewildered from the proceedings and this new knowledge of a previously unknown ancestry and sexual orientation. The prosecutor sat down, dejected. He was glad to see an innocent man go free, but he had a lot of other clever things to say. He sat at the desk, slumped and sulking. The other attorneys gathered up their materials, patting him on the back and trying to comfort him.

Winston Jones looked at the judge who was preparing for the next case, a murder case, and the real reason that the courtroom was so full. Judge Mike wanted to be really prepared for this one because the cameras would be there and there would be a lot of publicity. Jones cleared his throat.

Judge Mike turned toward the witness stand. "Oh, yeah. You can go. It's all over. He waved his hand dismissively and turned back to his notes. "You've been very helpful," he added after a moment, without looking up.

Winston Jones gathered up his notes and walked toward the back of the courtroom. The crowd began murmuring. The celebrity defense attorney walked in with his team and brushed past Jones. The crowd's murmuring got louder. A few cheers, a few boos. The celebrity attorney smiled, pointing at a few people in the crowd as he worked his way toward the defense table. The prosecutor from the previous case looked at the celebrity defense attorney with unhidden awe.

Following the celebrity defense attorney was the alleged criminal, escorted by several police officers. He raised his shackled hands to wave at the crowd. He was greeted by loud cheers and hisses as he swaggered his way to the defense table, not unlike a wrestler coming into a ring.

As Jones left the courtroom, a tall, thin figure in a dark trench coat stood from the audience seats and followed Jones out. He walked quickly but silently to catch up, until he was only a breath away. "Mr. Jones," he said quietly.

"Yes?" Jones turned around.

"I was impressed with your job on the stand."

"I only told the truth."

"Yes, and you're good at it."

"Well, it's my job, actually."

"Yes, I know."

The lights in the courtroom were turned low to save energy, but still the man's fedora cast a shadow over his face, making it difficult to discern his features exactly. "I'd like to talk to you again about an important matter," said the man.

"What matter is that?"

The man handed Jones a business card. "Call me. You'll like what I have to tell you. It's important. It's good. We'll talk."

"Talk about what?" But the man was continuing toward the door, silently and smoothly as if he were gliding.

Winston Jones looked down at the card in his hand:

Rom Automatic

(215) 555-3776

A Day at the Office

"The computer is sparking." Winston Jones told himself to be calm, stay calm.

"I'm sorry to hear that you're having trouble, Mr. Jones. I know that it's a great inconvenience and I sympathize with you. You know that we're here to do all we can to help you."

"Yes, thank you."

"No, thank you. For your patience. While we resolve this problem."

"OK."

"OK."

"Well?"

"I need your ID number and telephone number."

Winston sighed loudly and recited his ID and telephone numbers into the phone.

"Thank you for supplying your ID number and telephone number. And thank you for your patience. What seems to be the problem?"

"My computer is sparking."

"OK. I'm sorry to hear your computer is sparking. Can you tell me what operating system you are using and what program you are running, please?"

"Does it matter? There are sparks coming out of the back."

"I sympathize with your problem, Mr. Jones. I need to know what operating system you are using and what program you are running so that I can direct your call to the correct department."

A Day at the Office

Winston sighed and clenched his fist until it was red. "MicroGoogle 1000 and FaceHoo."

"I'll transfer you to the MicroGoogle Support Department. Just one minute."

"No, it's not the software…" It was too late. He heard the click followed by the easy listening version of *Don't Stop Believin'* that had become the standard on-hold music on government phones for the last decade or more. He slammed his fist on his cubicle desk.

"Do what, fren?" asked Stony Stevenson, popping his head above the cubicle wall like a human gopher.

"Trying to get my computer fixed. It's sparking."

"Sposed to do that, fren. Look aroun."

In the labyrinthine layout of cubicles that stretched out over the entire floor of the vast office space there were all kinds of sophisticated equipment from computers to coffeemakers, with interface screens, pushbuttons, cables, dials, and gauges. All of them had strips of duct tape, from very small to very large, in random patterns. All of them sparked at random intervals, creating a light show within the office space.

"No, this one's really bad," said Jones. Just then a large spark jumped from the back and set a paper on his desk on fire. He dumped his coffee on the paper to douse it, then moved the pile of papers away. "See," he said.

"Yeh, fren, that's worse. You need help. Call computer support."

"OK, I'll do that."

Stony sat back down, pleased to have helped. Jones sighed again. The on-hold music stopped and someone answered on the other end. He wound up being transferred thirteen times. Around noon he had rushed to the snack machine down the hall, which also sparked but not nearly as bad as his computer, to get lunch while he waited on hold. His desk had a few black streaks from the larger sparks, but he got all the small fires under control. The engineering department promised to send a repairperson right away.

Stony Stevenson popped his head up again abruptly from his cubicle. "Do what, fren? Get your 'puter fixed?"

A second later, Joe Bauers popped his head from the cubicle on the other side and sniffed. "What's cooking?"

"My computer is sparking," said Jones.

"They all spark," said Bauers.

"I told 'im, fren," said Stony.

"No this is worse. Look it's cooking my desk, that's what's cooking."

"Talk about cooking," said Bauers, nodding conspiratorially down the hallway. A tall, lithe blonde woman was walking in their direction. It was a good thing, too, because Stony and Bauers had about exhausted their conversation skills by then. The three of them watched her silently as she maneuvered through the cubicle pathways. You could see the tongues of Stony and Bauers drooping metaphorically, if not physically, out of their mouths and onto the floor. In their minds they made all kinds of cat calls that they would not dare make out loud for fear of a sexual harassment suit.

Jones felt an attraction to this woman also. Alisa Rosenbaum was beautiful and sexy, no question, but so were many women in the office. Alisa was different. She always dressed in business attire—dark skirts or trousers with white blouses and dark jackets or vests. The clothes were tailored and form-fitting, and while accenting her thin build, the clothes revealed little skin. What skin did show was surprisingly tattoo-less.

Alisa walked briskly, continuing toward them with a bulging folder in her hand. There were lots of cubicles she could be headed for, and at any time they expected her to take a turn one way or another, but she continued straight toward them. Stony and Bauers smiled as she got closer, but there were also signs of nervousness—a twitch of the corner of the mouth or a tremble of an eyelid. Alisa Rosenbaum had a confidence in herself that was obvious, something that unnerved some men but made her even more appealing to Jones.

"Gentlemen," she greeted them.

"Do what, fren?"

"Howdoo?"

"Hi Alisa," said Jones.

Alisa handed the folder to him. "Some newspaper editorials, letters to the editor, a couple magazine articles, and I think a research paper. You're supposed to categorize them and prepare alternate opinions for publication by the end of the week."

"Thanks Alisa." He was always pleasant to her, but she never seemed to notice him. She spoke very little so he had a hard time starting conversations. He had no idea what she was interested in. "Nice weather, huh?" He mentally kicked himself.

"Yeah, nice huh?" echoed Bauer.

"Global warming today. Global cooling in a few months, fren," said Stony.

Alisa looked at them, then nodded, but not at their comments. She started to walk away then stopped. "You were in court the other day?"

Jones didn't realize at first that it was a question. When he realized it was a question, he didn't realize it was directed at him. She turned to look at him like at a child who isn't paying attention.

"Oh… yeah," he said. She continued looking at him and he unconsciously bit his lip. "I was a witness to a crime. Well an alleged crime. Actually there was no crime after all."

"What kind of crime?" She seemed moderately interested.

"Hate crime. Well, it turns out the perpetrator had protected minority status after all so the hate crime charges were dismissed. I think he had to do community service and take sensitivity training classes nonetheless."

"We all have to do community service and take sensitivity training classes," said Bauer. "It's a civic duty and government requirement."

"Maybe extra ones. Maybe not. I didn't stick around to get the details."

"So you think the government has a right to control what we say and think?" Alisa Rosenbaum stared at Jones. He had never noticed that her left eye was blue and her right eye was green. How could he have not noticed that before?

"Not control, but make sure no one is hurt by words…"

"Hurt by words?"

Jones looked at her for a moment. "Well, this is the Department of Fairness. Our job is to make sure words don't hurt."

Alisa shrugged. She gave a short, condescending shake of her head. At that moment a spark shot out of Jones' computer with a loud pop. "What's with that?" she asked.

"It's sparking."

"So fix it," she said and walked off. Jones, Stony, and Bauer looked after her as if she'd told them to do brain surgery on themselves.

"What can I do fer ya?" A big, round guy stood in front of them. They hadn't noticed him walking up while they were talking to Alisa Rosenbaum. He wore a utility belt stocked with screwdrivers, pliers, rolls of duct tape, and all sizes of cylindrical and spherical plastic and ceramic cases with wires sticking out of them.

Just then another spark flew out of the computer with a loud pop, scorching the desk. The man seemed not to notice.

A Day at the Office

"It's the computer" said Jones, pointing at the smoldering desk.

"Gotcha," said the man. "Seems like you've got a capacitance problem." At that point Bauers and Stony lost interest and ducked once again below the partitions.

"OK. Which means what?" asked Jones.

"Means you've got too much electricity in this thing. So you need one or two of these." He pulled one of the plastic cylinders, about three inches long and one inch in diameter, off his belt. There was a wire going through the middle. He bent the leads to form right angles with the cylinder and held it between his thumb and forefinger, slowly approaching the computer like a crab approaching prey.

"Don't you need to power it down first?"

"Of course." The man grabbed the power cord and gave a quick yank. The computer died. Whipping out his screwdriver from his belt like a gunfighter pulling a gun from a holster, he quickly unscrewed four screws and popped off the computer's back panel.

Stony and Bauer both pronked from behind their partitions, their radars having been triggered.

"Here's a new assignment." It was Alisa again. She had returned silently without Jones noticing. It seemed like people were just appearing suddenly in his life these days. Was he just not paying attention anymore or was it something else? He took the slip of paper from her. "I thought about emailing it," she continued, "but was afraid of the consequences." She nodded at the computer.

"What is this? Seems like a rush. There wasn't any advanced notice."

"There was notice," she replied. "No one wanted it. So you're stuck with it. Maybe you'll like it. It's a little different."

"Why?" but she had already moved on. He saw her face above the cubicles, moving away. She looked back at him and smiled. Or was she looking at something or someone else?

"All done," said the computer repairperson. The computer backside panel was screwed back on but there were three of the capacitors duct-taped onto it, two large cylinders and one small disk. "This one was tough to figure out. As I said, sometimes electricity builds up in these computers. If you use it a lot, you get this buildup. So you need a capacitor in just the right spot to increase the electric capacity. It's as much an art as it is a science." He looked proud of himself. He plugged the computer back in and it started up. A few small sparks were accompanied by quiet pops. "Yeah, I seem to have gotten most of it. You should be ok now."

The repairman walked off whistling and swinging his large bundle of keys around his index finger. Jones looked down at the note that had been handed to him by Alisa Rosenbaum. He didn't have time to read it in detail because he was going to be late if he didn't leave right away. He grabbed his coat and ran toward the exit, wondering why no one else wanted this particular job.

A Day at the Office

Mr. Fix It

As he made his way to his assignment, Winston Jones thought about his computer and the computer repairman, and then about his dad. He had not really thought about his dad much, so it surprised him that his dad came up in his thoughts twice recently. His dad could fix anything. Well, anything mechanical at least.

Morrie Jones had gone off to fight in the war after high school. It was his patriotic duty, and it seemed like a good way to get out of the Chicago public housing, the Chicago ghetto known as Cabrini-Green. He wanted to see the world, have an adventure, do the things he was afraid he would never be able to do otherwise. And he could meet beautiful, exotic women who would be impressed with his clean and pressed uniform, the muscular figure it covered, and the suave mustached face above it. Morrie Jones had a lot of self confidence. He was outspoken and not politically correct at a time when that was considered a bit daring and exciting by young women. Morrie Jones was about average height, maybe a little below average, with a taut, angular build from years of regular weightlifting and high school sports—a big contrast to the tall thin son he would have many years later. He had a head of thick wavy hair that he slicked down every morning to keep from puffing up into a wool pad. He often slept in a Chicago Cubs baseball cap that was stained from hair oils and gels, but it worked to give him that thick black mane. His mustache was thin and short-trimmed with a soul patch below his chin that together looked like some ancient cuneiform. And the women did like him.

Morrie fought in the war but rarely talked about it afterwards except for a few stories about escapades with local women or some bar fight in a foreign setting. It was not that the war had affected him or that he was ashamed of his part. In fact, he was a practical young man who understood that it was important to stand up for what was right and that sometimes that was a difficult thing involving very difficult decisions. And he was an unquestioning patriot who believed in America and in the freedoms and opportunities it had afforded him and his family. Even in bad times, he was the optimist who believed in his own ability to change his life for the better. Mostly it was because he enjoyed himself too much to dwell on the kind of tough and sometimes terrible situations that every soldier faces. Morrie Jones was a fun-loving guy with a big bellowing laugh—the kind that made everyone in the room turn to look. He had a strong sense of fairness and was much more often breaking up fights than caught in the middle of them. And when he was in the middle of them, it was often protecting someone or challenging someone's hatred. But whenever he was in the fight, it always ended at his prerogative, and often with him buying the other party a beer. He could be quick to ignite, but quicker to calm down.

When Morrie Jones got back from the war he was too impatient for college. The government was offering scholarships to every veteran, but Morrie opted out. He was smart and well-read. He was unpolished and there were big gaps in his knowledge, but what he knew he knew well. He had a passion for life and a passion for work. Morrie Jones, after traveling the world, came back to Chicago and married a pretty young woman from the projects. Her name was Rita. She was petite and shy and like most young women was flattered that Morrie paid attention to her at all. They fell in love and Morrie promised her that he would provide for her and they would have children and live in comfort and security. And like most people who listened to Morrie, she could not do anything but believe him and go along for the ride. They married.

Morrie took a job at a heating, ventilation, and air conditioning (HVAC) repair company and learned the engineering skills on the job and by reading textbooks at night. On the weekends he would take apart machinery and put it back together again, often improved from the original. Eventually he quit his job and opened his own one-man company. No one was sure where this young man had gotten the funds to go off on his own, but they knew Morrie as an honest man, and if he had gotten the funds he had gotten them legitimately even if he never spoke about it. He used the money to buy equipment, an old Cadillac to haul the equipment in style, and a small brick building that had just barely escaped being condemned. The neighboring buildings had not been as fortunate and so this small building sat in the middle of an empty lot of concrete and asphalt rubble. But Morrie hung his sign and saw nothing but promise when he looked at the graffiti-covered building. GE—Galt Engineering was born. He chose a name that he thought sounded impressive. He did not want people to know it was his business unless he told them. That way he could always defer to Mr. Galt in negotiations. "That sounds like a fair deal to me," he would say, "but Mr. Galt has insisted that I not go that low on the bid. Mr. Galt is very demanding you know, but I'll talk to him and see what I can do." He and Rita saw nothing but a promising future.

The business struggled for years, but Morrie seemed to have undying optimism. He knew that he had to persevere. He knew that opportunity and success was just around the corner—if not this corner then probably the next. And anyway it paid the bills and paid his salary and allowed him to hire occasional help, even if it wasn't really the American Dream come true. Yet.

Winston was born a few years later and whatever doubts Morrie had about his future vanished. If Winston had been in any way less than perfect it would not have mattered much to Morrie, but that was not the case anyway. At least to Morrie. Winston was smart and inquisitive though a bit rebellious. Not in a bad way. Not in a way that anyone got hurt. Winston just liked to push the limits, bend the rules, and watch the reaction of those in authority. He was well-mannered so that few people suspected him of any unruly behavior. And he was smart enough to rarely get caught and then rarely suffer consequences.

If Morrie could save enough money to put his son in college, then his family's future would not be in doubt. Morrie had come to conclude that skipping college had not been a great idea after all. He saw competitors—not as smart, not as hard-working as him—often get awarded contracts over him. Morrie attended night school to get an Associate's Degree, but it took everything out of him to work during the day and study at night. And he felt that he was missing out being a bigger part of his son's life. He got the degree—he was not a quitter and did not even think about stopping short—but then focused solely on his business and his son. Rita loved Morrie but realized that she had become a third priority after the other two priorities and eventually came to accept that. She loved Morrie and she loved Winston and accepted her position in the hierarchy.

Morrie would often take his son to work with him and show him off proudly. "This is my helper," he would proclaim to anyone who came by—fellow contractors, employees, clients, or just passers-by. Winston would have liked to actually help, but Morrie told Winston that he was going to make sure that Winston went to college and got a good job. Winston was smart and was going to make something of himself, his dad would say. Still Winston watched the great machinery that his dad worked on and was fascinated by it. He would watch the fans whirl and the motors spin, and the meshed gears rotate, sometimes for hours. Winston could sit and stare at the machinery for long periods, trying to understand their principles or sometimes just hypnotized by their intricate motions. Occasionally someone passing by would get worried or frightened seeing this mesmerized young boy sitting and staring and would approach him cautiously, but Morrie would step out of some shadow where he had been working and claim Winston as his and try to put the stranger at ease.

At some point, Morrie's business did pick up. He had fought for, and won, a contract to install a central air condition and heating system for the Chicago Mercantile Exchange Building. It was a big, big job and Morrie had bid on it, not really believing he would get the job. But Morrie had a great reputation for precise engineering and uncompromising workmanship, and someone somewhere took a risk on him. "After all, this was what America is about, isn't it?" he thought.

Morrie started hiring employees. He moved out of his tiny building into a bigger, though still modest one. He was able to finally leave the small row house that he and Rita and Winston had occupied since Winston's birth, and move into a townhouse in the suburbs. It was nothing special, but to him it was a palace. There was a lot of work, but Morrie did not mind work—rather he liked it, and so it was no trouble. Yet with all of the work he found more time to be with his family. They even took occasional vacations, something that was previously alien to him and Rita.

Sundays were probably best of all. Winston would wake up early to watch cartoons but also keeping his ears tuned to his parents' bedroom door. Once he heard stirrings, he would fling open the bedroom door, run, and take a giant leap onto his father's big belly. By then Morrie's young, muscular physique was gone, replaced by a larger but imposing girth. Rita and Morrie would laugh, acting surprised at this regular tradition. Morrie and Winston would laugh and talk and eventually get into discussions of all kinds of things—engineering and science but also history and even politics. Morrie was well read but Winston was catching up even though he didn't realize it and still felt that his father knew more than any human being could possibly know. Rita would listen to the conversations, and occasional debates as Winston grew older, and eventually slip out to prepare breakfast. She too was happy.

Things seemed good. The job at the Mercantile went well, it seemed, and brought in enough money to expand the business a little more. GE hired more people from the neighborhood—even from the projects—trained them and put them to work. Morrie Jones was a tough boss, but a rewarding one too. Some people quit. Some people were fired. And those that remained worked hard, were rewarded, and were fiercely loyal.

But after a couple years, things took a turn for the worse at GE. It was not clear why, because things had seemed to be going well. Big contracts started going to other companies. GE started bidding lower in an attempt to win back business, but those contracts that he did win were bid too low to cover the costs. Morrie believed in hard work and seemed to work harder each day in an attempt to work his way out of the quicksand in which he now seemed mired. Morrie believed that every problem could be solved and that he could solve it by working harder. Rita and Winston saw him slipping away from them—working more, seeing them less. The material things that they had earned, they started losing. People say you should not get attached to material things, but once you have lived in a townhouse it was hard not to regret going back to a row house. They survived. They accepted their condition. Winston was smart and a realist and he understood why they had to sacrifice, but it still hurt. It probably hurt more that he rarely saw his father any more, not even accompanying him to work as his dad's "helper." For an eleven year old boy it was hard to know what hurt more—losing the toys and the vacations or losing the time with his dad—but he knew it hurt and he withdrew.

Morrie became depressed. People did not recognize the morose man who had once been so confident, so joyful even when he was not well off, even before he was a neighborhood success. Morrie withdrew to his office more and more often, and withdrew into himself.

The day that Morrie did not come home, Rita was afraid to call the police. She knew what she would find out and she just did not want to find it out. Winston called the police. They went to Morrie's office and found his body there. No note. Only the insurance policy in his hand that he had signed up for many years ago when his future had seemed so unsure but so promising.

Rita took it particularly bad. She had never lived on her own. The sweet, undemanding woman drew Winston close to her for fear of losing him. She became stern and serious. She watched over Winston and set boundaries for him. She needed him to grow up strong and independent, but her engulfing him, physically and emotionally, had just the opposite effect. Winston became more serious, more studious, less rebellious. But that was ok with Winston. He had lost a big part of his own spirit when his father died. And he was angry at his father for taking his life— cowardly—and leaving his mother and him on their own. How selfish! Winston wanted to just follow the rules and fade into the background. His father had taken risks. His father had pushed boundaries. His father dreamed of better things. And look where he had ended up. Winston swore to be a different person than his father. And from then on he was.

Fair and Balanced

This was the one that nobody wanted. That's ok, Winston Jones thought, his job is to do his job, and this is his job no matter how repulsive.

This time it was a subway station. The acoustics could be a little tricky. That was a challenge, but Jones liked challenges. It was a skill, an almost mathematical determination of where to stand so that he could be heard without drowning out the words of the other speaker, because that wasn't allowed. We do still have free speech in this country, with only a few exceptions.

Jones could hear the speaker's voice emanating from the subway entrance as he approached. The sounds echoed slightly and came in blips and blurbs as crowds entered and exited the subway, the sound waves bouncing off people's heads and absorbed by their padded clothes.

As Jones walked down the stairway, the words became clearer. He followed the sounds, occasionally making a wrong turn that was easily corrected when the words dimmed rather than brightened. At last he saw the man, dressed in tattered clothes and unshaven, standing in a corner. A small crowd had formed, but most people were too busy to pay attention.

Jones surveyed the area. This was a rather large open area where several passages connected. It was open and empty except for the people on their way from one place to another. In his mind, Jones drew lines and angles representing moving people and sound waves emanating from the speaker and bouncing off the tile walls at equal angles. Jones had really liked geometry as a boy and used it on those few occasions when he had some opportunity. Jones had originally wanted to study engineering in school, but since the great "Engineering Degree Giveaway" to encourage engineers, there came to be too many of them. It turns out there was a shortage of Tuvaluan philosophers, so he was "encouraged" to enter the field with a scholarship and a promise of a job upon graduation. It was hard to turn down, so he got his degree in philosophy and began work for the government as a community organizer, like most of the other philosophy majors.

Jones mapped out in his mind the perfect spot, optimized for the acoustics and for the most traffic, and headed over to it. He held off setting up his standard sign that read "Alternate Opinion Courtesy of the U.S. Government." He held up his PDA above his head, aimed at the speaker, to record the words and begin generating an alternative.

"The Government," the speaker was saying. He was tall, nearly as tall as Jones. But bigger. Wrapped in layers of clothing, the man appeared like a bear. His hair was jet black and slicked back. His beard also jet black and wild. His whole appearance was wild, except for his eyes that were a penetrating steel blue. They looked sharp. They looked clear. They looked like they belonged on a face much different than that of the wild man in the subway. "The Government," the man repeated after a pause. "The Government's job is to protect the people from the people." He spoke clearly and thoughtfully, pausing often for effect. It caught people's attention as they walked by. "As civilization had advanced over the centuries, people have advanced from one stage to a more advanced stage. Humans began as nomads who wandered from place to place, taking from nature as long as nature supplied its goodness. When resources were exhausted, humans moved on. As long as nature, in her mysterious goodness, provided for the few humans that walked the earth, this worked out fine. Nature was happy. But humans are rarely happy and wanted more.

"Always wanting more than Nature was willing to provide, humans began growing in number. Procreating without control. To support this growth, humans settled down into agrarian societies. Farmers. These farmers ran small farms to feed their families and this was good. Nature was happy to oblige. Villages grew up around the farms and people had stability and were happy. They traded what they could for services that they needed. There was little excess. They supplied their families and they supplied their neighbors. Nature was pressed to its limits but happy to oblige. Nature worked hard and humans worked hard. All was good.

Good Intentions

"But then some humans got greedy. They wanted to produce more than their neighbors. They wanted more money. More materials things. A house that stood up to the rains or the winds or the snow. They wanted to travel to faraway villages. So they began to produce more than their share and more than they needed even to supply their neighbors. This led to competition between farmers. One farm overproducing caused others to fail. Caused farmers to lose their farms, lose their jobs, find work in other sectors where they were unprepared. Governments began forming to help these out-of-work farmers. To assist them and their families. Keep them from starving and dying out.

"Then, of course, came the Industrial Revolution. A few greedy humans pushed Nature beyond its capabilities. Machines were developed so that a few men—yes, mostly men—could control production of necessary resources and hold them hostage. And resources amassed in the hands of only a few men—mostly men—that controlled the world. Only Government, that benevolent congregation of peoples of all classes, could rescue civilization. Government set limits. Government distributed resources fairly. Government kept the poor from dying and the rich from their riches.

"The Industrial Revolution was followed by the Computer Revolution that created the largest resource gap in world history. The rich got richer while the poor got poorer. Those who learned technology could exploit its power while those who did not learn technology were doomed to poverty.

"And as you know, Nature started to tire out. It was overworked. It was supplying more and more resources to a small group of people while the rest of humanity suffered. The result was Global Cooling. Followed by Global Warming. Then Global Climate Change. Followed by our current period of Global Climate Unpredictability where even our best scientists can't figure out if the world is warming or cooling or both. Nature is taking delight in fooling us. Paying us back for working it to death over the millennia.

"And while Government is fighting back against those who would further drive Nature like a slave, and while Government is taking over businesses that produce too much or compete too harshly, it must start doing more. Much more. We know business is evil. We know Government is our salvation. We must now ask, or even demand, that Government force all businesses to reduce productivity so that we can give Nature the rest he or she deserves and bring humanity back to its long lost harmony."

Normally Jones would have started his counter argument long before this, but his PDA kept coming up blank. Words and phrases appeared but then disappeared quickly. That was a problem with a speech like this. It was so unusual to hear this kind of thinking that the government and the government's computers were not prepared with counter arguments. That was the reason that no one in the department really wanted this job. It occurred rarely, fortunately, but required some on-the-spot thinking. The government had considered just letting these kinds of speeches go without retort, especially since they were not harmful in any way, but the government was required by law to provide a balanced opinion.

"Ladies and gentlemen," started Winston Jones, "lend me your ears." Well it wasn't original but it was a good start and few people would have heard it before. Winston also paused often, but less for effect and more to figure out his rebuttal on the fly. "Yes, civilization has progressed from nomads to farmers to city dwellers. I use the word 'progress," because we must not forget that this is, indeed, progress. When people roamed from place to place, they ate what food there was and died when the food ran out. Life expectancy was short and tribes fought over the few resources that were available. Murder was acceptable, sometimes encouraged, and often necessary to survive."

Jones tapped his forehead furiously, thinking. "Eventually people learned how to farm. Animals have their natural survival mechanisms. Humans cannot run as fast as lions or tigers. They cannot fly to escape lions or swim from sharks. They cannot wrestle bears or alligators. They are slower, softer, and more limited than every predator large enough to devour it. But the skill that Nature did supply to humans was that of intelligent thought. And so people used that natural skill to create farms so that people were not at the mercy of weather or seasons. Farms allowed villages to grow where everyone could survive and prosper. Those who could farm did so and those who could not found their own skills to trade for food. Each person had the ability to excel and to contribute.

"But life was difficult. Life expectancy was higher than before, but still low. There was little leisure time and that was only for royalty, nobility, the wealthy few.

"But humans continued to use their one natural talent—the ability for intelligent thought. They invented new ways of making life better. This reached its first peak at the Industrial Revolution when advances began occurring at a higher rate than ever before. Yes there were problems. Sweat shops. Child labor. Accidents. Greed. But human inventiveness also produced miracle drugs that expanded life expectancy around the planet. Machines that made everyday life easier. Automobiles. Airplanes. Washing machines. It created great wealth for a few hard-working, intelligent, exceptional business leaders, but it also raised the standard of living for all. And it created leisure time even for the ordinary worker for the first time in history.

"The Computer Revolution provided new improvements to everyone's lives. It gave power to individuals with their intelligent personal assistants as well as the ability to communicate, and gain knowledge from any worldwide source, almost instantaneously. Personal fortunes churned. An inspired, industrious person could take a risk—yes a risk that could fail in ways that meant serious repercussions for the entrepreneur—and could succeed in creating a better place for all people. And that person could amass a fortune, but that fortune could just as easily disappear when a competitor took a risk and succeeded with something even better.

"It used to be that government encouraged competition by staying the hell out of the way." Jones surprised even himself at this point with his own enthusiasm. "Government kept the playing field even, attempted to root out corruption and cheating, and then let business do what business does. And it provided a cushion, a safety net, to those individuals who needed temporary help getting back on their feet and once again producing, whether in a large way or a small way, to the benefit of everyone in society.

"It is time for government to once again get out of the way. Do the job it was intended to do. Do the job of being a referee in the game, not the player."

Jones had been deep in thought to produce this counter argument and so he barely noticed the crowd that had formed around him. A few people had actually begun applauding, which brought his attention back to the subway in which he was speaking. More of the crowd joined into the applause. Perhaps it was just his enthusiasm that caught their attention and earned their appreciation. The applause died down and the crowd began dispersing. A few people remained for a while and talked about the speech and the points he'd made. There was not agreement, of course, but there was food for thought and people nibbled on that food.

Jones felt breathless and more excited than he had in a while. His heart was racing, but from excitement. He had actually enjoyed this. He reached down and picked up his sign to leave. He didn't notice that the speaker, the bear of a man whom he had come to rebut had stopped preaching shortly after Jones had begun and had instead listened to Jones. At the end of Jones' speech, the man had actually smiled, nodded slightly, and seemed to make a soft clapping gesture.

Jones had also not noticed the tall man in the dark black trench coat and fedora in the background. Rom Automatic also nodded slightly and smiled.

The Electoral Committee

Smoke filled the air and swirled around the figures surrounding the large, round oak table. They each wore the same dark black trench coats. Many of them puffed on their cigars. Others' eyes watered while some struggled to keep their coughing as inaudible as possible. Cigars were, of course, illegal. But these people took a few special privileges. After all, the entire country depended on them, so they could allow themselves a few small, extra perks.

Embedded in the tabletop was an interactive screen showing colorful graphs and charts that threw bright colored projections onto the smoke above. The rest of the room was dark, the faces of the Committee members hardly visible.

One short man waved his hand over the table, making the charts and graphs dance, expanding, shrinking, and morphing into other charts and graphs. "The demographics are changing," he said. "Look. The percentage with European ancestry has taken a tick upward. The low birth rate of Hispanics has caused a slow decline."

There was some murmuring as he continued. "We can look at skin color and zoom in on white vs. non-white or, more telling, off-white vs. light brown." He continued to wave his hands frantically over the table bringing up more graphs and charts. "And there's religion. Muslim on the increase, Christian on the decrease, though the distribution among the denominations is bouncing all over the place. Buddhism is showing a huge jump, though the percentages are still small. Judaism is fairly stable but Environmentalism is on a steep upswing."

There was more murmuring and more sucking and puffing as he continued. "We can look at sexuality." Several members leaned in closer, disappointed when only more graphs and charts appeared. "Heterosexuality continues its decline while homosexuality increases linearly. But bisexuality keeps jumping up, down, up, down. Transgender is increasing with the advent of at-home medical procedures.

Polysexuality is gaining favor, especially among the younger generations and zoophilia is still small but increasing in remote, rural areas."

A few of the members made some disapproving noises at the last category. The man paused and looked around for the offended, offending members. "Look, we're not judging here. We have no right to judge! I'm just talking about representation. And fairness."

One of the members spoke up. "Are you going to take us through every chart and graph in the census?"

"I haven't even gotten to most of them. Age, height, weight, hair color, eye color, infirmities, outfirmities."

"So what's your point here?"

The man looked on the verge of tears. "We're not truly representing the population as it currently exists."

"So?"

"So? So!" A vein on the man's forehead throbbed, about to burst. He was on the verge of an angry outburst or tears, he did not know which. He tried hard to control himself, swallowing his initial words, and thinking of better ones. "So what's the name of this society?" There was silence. He repeated louder, "What's the name of this society?"

"We all know the name…"

"It's the Fairness for EveryBody Society! It's not fairness for some; it's fairness for every single person!"

There was silence. The members of the FEB stopped sucking and puffing or coughing or tearing. They stared at the small man who had just lost his temper. From the shadows, a tall figure in a black trench coat appeared behind the small man. Rom Automatic put a firm, calming hand on the man's shoulder. "We all know the name of the society, Hector."

Hector calmed down. He looked up at Rom. "It's just that we're no longer representative," he said. The last time we reviewed the makeup of the society was several years ago. When I was brought on. Even then we weren't precisely representative, but we were close and you promised changes."

"I understand Hector, but there are very important issues to take up. Not that perfect representation isn't an important issue…"

"There's not a single member in the society with an infectious disease. Not one. How can we represent everybody if we don't even have one?"

Rom paused. Several members had objected to Hector's invitation to the committee, but Rom saw a quality in him that the others didn't. Hector was truly concerned with the goals of society. Sometimes it felt like the society had wandered and it would be good to have an idealist among them. And Rom owed a favor to Hector's dad, but that was really secondary. However, Hector's idealism seemed to get in the way more often than it helped. This committee had to run the society, which in turn had to run the greater society. Idealism was great when it was useful. When it helped get important decisions made. Rom had decided to ask for Hector to be removed from the committee because he slowed things down at a critical time when there was still so much to be done. Removing him would be a difficult task involving a lot of one-on-one discussions with other committee members. It would take promises, most of which he could keep, and a number of secret meetings. Even more secret than the normal meetings that were always highly secret from outsiders. These secret meetings would be secret from other members of the committee, particularly Hector. Rom sighed at the thought.

"Hector, we all respect your idealism. It's the trait that persuaded us to bring you onto the FEB and the into this committee. It's a trait that we all admire—the ability to remember principles, and fight for principles, amidst everything else that goes on. I think that you've made your important point and we all need to consider it in more depth. For now we need to move onto agenda item number one. I suggest that all members consider Hector's important points on their own time and according to their own schedule, and that we have a full discussion at a later meeting."

The Electoral Committee

There were a number of grunts and murmurs around the table. Hector hoped they were noises of approval, but he doubted it. His motions were always tabled for the next meeting, but there was always a more pressing issue at the next meeting. And the issues were important and critical, but he still thought there should be more time for his concerns. No one else raised these concerns, and he often wondered why. Aren't the others worried about these kinds of grand issues? But the committee was run by consensus, the way it should be. Rom always seemed to understand the consensus of the group. And the consensus of the group never swung in Hector's direction.

Rom walked to his place at the large table, and all eyes pivoted toward him. "Fellow committee members. As you know, the drawing is approaching and we must locate a candidate."

There were nods of agreement and the sucking and puffing became more intense. As did the suppressed coughs and tearing eyes.

"I have located one excellent candidate. He is tall and thin and above average in appearance without being handsome. You know that this fits the criteria that the American people love. His skin is dark brown, but not black. He is racially mixed including—get this— Tuvaluan." A murmur went up. "And yet, he is solidly middle class."

"How can that be?" asked one of the committee members.

"I can explain it later, but trust me it's true."

"That's perfect," exclaimed another committee member.

"It's better than that," continued Rom. "He is eloquent. He sounds intelligent. He can read scripted commentary and yet also create his own arguments, his own speeches."

"Isn't that… possibly dangerous?" asked one committee member.

"He stays on point, always. I've seen him. I've heard him. I think he's our candidate."

There were more murmurs throughout the dark room now almost invisible in a fog of cigar smoke. Hector had met one or two people he liked as potential candidates, and he had intended to raise their names tonight, but he changed his mind. It was clear, as always, that the consensus of the group never swung in Hector's direction. It swung in Rom Automatic's direction.

Rom waved his hands over the table top, clearing away the smoke and also bringing up a slideshow of candid pictures of Winston Jones. The committee members nodded and murmured in consensus. Even Hector was impressed.

"Ladies and gentlemen of the Electoral Committee of the Fairness for EveryBody Society, I give you the next President of the United States, Winston Jones."

The Electoral Committee

Another Day at the Office

Winston Jones walked slowly toward his cubicle. There hadn't been any physical activity, just some walking and talking and no more than usual. So why did he feel so worn out?

He sat at his desk and opened the folder full of articles and papers that needed fair rebuttal. His mind kept going back to his last rebuttal in the subway station. It felt different. It actually felt good to have to think of the reply on his own without the help of the PDA. A feeling of accomplishment. But exhausting.

He went back to the papers. Glancing at them he knew they would be easier. The normal right-wing clap trap. Those were always easier to rebut because he just had to speak the truth and use well-documented facts that were right here in the computer. That's when he noticed the computer had been tampered with.

"How's it working for you?" Alisa Rosenbaum was standing in the cubicle entry. Why do people keep appearing and disappearing these days?

"What?"

"The computer. How's it working?"

Jones looked again at the computer. The duct tape and capacitors were gone. And it wasn't sparking. Not even a little. "Oh. Works great."

"You're welcome."

"You did this? You fixed it?"

"Yeah."

"How?"

"I figured it was the power supply because the rest of the circuitry is pretty low voltage and wouldn't cause that powerful a spark. I put an oscilloscope probe on the power supply terminals and found that the output had an intermittent spike. Probing around the board I found that the spike coincided with accesses to a specific region of the L1 SRAM cache on the instruction bus. A visual examination showed that the power supply damping inductor had worked loose and connected with the L1 cache address bus. Shoddy workmanship. So I re-soldered it and removed those stupid capacitors."

Jones stared at her blankly.

"You probably meant how did I get the time to do it? I finished my workload early, saw you weren't here, grabbed my tools, and went to work on it. I hope you don't mind."

"I meant how did you know how to fix it? How do you know about computers and electronics?"

"Oh. I've always been interested in building things, fixing things. How things work. It can become an obsession. I want to understand the inner workings of things and improve on them."

"But you're working here. In the Department of Fairness. Why aren't you in engineering?"

"I studied engineering. At Stanford University. The Palo Alto campus. You know the big push for women engineers? I got into that program. Seemed like a great idea. I'm a woman. I love engineering. Thing is, I had to take the women's engineering courses. As if mathematics is different for men and women. As if women experience different physical laws of nature from men. Our courses emphasized group dynamics and solving problems without math. Our courses were friendlier, less competitive, sweeter –just like us. How stereotypical.

"Did you know that in the last century when universities started accepting women, they had entire women's colleges or departments dedicated to home economics? All the math you needed to get a good deal at the supermarket. They taught cooking skills and cleaning skills but gave them names like food science and sanitation engineering.

"Now they do it with Women's Engineering programs. They dumb it down. They dumb everything down, but it's worse for women. I wanted to learn engineering not some bureaucrat's idea of what a female should learn. I found some like-minded women and we formed a group. We snuck into the men's engineering classes. It didn't hurt my self esteem for a man to do a better job than me. Just the opposite. It made me want to work harder. It made me feel great those times when I came out ahead. I loved the competition. It's a rush. Getting a bad grade or a mediocre grade or seeing someone solve a problem in a better, more efficient, more elegant way than you made you want to work even harder. At least it did me. And my girlfriends. We had a blast."

Jones seemed confused at Alisa's extensive monologue. "But you're not in computer services. Or engineering. You're not doing engineering."

"I got caught. The administration found out. The other women were sent back to the women's engineering courses. I was the ringleader. They told me how proud they were of my achievements. You know, they didn't want to hurt my self esteem. They told me they needed me to be a role model for other women to enter the field. They needed to get the message out to young girls about the women's engineering programs. If the women entered the men's engineering program, the women's engineering program would disappear and that wouldn't be fair to those girls who didn't want to study men's engineering. Their logic was... interesting.

"Anyway, they didn't feel comfortable with me anymore. The feeling was kind of mutual. I was asked to transfer to the University of the Nation at Berkeley on the other side of the Bay. The women's engineering classes there were no better. I wanted real engineering not the fuzzy, feel good, close-enough engineering they offered. So I dropped out of the program."

Jones looked at her for a moment, not knowing what to say.

"What's your story?" she asked.

"I went to Harvard."

Another Day at the Office

"Which campus?"

"Ithaca, New York."

"That's a good school," she said. "I know we're not supposed to pass judgment. Every Harvard campus is as good as any other. And those are as good as any Stanford campus and as good as any University of the Nation campus. But Harvard-Ithaca is good. Has a very good engineering school."

Jones shrugged. "I studied philosophy with a minor in community organizing at the Industrial and Labor Relations School. When I was young I thought I'd go into business but it's a lot of hard work and risk without any real reward. And my dad was in business and it didn't go well for him." Jones felt his face flush, regretting mentioning that last part.

Alisa was silent, listening, so Jones continued. "I thought of going into sports. I was pretty good at basketball. Only thing is that most spots on teams are reserved for white guys. Which is fair. So I studied community organizing. I originally wanted to be an engineer. But since the great Engineering Degree Giveaway to encourage more people to go into engineering, there were too many of them. It turns out there was a shortage of Tuvaluan community organizers, so I was 'strongly encouraged' to enter the field. I'm part Tuvaluan."

Alisa continued to look at him, silently. Jones continued to fill in the silence. "I was a community organizer for a while. But it wasn't challenging. It's pretty easy you know. I've always been a good speaker. So I'm told. And I like debate. When an opportunity opened up here I took it. I have to admit that my Tuvaluan ethnicity opened a lot of doors. Anyway, this isn't nearly as challenging as I thought it would be. There's not much debate and the facts are fed to me. But I get to put them together into coherent arguments. I get to influence people. I do good. I get to counter dangerous speech."

"Dangerous?" asked Alisa.

"Whoops. I mean controversial speech." The term 'dangerous' was dangerous to use. Employees of the Department of Fairness went through vigorous training consisting almost entirely of learning how not to use the word 'dangerous.' No speech is dangerous. Only controversial."

"Do you think any speech is dangerous?" she asked.

"No, no. That was a slip." Jones was embarrassed.

"I don't mean what does the department think? Or what does the government think? I mean what do you think?"

Jones looked around again. "I'm on company time," he replied. "While on company time I'm a company man and repeat the company creed." He smiled as if he were joking.

Alisa stared at him for a moment. He imagined those blue and green eyes were the flashing lights on top of a police car. "I'll ask you again when you're off company time. Let's hope you have a better answer then."

"Sure," he replied a little nervously. Alisa turned to go. "When?" he asked.

"When what?"

"When are we meeting off company time?"

She smiled. "Next Thursday? Right after work?"

"Sure." He watched her turn again and walk away. She made him a little uncomfortable. And a little nervous. But she also made him feel good. He smiled to himself. It was an interesting week so far.

Another Day at the Office

Maple Leaf Rag

Winston Jones walked home thinking about Alisa Rosenbaum. She was a mystery. She seemed out of place. Wherever she was, she seemed out of place. Too well-dressed; no one dressed up anymore. Why be so uncomfortable? He thinks:

I dress nicely because I go out to speak. I need to get people's attention. But I don't go overboard with it. I don't need to have my clothes perfectly pressed or stain-free. A wrinkle here, a spot of ketchup or mustard in a corner—it shows people that you're not better than them. We all have our imperfections. We all have a wrinkle or a spot somewhere, whether it shows or not. But Alisa looks perfect. Perfectly dressed. Perfectly groomed. Her hair is always combed when the style is to be loose and free and tangled. No one should pretend to be perfect, that's what we've learned. Striving for perfection is striving. Striving is competing. Competing means someone loses and feels really bad. No one has the right to make any other human being feel bad about something. About anything.

Yet Alisa looks perfect. She acts perfect. She even fixed my computer and made it perfect. Even her blue and green eyes are perfectly imperfect. And that perfection is perfectly appealing. Should I feel guilty about being attracted to perfection?

And what did she mean about dangerous speech? We all know that speech is not dangerous. We all have freedom of speech. But some speech hurts people and no one has the right to make any other human being feel bad about something. We have a society where no one gets hurt. The government makes certain of that. No bullies, no haters, no meanness. A virtual utopia. We still have a way to go—not everyone is happy. And certainly outside the United States there are many people who are unhappy. It's our job to make them happy. And to make sure the world is fair. And that people get balance and hear all sides of an argument. Particularly the right side. The happy side. That sounds funny. Childish. The happy side. Well, the fair side. It's important that people hear the ideas that are fair and just and that will make them happy. And that's called freedom of speech and is the very first of the 37 amendments to the U.S. Constitution.

The buildings got suddenly a bit cleaner, a bit better kept, and Jones knew he was on his block. He felt pride that his block was a little nicer, but why did those things that made him proud also make him feel guilty?

He had seen the flashing lights as he approached but he had filtered them out until he started getting closer. Several police cars were parked in the street and on the sidewalk at random angles like they had pulled up in a hurry to answer a dangerous call. Like in the movies. Jones got a little worried. Police cars were fairly common, but so many, all with their lights flashing, were not common. And in front of his building.

Gertrude Meyerson, in a flowered frock and bare feet, was yelling at one of the officers and he attempted to usher her away from the building and behind some sort of protective screen. About a dozen police officers milled about nervously, keeping their cars between the building and themselves.

An officer came up to Jones as he approached. "Move away from this building sir. You need to turn around and take a different route."

"I live here. This is my building. What's going on?"

"OK, OK. Do you have some ID? If you don't have any ID, then one will be provided for you because this is a free society and no one has the right to demand ID. You are aware of your right not to show ID?" Jones nodded but pulled out his ID card. The officer didn't look at it because of course he was not authorized to examine ID without a court order. He could only request it. "Good, good. Let's move you to a safe position behind this protective shield. Nothing's wrong and nothing's going to happen. This is just a precaution." He guided Jones toward the partition. Jones could make out Gertrude's words.

"He's got a gun! He's got a gun! You need to get him out of there!"

"Who has a gun, ma'am?"

"The teenager! The Canadian. The illegal damn Canadian teenager who took over my house!"

"OK, ma'am, you don't want me to cite you for hate speech, now. I realize you're upset so I'll let this go. Remember that no one is illegal or illegitimate. We're all created equal and are all equal in every way."

"He's got a gun! And he's in my house! He's illegal, damn it! He's in this country illegally and he's in my house illegally! And he's got a gun! And my babies are in there! Go in there and get him out!" Gertrude's ears were red from the cold. Or from anger.

"Ma'am, please calm down. Nothing good happens in anger. First we need to evaluate the situation. We're going to resolve this, but you need to calm down first so we can get the facts. Just take a few deep breaths. Calm down. We have this under control."

Gertrude took a few stuttered breaths. She wasn't calm but the officer was following procedure and sometimes that's the best you can do. "Now tell me the situation," said the officer.

"He came in this morning…"

The officer cut her off. "Who? Who is he? We need all the facts, ma'am."

"He's a lousy Canadian. He and his parents just moved in a few weeks ago. I complained to you people about it but you wouldn't do anything. "

The officer made a mental note about "lousy Canadians" and "you people." After this was all over, he might need to make a report on Ms. Meyerson. She sounds like she requires a little more sensitivity training. But for now, there was a more important situation to understand and act on.

"They just moved in and started cooking and rearranging furniture and… and… just living in my house."

"OK. There's nothing wrong there. A little uncomfortable, perhaps, but nothing wrong. When did the trouble start?"

"It started when they moved into my house!"

"I mean today's trouble, ma'am." It disheartened the officer to deal with someone so selfish and hateful, but he was trained to deal with such things.

"The kid, the teenager, came in this afternoon in a bad mood. I mean really bad. He and his parents were yelling in French. They don't speak English or Spanish. Only French. I don't know what the hell they were saying. If they're going to live in this country they should speak English or Spanish."

"So if he only speaks French, and you don't speak French, how do you know he has a gun?" The officer had a keen mind.

"He said he has a gun. He started yelling something in French and his parents ran out of the building. I came downstairs to see what was going on and he started yelling at me. He said in English, "I have a gun! I'm going to shoot someone! I have a gun!" I saw you passing by so I ran out to flag you down.

"I thought you said he only spoke French."

"He speaks some English. I guess. In the house he spoke French."

"So maybe he said something in French that sounds like 'I have a gun.' How would you know?"

Gertrude stared at the officer blankly.

"Did you do something to upset him? He's from Canada you know. His life has been terrible up to this point. He came here to find a better life and you try to kick him out of your house and insult him with your racist epithets. Of course he's angry. You would be angry if you went to Canada and they treated you that way. His anger is perfectly understandable."

Gertrude continued to stare blankly.

"The question now is whether he really has a gun or not."

"He said…"

"I know what you say he said. What if you heard wrong? What if he is only pretending to have a gun? To bolster his self esteem. To empower him against your disparagement. Do you know what would happen if I sent in a squad of armed officers and it turns out he doesn't have a gun? That he wasn't a risk whatsoever? I'd be fired. I would lose my job, and deservedly so."

"But my babies are in there…" Gertrude's voice was weak and hoarse.

"Yes and you seem to think that just because he's a Canadian, that he's dangerous. That he's going harm your kids, He's probably taking better care of them than you are. Canadians are very family oriented."

"But…"

"And do you know what would happen if one of my men got scared and shot this Canadian? Don't think that just because he's a Canadian that his life is worth any less than yours or mine. In fact, just the opposite If we shot an unarmed Canadian, and he died, I'd be in jail. And so would you. We'd all be in trouble for taking the life of an innocent person."

"But my babies are in there…"

At that moment a gunshot came from the building. The police officer turned to look. Gertrude Meyerson grabbed the gun from the officer's holster and ran toward the building, her frock flowing behind her like a cape. The officer called for her to stop, but she did not stop. He radioed the other officers. Another gunshot rang out. The officer yelled into his radio, "Go in! Go in! She has a gun! I repeat, she has a gun!"

Several other officers ran into the building. There was silence for ten, fifteen minutes. The front door opened and several policemen brought out Gertrude Meyerson. Tears streamed from her eyes, but she didn't make a sound. Her hands were cuffed behind her, but she walked out with her head high, defiant, as they walked her to a police car and put her inside.

"She's in trouble. She killed a man. Poor old lady, she's really in trouble. We could have handled the situation but she took justice into her own hands. Poor old lady. She's really in trouble."

Winston Jones learned the next day that the Canadian teenager had shot and killed Gertrude Meyerson's son-in-law when he tried to wrestle the gun away. Gertrude had found the Canadian with his gun pointed at her granddaughter when she shot him in the back. He died instantly.

The Doctor Is In

Winston Jones' night was rough. The scenes kept flashing into his head—the police cars surrounding the house, the first gunshot, Mrs. Meyerson running inside with gun in hand and cape flowing behind her, the other gunshots, Mrs. Meyerson handcuffed and walked outside but with her head high. He kept imagining the scenes inside the house—the Canadian yelling and threatening, waving his gun, struggling with Mrs. Meyerson's son-in-law, shooting him, being shot by Mrs. Meyerson. Bodies on the floor. Blood on the walls and floor. Her kids cowering, crying.

Jones tossed and turned all night trying to erase those scenes. The morning alarm finally rang. His eyelids were closed but he was fully conscious face up in his bed, his sheets damp with sweat. The alarm music faded up gently; it was classical music. Vivaldi's *Four Seasons*. It was his guilty pleasure, the music of old, dead, Western, white men. Not very popular these days, but strangely enough it soothed him. He always programmed a classical wakeup when he expected a difficult night.

The aromatherapy was set to lilac and pine. It was set to "subtle" so it smelled like lilac bushes and pine trees off in the distance. He lay on his back and envisioned himself lying in a field of grass on a late spring afternoon, the sun shining on his face, lilac bushes and other shrubs scattered throughout the field and pine trees surrounding it. His pounding heartbeat began to slow though it was still loud in his ears.

He imagined small birds—chickadees chirping among the trees and hummingbirds flittering among the bushes. A couple of deer grazed gracefully near the northern edge of the field. There was then a rustling in the bushes. A large bull moose appeared and began grazing with the much smaller deer that seemed not to notice. The moose moved closer to the deer, nudging one with its antlers. The nudged deer moved aside and continued grazing. The three seemed content for a while, but the moose moved again toward the deer, nudging it with its antlers. The nudged deer moved away but the other deer moved closer to the moose, puzzled.

The Doctor Is In

The moose pushed that deer away with its antlers and snorted at it. The second deer looked curiously at the moose, nodded at it, shrugged its shoulders, and moved away to join the first deer. The moose snorted again, its eyes fixed on the deer that were grazing a short distance away at this point.

The moose seemed frozen. Frosted air emanated from its nostrils despite the pleasantly warm, sunny atmosphere. The moose let out a deep, frightening growl and charged at the deer that looked up slowly to see the moose bearing down on them. They turned to run, but one was not quick enough. The moose pounced upon it, raised its antlered head to heaven, and once again roared. Then it brought its massive head down and bit into the deer under its hooves. Blood flowed onto the ground, spurted into the air.

Behind the moose the bushes began rustling again. The entire northern edge was rustling. Hundreds of Canadians appeared, their baguettes raised threateningly as they rushed toward him. He tried to get up but he was frozen in place. He turned to look southward to see the bushes rustling on that side too. A large furry creature, the size of a small bear, with a row of spines reaching from the neck to the base of the tail leapt over the jasmine bushes and hurtled toward him.

The beast from the south screeched as it ran, its fur matted and greasy, its spines sharp and glistening. The moose at the north growled as it tore into the deer with its powerful teeth, thrashing its head and throwing bloodied deer flesh all over. The Canadians shouted unintelligible French words as they ran toward him. The rest of the bushes and trees on all sides began rustling as people and beast prepared to enter the field when the field itself began to move and shake.

Jones woke up. He had finally dozed off but wished he hadn't. The sheets were soggier and wrinkled with his perspiration. The events of yesterday were weighing heavily on him. Actually he had been feeling down for some time now, but yesterday seemed to take a particular toll on him. Of course that made sense. He needed to talk to someone, to a friend. He would take a wellness day. That was justified for sure. He would call in unwell and talk to a friend.

Good Intentions

Jones got up slowly. Stooped over, he folded his hands behind his neck and tried to massage out the tension. He brought his hands up, wiped the sweat from his brow, then balled his fists and rubbed his eyes before spreading his hands over the stubble of hair on his head. He stood slowly and took a deep breath before moving into the bathroom where the cold water felt good on his face.

After brushing his teeth, showering and shaving, he felt a bit better. Breakfast tasted bland and he knew things were still not right with him, so he called in unwell, put on his hologoggles, and logged into MyFace. He was greeted by the MyFace receptionist, a sexy Puerto Rican blonde, very thin in low cut top and short dark hair that swept across one eye.

"How can I help you?" purred the receptionist with a slight accent.

Jones tapped through a few variations until he found one he liked better—an elder Asian lady, soft spoken and heavyset. This avatar seemed more appropriate to his mood.

"How can I help you?" said the lady soothingly with a slight accent.

"Friend please," he said.

"Personal or professional?" asked the lady.

"Professional."

"Please select from these common types," she said as a book appeared in front of his face on the left, "or select from these custom attributes." She pointed to his right and another book appeared. Both books floated in front of him. Had he asked for a personal friend, a directory of his online friends would have appeared. He had over five thousand online friends from all over the world. But today felt like he needed a professional, so he scanned the list before coming to one that sounded particularly good:

Dr. Eliza Weizenbaum

Interactive, Non-Judgmental Psychiatry

The Doctor Is In

The description did not say much, but it felt good. And even the doctor's name felt good for some reason. He tapped on her name and was immediately transported to her office.

Dr. Weizenbaum's default avatar was a woman in her sixties or seventies, Caucasian, gray and white hair with a slight wave that reached just above her shoulders. She had soft, rounded features and wore glasses with a frame so thin the lenses appeared to hover above her nose. Or maybe they were hovering. She was average height and average weight, and she wore a flowered frock that fit loosely and draped to just above the floor. She held a notebook and pen in her hand, which was quaint since no one ever used a pen anymore.

"I'm Dr. Eliza. I'll give you a minute to get comfortable," she said smiling. Her small teeth were perfectly even.

A menu hovered to the side and Jones could have chosen several other characteristics—race, age, height, weight, sex, sexual preference, sexual orientation, sexual proclivity, and many other characteristics on various menus and submenus. He found her to be soothing so he made no changes. Anyway, he often liked the randomness of a new avatar. He liked the feeling of adapting to a new person—a new personality—rather than customizing every new encounter to meet his own expectations. But he was unusual that way.

The room was modern and bright with lots of primary colors. It was too happy, too cheery. He wondered if it was adjusted to some aspect of his personality or meant to remind him of some other place he visited online. Possibly the search engine had kept track of his online visits and created some Roschian prototype of his most comfortable surroundings. More likely his online surfing had been tracked by advertisers and this office configuration was most conducive to his buying habits. Or maybe this was just the default office setup. Regardless of the reason, it wasn't what he wanted right now, and it didn't seem to fit with Dr. Eliza anyway.

So he tapped a button in front of him; the room dissolved into a pleasant grass field on a sunny day that made him gradually more uncomfortable as it reminded him of his dream. He tapped again and he was floating on raft on a deep blue sea and Dr. Eliza hovered above him, smiling. It felt odd—like a religious experience—and he was getting a little queasy anyway. So he went through the menus and found what he wanted, a décor from the early twentieth century. It had lots of earth colors. There was a mahogany desk, a padded leather chair, and a couch. The couch felt right. It was draped with a busy Persian carpet with dizzying patterns of angular red and black lines surrounding flower-like abstract designs. On top were plush cushions. Unlike the more antiseptic leather couches in old movies, this one was the actual one used by Sigmund Freud himself. Well, at least a digital reproduction.

Jones sank into the couch; Dr. Eliza sat on the chair and began, "Please, describe your problems."

"I witnessed a shooting," said Jones.

"Go on," said Dr. Eliza.

"Well, people were killed. In the house next to mine."

"And how did that make you feel?"

Jones thought that was an odd question. "Umm… not good."

"And why do you think that made you feel not good?"

"Mrs. Meyerson's son-in-law died. The son-in-law was killed by an intruder."

"And who is Mrs. Meyerson?"

"The lady next door. A nice lady." He paused. "She's going to jail now." He noticed that Dr. Eliza held onto that notepad and pen, but never used them.

"Why is she going to jail now?"

"For killing the man who shot her son-in-law."

"Killing is wrong."

The Doctor Is In

"Yes, of course killing is wrong. But isn't it right sometimes?"

Dr. Eliza suddenly made a note in her notebook. It was probably for effect, Jones thought, because she's a digital avatar. It bothered him, though. Maybe that was the desired effect? Now he was getting paranoid. Seems ironic—getting paranoid at the psychiatrist's office.

"Go on, Mr. Jones," prompted Dr. Eliza.

"I just think she was protecting her family. That should be ok."

"Maybe the police can protect them better than an ordinary citizen. The police are trained in empathetic behavior and restraint."

"But the police weren't doing anything. Her son was killed."

"The police are trained in empathetic behavior and restraint. We mustn't take the law into our own hands."

"Don't we have a right to take action on our own behalf? Isn't that a requirement for survival?"

Dr. Eliza suddenly was scribbling in the notebook. She looked up. "Our emotions can get in the way of our judgment. The police are trained to be fair and balanced. You may do your best, but you have prejudices of which you aren't even aware. Perhaps one dislikes undocumented immigrants and so is inclined to take unlawful action against one."

"How did you know the man was undocumented?"

A little more note taking. "Who was undocumented?"

"The intruder. The man that Mrs. Meyerson shot. How did you know?"

"You see, your unconscious prejudices have led you to believe I was talking about you when I was giving a generic example. This is why we trust important decisions to the government." Dr. Eliza stared at Jones and smiled. Her arms relaxed and dropped to her sides, notebook in one hand, pen in the other. "Go on," she said.

"It's not just the shooting yesterday. I've felt uncomfortable for a while."

"What makes you feel uncomfortable?"

"I was in court a little while ago."

"Did you commit a crime?" Dr. Eliza's arms started to rise slowly.

"No, I was a witness to a crime."

Dr. Eliza's arms relaxed again, down at her sides. "Go on."

"Actually not a crime. An incident. A young man was accused of a crime. A hate crime."

"How do you feel about hate crimes?"

"They're wrong of course."

"Good. Go on."

"But the young man didn't do anything wrong."

"And he was acquitted?"

"Yes."

"Then justice prevailed."

"He was acquitted because of his race. Or his sexual orientation. I'm not really sure."

"He was innocent, correct?"

"Yes."

"Then justice prevailed."

"Shouldn't a person be judged by their actions? By the content of their character?"

Dr. Eliza's arms came back up and she began scribbling once again.

The Doctor Is In

"The Reverend Dr. Martin Luther King Junior was a great man, wasn't he?"

"Pardon?"

"You just quoted him. 'I have a dream that my four little children will one day live in a nation where they will not be judged by the color of their skin but by the content of their character.'"

"Oh yes, I hadn't realized."

"Perhaps one day we will reach Dr. King's goal. But we live in a different time. We can now trace racial information using clouds of supercomputers performing sophisticated DNA analysis with giant databases. We do not judge people by the color of their skin, but we can trace even the smallest bit of racial inheritance and then right wrongs proportionally. We have transcended Dr. King's society. Judging people by their skin color is wrong. And simplistic. We can now trace racial characteristics, and sexual characteristics, through multiple generations and equalize everyone in every way. We can compensate for prejudice 120 years ago against your great-great grandfather who was denied a job because of prevailing prejudices at the time."

"But everyone has hurdles to overcome, don't they? Can we really make every outcome equal? Can we really make every person equal? And do we want to? And who has that authority to do it? You? Me? The government? Who decides and why should they?" These questions had been going around in his mind for some time but he hadn't been able to verbalize them. He looked up at Dr. Eliza. Her eyes were closed. Her pen was pressed unmoving into the notebook. Her smile was wide, her teeth like a perfect row of white corn kernels on a cob. She was silent.

"Dr. Eliza?" he asked.

She did not move.

"Dr. Eliza?" She was frozen. He tried to get up but found himself frozen. His arms would not move. His legs would not move. It was difficult to breath. He felt a panic.

Good Intentions

He tore off his hologoggles. His computer screen was a solid blue with small white letters. His computer had crashed. He sighed and his heart rate slowed gradually. Reaching over to his keyboard, he pressed the familiar Control-Alt-Delete key combination to reboot.

The Doctor Is In

Drifting Off

The psychiatrist consultation hadn't really worked its purpose. Winston Jones was still edgy, maybe more so than before the visit. That night the visions of Mrs. Meyerson running into her house and the subsequent sounds of gunshots still played over and over in his head. Then the psychiatrist's statements started getting mixed in. Following the gunshot sound, he heard the echo of "killing is wrong" and "we mustn't take the law into our own hands." Of course these things were true. So why did it sound wrong? Simplistic? Was Mrs. Meyerson wrong? Of course she was wrong. Important decisions must be left to those experts who are trained in making these kinds of important decisions. What if everyone just went around killing people? What if everyone tried to make important decisions about their lives and they screwed up their lives? Or they screwed up society? The government can make decisions that are right for everyone and then we're all happy. So why aren't I happy? Maybe we're all happier than we'd otherwise be. On average. Maybe some are happier and others not. Weren't we taught the answers to these questions in school? And why do all these simple questions lead to complicated questions?

Jones took a sleeping pill—he needed his sleep to be sharp for work. He could take another wellness day tomorrow, but he felt a responsibility to work. And maybe work would take his mind off things. As the pill kicked in, the images and sound bites begin to fade. Alisa Rosenbaum faded into view. He was back in the psychiatrist's office, lying on the couch in pajamas. She was the psychiatrist, sitting upright in the chair, notepad in her hand. She was dressed in her typical blue blazer and white blouse. The blouse was unbuttoned and he could see just a glimpse of enticing cleavage. "I'm worried," he said to her. He felt on the edge of crying. She stood up, placed the notepad down gently, and smiled at him. He was nervous. And excited. He knew where this was going, and he felt good. And bad. Nervous. And obviously excited. She walked toward him slowly, sensually. She continued past him, to the bookshelf and pulled a thick book from the shelf. She hesitated for a moment, thinking, then ran her finger sensuously over the books to another, thin one, and pulled it out.

Alisa walked back to Jones and bent down to face him. Her lips were cherry red. She leaned in and he thought she was going to kiss him. The pill's magic began working stronger and he lost hold of the realization that this was a dream.

"This will help," she said slowly, her lips forming each syllable perfectly. Her breath was hot. His eyes widened and his pulse picked up. She handed him the larger book. He had trouble focusing. The title was "Capitalism and Freedom." He took it from her and she immediately handed him the smaller one. By now his ability to focus was just about gone as he drifted further into unconsciousness. He could make out cartoon animals on the cover. It looked like a children's book. The books and Alisa and the bookshelves and the entire room floated away. He still had more questions.

"Five, four, three, two, one," called out Morrie Jones and Winston Jones in unison. Eight-year-old Winston pressed the switch that sent an electrical signal to ignite the rocket engine in the model Atlas rocket. Nothing happened. Winston shrugged. "What's with that, Dad?" he asked.

"I don't know," said Morrie Jones. "Sometimes things just don't work out as planned.'

Sometimes Winston thought his dad made everything into a life lesson. Most of the time that was ok, but sometimes it was annoying. Just sometimes it was really transparent. He didn't think his dad had planned this to go wrong—just to teach Winston a lesson—but it was a possibility. "What now?" he asked.

"Well, we wait a minute. If nothing happens I walk over carefully and take a look."

"Me too."

"It could go off."

Good Intentions

"So?"

"Let's wait first and see." Morrie and Winston waited a few yards away. The miniature Atlas rocket was frozen on its launch platform, pointing straight to the sky, unmoving. A minute or two passed.

"OK, we're going in," said Morrie. "Stay behind me," he added.

Morrie moved forward slowly, continually crouching as if they were sneaking up on the rocket. Winston was behind him, a miniature duplicate of Morrie, his arm and leg movements nearly synchronized with his dad's. As they walked, their sneakers stirred up small clouds of yellow mud dust from the dry, dead park. Perfect for a rocket launch site, but only slightly reminiscent of the playground it had once been. The sun was bright on this summer day. The sky was blue and cloudless, inviting the rocket that would not budge.

As they got closer a little stream of smoke drifted out of the rocket's butt.

"The rocket just farted, dad," said Winston giggling.

"Hold up," said Morrie, putting both arms out like a crossing guard.

With suddenness the rocket's tail let out a big burst of smoke and with a whooshing noise shot off its launch pad and into the sky. "Head for the hills," said Morrie, laughing, turning, scooping up his son, and trotting backwards, both of them keeping their eyes on the rocket.

The rocket was spiraling rather than shooting arrow-like upward. The spiraling grew more pronounced as it gained altitude, then suddenly flipped over into a tight arc and continued its engine-propelled flight downward. Toward the two of them like an angry Frankenstein monster bent on it creators' destruction.

Morrie Jones let out a rare obscenity. Their laughter stopped and he began running for real, carrying little Winston on his shoulders. He kept his head turned, looking upward and over his shoulder at the missile above them. "Hold on," he yelled. Morrie tried to zig and zag but it felt pointless because he could not predict the rockets trajectory. It just seemed like he had to take some action.

In the few seconds as the rocket approached, it seemed to be heat-seeking and actually targeting them. "Hold on!" shouted Morrie to Winston who did not need to be told but was actually choking the air out of his dad's throat. Morrie fell to his knees just as the rocket whizzed by Winston's nose and slammed into the dry earth in front of them. A cloud of dust flew up everywhere, blinding them. It took several minutes to clear, revealing a three-foot ditch right at their feet. Winston started sobbing. Morrie pulled Winston off his shoulders and held him in front of him. Little rivulets of tears flowed through the dust mask on Winston's face. "Are you hurt?" asked Morrie. "Are you ok?"

"The rocket is broken," said Winston through his sobbing. "We spent all that time building it and it's gone. All that time wasted. The rocket wasted. Everything wasted."

Morrie was silent for a moment, then burst out laughing—his deep, booming, echoing laugh.

Winston was puzzled, stopping crying long enough to contort his face into a terrible pout.

Morrie said "If everything had gone right, we would have shot a rocket into the sky like we usually do. It would have parachuted back like it always does. We would have packed it up, gone out for ice cream, and gone home satisfied."

"Yeah," responded Winston.

"Instead we were just attacked by a crazy rocket from outer space," said Morrie. "It chased us down and blew a gigantic hole right in front of us. We could have been hurt but we're fine. We just had one of those once-in-a-lifetime experiences. I'd say this was a very successful day."

"But the rocket is gone... And we failed."

Morrie grew momentarily serious. "It's only a failure if we didn't learn anything from it. Did you learn anything?"

Winston thought for a moment. "I learned we need to have a more reliable ignition system. Maybe more voltage. Or a lower resistance triggering wire."

"Good," said Morrie cheerfully. "I think the rocket fins may not have been as straight as they should have been. Or maybe they were too close to the center of gravity making it unstable. We can test that when we get home."

"How?" asked Winston.

"I don't know. We can grab some ice cream and brainstorm about it."

"OK," replied Winston. How did his dad turn everything into a life lesson, he wondered as they walked toward the launch pad to pack everything up.

Ten-year-old Winston was accompanying his dad to work and skipping slightly with pride. He liked when his dad took him to work. He liked the cool machinery and could not wait for the day when he could build and fix some of those machines. Right alongside his dad. Right now his dad let him watch and sometimes, under very careful supervision that Winston regretted, adjust some valve or connect some wire.

Morrie and Winston Jones walked side-by-side along Wacker Drive. Winston had no difficulty understanding why Chicago was called The Windy City because the wind was strong enough to cause a physical impediment to his walking. His dad, who was much larger and thus offered more wind resistance, did not seem to be effected, and so Winston kept looking up to see his dad ahead of him. Winston would scurry up to his side, only to lose ground again later.

Morrie Jones was deep in thought about the projects on which his small company was working. He thought about cash flow issues and personnel issues and taxes. His mind was running through various scenarios, rethinking them, and rerunning them. A flurry of snow started. The sparse flakes pinged his face and bounced off without him noticing. Winston noticed when they hit his own face, each one stinging a little bit. He pulled his collar up around his chin.

A crowd of people were gathered ahead on the street. They were waiting for taxis or in line to get into a building or just milling around—Winston could not tell. But he saw them ahead and saw his father, lost in thought, heading for them. Winston could almost see the events unfold before they actually did. His dad barreled his way through the crowd, bumping hard against a couple of the men.

"Hey," shouted one of the men.

Morrie Jones turned around, still mostly lost in thought but also looking for Winston to make his way through the crowd.

"Hey," repeated the man, looking at Morrie.

Morrie was staring back, but still his mind was going through business scenarios, bidding on new customers, examining ways to bring down costs, thinking of ways to attract new business. Morrie was also thinking about Winston and when he saw Winston wiggle through the crowd and approach him, Morrie turned around to continue his march along Wacker Drive. But the man's near whisper drifted into his thoughts and abruptly interrupted them. "Stupid nigger," he heard him say.

Morrie stopped, turned slowly, and faced the man who had said those hateful words. Morrie stood glaring at the white man. He took three long steps up to the man and inches from his face said quietly but unmistakably, "Don't ever say something like that to me. Ever." He paused and continued to glare at the man.

The crowd around the man had gone silent. The man held his ground and attempted to look unfazed, but it was clear from the twitch in his cheek and short, sudden intake of air that he was not so calm, at least a little afraid. He said nothing.

Morrie was about average height but broad and muscular and with his deep voice and chiseled features he was intimidating. When he wanted to be. And he wanted to be now. "Ever," he repeated. "Especially not in front of my son," he said slowly, grinding his clenched teeth at the end of the sentence and pointing down toward Winston but not taking his eyes off the man.

The man blinked and Morrie was aware of the water accumulating at the bottom of his eyes. Morrie knew he had had an effect. He turned slowly, his back to the man, walked toward Winston, and kept going along Wacker Drive.

The muscles of Morrie's body had all tensed as could be seen from his now stilted gait. Winston followed him down the street, partly scared from the incident, partly proud of his strong, fierce dad. As they continued walking, Morrie's gait smoothed as his muscles relaxed. He slowed his pace and it became less mechanical. Though he tried to continue thinking about his business, his thoughts kept returning to the white man he had just confronted. Eventually he stopped walking. Winston caught up as he saw his dad press the palms of his hands on his forehead and wipe them down his face as if clearing away some film. He turned to his son and crouched down to face him.

"You see what I just did?" he asked.

"Sure dad, you stood up to that man."

"Don't you do that," he said. "Learn from my mistakes."

Winston was confused. "But dad. You always told me to stand up for what I believe in."

"Yes, but I stood up for nothing just now."

"He called you the N-word."

"You know what. I bumped into him and didn't say anything."

"But dad… the N-word!"

"You know, maybe that man's a bigot. Maybe he's stupid. Maybe he got angry and something stupid just popped out of his mouth. Whatever the reason, I let it control me. I let it drive me to do something stupid. What did I prove by confronting him like that?"

"That you're stronger than him. Braver than him." Winston was on the verge of tears. He had just seen his dad at his best—strong, powerful, uncompromising—and here he dad was telling him it was wrong.

"No I told him that I was weaker than him. Because I couldn't control my emotions. Because I let a word bother me."

"But…"

"You know how we show people we're as good as them? You know how we show people we're better than them?'

Winston stared blankly.

"By being better than them," answered Morrie Jones to his own question. "By being more successful in school. By being more successful in sports. By being more successful in business. By being successful."

"We're taught that people like that are holding people like us back."

Morrie started to get angry, then calmed himself. "You know what holds us back? We hold ourselves back."

"But some people *discrimate* against us," said Winston. "They teach us that in school. The white people made us slaves. Held us back."

"Are you a slave?"

"No. But my great grandfather was a slave. You told me that."

Morrie Jones looked around before noticing an Asian man hailing a cab. He pointed at him. "See that guy? A few generations ago his family was probably taken from their home and sent to an internment camp during World War II."

Winston looked at the man carefully.

Good Intentions

Morrie Jones looked around again and saw a man in a black overcoat with a thick beard and long side locks curling from under his wide-brim black hat. Morrie pointed at him. "See that guy? A few generations ago most of his family was probably taken from their homes in Germany or Poland and murdered for no reason at all."

Winston shuddered.

Then Morrie Jones pointed at a nicely dressed white man as he walked by carrying a leather briefcase. "See that guy? You know what he and his family went through?"

Winston shook his head.

"Neither do I. But everyone has gone through something. We don't go through life feeling sorry for ourselves or making excuses that we have it worse than the next guy. We go through life being the best we can. And for all the people that try to hold us back, we work harder and don't let them. You got that?"

Winston nodded.

"Good," said his dad and smiled. "Then let's go and be successful—do a great job, build something useful and reliable, give people jobs, and make a heck of a lot of money. OK?"

"OK!" said Winston cheerfully.

Morrie put his hand on Winston's shoulder. "Maybe you can do some electrical work today. You like electrical work, right?"

"Sure do," said Winston smiling, and skipping to keep up with his dad's quick pace.

Twelve-year-old Winston knocked on the door to his dad's office. "Come," he heard his dad say just barely audible. Winston opened the door slowly to see his dad behind his large wooden desk amid piles of papers and books. A large computer screen on the desk partially hid his father's face, which rested in the palms of both hands.

Drifting Off

Morrie Jones' stern, imposing features had softened and drooped in the last year. His once sturdy build was a bit pudgy and he had developed a paunch. Part of growing old, thought Winston, but it had seemed to happen so quickly, not unnoticeably slowly as he had expected. His dad's movements had slowed too and he often seemed tired these days. Too tired to do much together. Anyway Winston was growing older and hanging out with his dad was not as high on his priority list.

"Hey dad," said Winston softly.

His dad looked up wearily.

"Just came to see if you want to watch some TV tonight."

"No," came his dad's reply. The speed of the reply hurt a bit.

"OK. Just checking." Winston stopped and looked at his dad. He wanted to say something else, but was not sure what. "What are you doing?" he eventually asked.

"Nothing," replied his dad then added, "just trying to make ends meet. How did I do this? Things seemed so good. How did I let this happen?"

"What dad? Let what happen?"

"You know son, sometimes things don't go as planned. Remember that. Make your plans and have your contingency plans, but sometimes even those don't work out. Sometimes you have to take drastic measures."

"What do you mean, dad?" Winston was getting frightened but he didn't really know why.

Morrie looked at his son silently. Sadly.

"Good night dad," said Winston, unsure of what to say. He turned and started to leave.

"Winston?"

Winston turned around.

"How about a hug?'

"Sure, dad." It seemed like an odd question. His dad had never asked him for a hug, he just took it. But Winston obliged and walked to his dad who stood up and gave him a strong, squeezing hug. Winston was about to complain—it was a little too tight, a little uncomfortable—but then it ended and his father sat back down, staring at the papers in front of him on the desk. Winston quietly left the room. As he closed the door he heard his dad softly humming some song. What was that song?

Winston's dream turned to darkness. He was floating in darkness. A gunshot broke the silence. Winston Jones woke up abruptly, heart racing, frightened. He wasn't sure if the gunshot in his dream was the one that killed Gertude Meyerson's son-in-law or the one that killed the Canadian in her house or the one that his dad fired into his own head. But he was sure it was one of them.

Drifting Off

Winning the Lottery

The next morning, nearing his office building, Jones still felt uncomfortable. His thoughts from the night before, including the dream, were vague and shadowy—a result of the sleeping pill. He also had that feeling of being watched that he seemed to be having more often these days. It bothered him. Was he becoming paranoid? Living in utopia and not happy. Something was definitely wrong. Maybe he should schedule a visit with a real psychiatrist. Of course, that could be weeks or more before he could have an appointment. Scheduling time with real, live medical practitioners was discouraged, but since he worked for the government, maybe he could pull some strings and get an expedited approval. Then again most people worked for the government, so it probably wouldn't matter.

Jones pulled his overcoat collar tighter around his neck. It was sunny out, but not warm. Throngs of business people filled the sidewalks bustling toward their jobs in one of the many skyscrapers along Broad Street. Everyone had a job. There was a rumor that the government paid homeless people to put on suits and coats and just walk back and forth along Broad Street, looking intent on reaching their destinations and getting down to work. Some of these business people did look a little shaggy, but not everyone made hygiene their first priority. The homeless had disappeared from the streets over the last decade due to government assistance for job training, medical care, self-esteem workshops, and government jobs. All those years of politicians deriding these efforts, and more importantly throwing up roadblocks. When those politicians had finally been defeated, and the government was unified under a single political party following the Warm War, these programs could take full effect and raise all of society. Well, not raise all society, but equalize all society. We are all equal in all ways, he thought, echoing the government's slogan that appeared on currency and government buildings, and legal documents, and, well, seemingly everywhere.

"Mr. Jones."

Winning the Lottery

Jones stopped and turned to see a tall, thin man in a dark black overcoat and a fedora that hid most of his face except for his eyes, two bright white orbs seeming to float under the hat. At first Jones thought he had misheard, and anyway Jones is a pretty common name. So he began to walk again.

"Mr. Jones I'd like to talk to you." Jones turned back to the man. A Cheshire Cat smile appeared under the fedora and under the floating eyes. Or was it a grimace? Hard to tell. "Would you come with me, please."

The man said it ominously. It was a statement, not a question. Jones would always wonder why he complied so easily. Something in the man's manner spoke of power and persuasion. Everything he said seemed official. And though said without much volume or inflexion, everything he said seemed final and not to be disobeyed.

The man motioned toward a big, limousine, perfectly shiny and clean and boot black. As Jones watched, the rear door of the car opened slowly. The inside was also black. A large hand reached out, grabbed the roof of the car, and physically pulled the rest of a very, very large man out of the car, like a crowbar plying this massive human mound that had been squooshed inside. Jones thought he heard a pop like a wine cork and a whoosh like the rush of air into the car. The man was big and round and dressed in a fine, expensive Italian suit. He looked at Jones, his eyebrows forming a V. Jones shuddered.

Rom Automatic, the thin man in the black overcoat, nudged Jones. "Over here," he said, motioning to the small, yellow, electric Teslius minicar in front of the limo. The big man walked slowly past Jones, still staring at him, then smiled and nodded as he passed, and let out a laugh.

Rom gently touched Jones' elbow and maneuvered him toward the minicar. It was one of the four-seaters, but not much larger than the two-seater. Rom opened the passenger side door and motioned toward the backseat. Jones pushed up the front passenger seatback and climbed into the backseat. His tall, lanky frame barely fit and he had to make several starts and twists and turns before being able to place his butt in the seat.

His knees rode up into his face and his right foot was wedged in between the seat and the door. He made subtle attempts to wriggle it free, not wanting to draw attention to himself.

Rom Automatic entered from the other side of the car and though not as tall as Jones, he still struggled to get in, attempting to coordinate with the driver who was pressed against the steering wheel but wriggling his shoulders back and forth. After some brusque instructions and commands between the driver and Rom, he was able to settle into the back seat next to Jones. He brushed down the creases in his overcoat and twisted his fedora back on straight, obviously annoyed at the effort. He had wanted this to go smoothly, coolly, in his complete control.

Jones was silent.

"This is a good day for you, Mr. Jones. A very good day. Maybe your best day ever."

Jones nodded uncertainly.

"Have you ever thought of making things better in the world, Mr. Jones? Ever thought of doing something for the general good?"

"Yes, my job…" Jones' voice trailed off.

"Yes, of course. Your job is very important. Fair and balanced. Getting out the word. Getting out the opposing views that may not otherwise get heard. Making sure the people hear the truth. Very important indeed."

"How do you know about my job?" asked Jones. He realized he'd seen the man before at some of his speeches. And that day in court when he gave Jones his business card. Was the man a fan? Or something more sinister? He rubbed the dampness from his palms.

"I've been watching you, Mr. Jones. A number of us have been. We're very impressed."

"Impressed?"

"Yes, yes. You'll find out more when we get to our destination. I appreciate your patience."

The city was crowded and traffic was slow. The car moved in fits and starts and made little progress. A car was stalled in the intersection bringing even this molasses slow pace to a complete stop. Both backseat travelers were getting uncomfortable with the silence. Rom broke the silence with a sharp command to the driver. "Fred, get us going. Just go around this. I see openings—just gun it."

"Can't do that," said Fred, a skinny man but with a pot belly and a strong Brooklyn accent. "Electric, remember? And it's got the mandated acceleration controls. Can't just gun it."

"This has the a-controls still active? You didn't disconnect it?"

"Course not. That's illegal." Fred gave a goofy grin and nodded in the direction of Jones.

"Of course, of course. Sorry for implying…"

"I'll try signaling. Someone'll let us in." Fred put his left arm out the window and began pointing and waving at passing drivers. Their faces were positioned straight ahead, but their eyes sometimes glanced furtively at the car. They all kept going.

Rom looked at Jones who was watching him the whole time. Rom smiled uncomfortably. Turning to Fred he said, "Gun it."

Fred pressed the accelerator and the car lurched forward. The passengers slammed their heads back against the headrests. It wasn't that the car moved fast, it was mostly just unexpected. Fred found an opening, or made one, and continued. The pace of traffic was still slow, though.

The car eventually pulled up to one of the large steel and glass skyscrapers in downtown Philly. Workers filed busily in and out of the building whose façade looked like a blowtorch was taken to it, the steel and glass dripping down toward the workers below. Above the entrance a sign declared in big, bold, black letters, "Stephen Holl Government

Building Number 17." To Jones, the building was a nightmarish block that was dark and disturbing.

The ride had been eerily quiet. Rom and Jones had stared out their windows, faces turned from each other. Jones had attempted surreptitiously to wriggle his foot free, to no avail. Upon reaching their destination, Rom simply said "We're here" and exited the car. He came to the passenger side and opened the door, freeing Jones' foot that had gone numb. Jones exited the car, stumbled, and fell to the sidewalk. Rom picked him up, explaining, "This is impressive. The building, the people. But there's no need to be nervous," and led him into the building. They passed the security guards at the front, who both nodded to Rom, and continued through the scanners and turnstiles. They rode an elevator to floor 102, but the doors did not open. They waited a moment before the elevator started up again and continued to the unmarked 103rd floor.

The elevator doors opened to a brightly lit hallway ending in two large, elaborate marble doors. As they approached, the doors slowly swung open to reveal a room with a large, round oak table in the center. People in grey suits sat at the table, smiling vacantly and looking in his direction. Jones smelled something in the air, something vaguely familiar, slightly caustic, slightly stinging his throat causing a sudden coughing fit. The people in the room patiently waited for him to recover, their grins not fading, their eyes locked onto him.

A woman stood. "Welcome, Mr. Jones. We're honored to have you here. Please take a seat." She motioned toward the empty chair at the table. Jones sat hesitantly. Rom Automatic took the empty seat opposite him. Each seat at the table was then occupied.

The short man rose. "Before we begin… Mr. Jones what is your opinion of national monetary policy? Do you have a position on monetary policy?"

The others looked annoyed at the short man. Rom spoke: "Hector. We'll have time for that later."

Hector took a breath to speak but reconsidered and sat down.

"Mr. Jones," said Rom, "we have been watching you for some time and we are impressed. Very impressed." Murmurs and nods around the table. Excerpt for Hector who was pouting. "We have seen your poise and composure in difficult situations. We have seen how you can quickly and flawlessly debate an ideologue, even when it requires reaching for arguments that may seem, well, distasteful or bizarre. We've seen how you can put together words eloquently to present ideas in persuasive form. "

Jones blushed and felt awkward at the praise.

"In addition to being articulate and bright, you are clean and a nice-looking guy." More murmurs and nods around the table. Jones was not only uncomfortable, but the description struck him as odd, maybe insulting but he wasn't really sure. It seemed out of place. But then what was this place? How could something be out of place in a place he did not understand in the first place? Why was he here?

The woman who had greeted Jones stood up; Rom nodded to her and sat down. She was older, maybe in her seventies, though well-preserved with bleach blonde hair and only a few wrinkles probably placed strategically by the surgeons to appear natural rather than sculpted. Her figure was stocky under the dark faux fur-lined coat that seemed like it should be too warm in the comfort of the temperature-controlled room. "Mr. Jones, we believe that you have a great destiny. A great purpose in life. Have you ever felt that?"

Jones thought for a moment. "Not really," he responded.

That's odd, she thought. Most people feel they have some great destiny. We teach our children that they all have some great destiny. This man truly is unique. She continued. "Well you do, Mr. Jones. You have the ability to change our country for the better. You have the chance to change the world for the better. That would be good, yes?"

"Well, yes," said Jones hesitantly.

Hector stood up. "And monetary policy. And foreign policy. And military and social policy." The woman looked at Hector scornfully and he sat down.

"Mr. Jones," continued the woman, "you know that The Lottery is coming up in just over a month."

"Of course, but…"

"What if we told you that you have won The Lottery?"

Jones swallowed hard. He was now more confused. "How could I have won The Lottery if it hasn't occurred yet?"

There were chuckles, winks, and nods around the table. "Mr. Jones, what do you think it takes to be the leader of the free world?"

"Nothing," replied Jones immediately, wondering if this was a test of some sort.

"And why do you say that?"

"We learn that in school."

"Do you think it takes no skill at all to run our country?"

Jones continued. "In the early twenty-first century people realized that anyone could become president. That the president simply represented the people and it was the people who made the real decisions. The president had to represent those decisions to our citizens and to the other politicians and to the world. So yes, it takes no skill. And in that case, in order to be fair to the population, everyone is entered into The Lottery, regardless of race, religion, creed, gender, sexual preference, sexual orientation, heritage, political affiliation, height, weight, skin color, ability, or citizenship status. And the president is then chosen fully at random. It's perhaps the most egalitarian act in all of the civilized world. It proves the fairness of the United States not only to its own citizens but to those of the rest of the world." Instinctively, a tear welled up in the bottom of Jones' eye and overflowed down his cheek.

Winning the Lottery

There was silence in the room for a moment before the woman continued. "Yes, yes. The Lottery is one of the great achievements of our great country. Yet you stated that the president must represent an entire country, an entire citizenship, even represent non-citizens. The president represents an ideal. What good would it do if the president could not articulate important ideas and policies?"

Another person at the table added, "What if the president were so disfigured that people could not concentrate on his important words?"

Yet another person asked "What if the president had a voice like fingernails on a blackboard?"

"What if the president never washed?" added another.

"What if the president had no concept of foreign policy or monetary policy?" asked Hector, followed by a brief silence in the room.

"Well, if the president did not have a good 'face' so to speak, then the message might not get out. After The Lottery was instituted, and after a few failed presidencies, the Electoral Committee was formed. To guide the process. To make sure that the leader of the free world is a person who can actually lead the free world. Oh, and the president does have to be well-spoken and smart and present a good appearance."

"But what about fairness?" asked Jones.

"This is fairness," replied the woman. "We choose a person who has maximal 'demographic satisfiability.' This includes appearance, expressiveness, and likeability. We have computers calculating multidimensional correlation of over 271 characteristics to find potential candidates. Of course, we also surveil the candidates. Our computer chose you and we agreed. You are well-spoken, attractive, and you have a unique and positive mix of racial and ethnic characteristics including Hispanic and Tuvaluan, both of which are in high regard this year."

"But what about The Lottery?" asked Jones.

"We take care of that for you," said a voice from the back of the room.

"Yes, continued the woman. Understand that The Lottery is still random. The lottery is processed by our computers, the same computers that found you to be an ideal candidate, so in effect it is all the same."

Jones tried to wade through that logic. "But I have no experience. And no knowledge of government policy."

"Exactly. You're fresh. You have new ideas. We can help you with that. We have great ideas, but you can add your own perspective. Anyway, ultimately these things are determined by the voters anyway."

Jones thought he saw a few smirks, winks, and nods around the table, but could not be sure. "I just don't know," he said. "I just don't know."

Rom Automatic rose and the woman sat down. "It's a great privilege," said Rom. He walked over to Jones.

"I just don't know," repeated Jones.

Rom put his hand on Jones' shoulder. "Of course, you need time to absorb all of this. It's a lot to take in. Let me walk you to the door."

Jones stood and Rom led him back through the great marble doors that closed automatically behind him. Short wisps of smoke snaked out from behind the doors. Rom led Jones to the elevator and pressed a button.

"Sleep on this. Process all this. Take your time. But remember that this is a great honor and a great duty to your country."

The elevator door opened.

"Take this down to the first floor. The driver will take you back to work. Or wherever you want to go. I'll be in touch very soon to work out the details." Rom shook Jones' hand. "We are all very proud to have you lead us into the future."

Jones headed into the elevator, turned to face Rom. "I'm just not sure."

"You'll be sure. You just need a little time. We know where to contact you. Where you live. Where you work. Where you hang out. Who you hang out with. We'll find you when we need you."

The words chilled Jones. The elevator doors started to close but Rom reached in to stop them.

"Sorry about your neighbor, Mrs. Meyerson," said Rom. "Associating with a criminal will not be good for a future president of the United States." He paused to let the words sink in. "But we can take care of that, don't worry. We control clouds of computers dispersed throughout the world. It's amazing how each little bit of personal information can be dissipated in that cloud so that the connections between them are impossible to trace." He paused again. "When you're president, no one needs to know about it." He pulled his arm back and let the elevator doors close in on Jones silently.

GovMintBucks

Jones walked down the busy street, seemingly in slow motion. People walked by quickly, all appearing intent with some purpose. Where were all these people going? He was usually in his office at this time of day, so he never saw that the city streets were still crowded with people going here and there. He noticed very few of them actually entered or exited a building. They just kept walking, but looked very serious. He looked into the eyes of a few passersby, and they seemed blank. He shivered. He usually didn't look into people's eyes. He was too busy.

The minicar had been waiting for him when he left Stephen Holl Government Building Number 17. The driver had smiled and opened the door for him, but something made him uncomfortable so he waved at the man but kept on walking. He wanted to be alone with his thoughts. In that car he wouldn't be alone, and he had this weird feeling that he couldn't think freely there—a paranoid feeling that maybe his thoughts could be read and recorded in that car. He had shivered then, too. His thoughts kept flipping between a fear of this new paranoia of his and a fear that people were actually keeping track of him, which he now knew was true.

Jones came to his office building but stopped in front and brought his head up slowly, noting each identical row of windows, until he got to the spire at the top. The building loomed over him and he felt a little dizzy. There was something else. He just didn't want to go to work today. His mind was still jumbled, but with sudden disturbing flashes of clarity like lightning on a perfectly dark night in the woods. These sudden thoughts came and went so quickly that he couldn't quite grasp them, but they seemed important.

In the building next door there was a GovMintBucks coffee shop. A cup of hot, smooth coffee might be good to help him focus. He walked in and immediately spotted the caffeinator in a corner. The young man's purple bowtie and black t-shirt marked him as a caffeinator. Jones ordered the coffee and walked to a table. He passed the caffeinator and hesitated, then turned toward him.

"Hey man, good to see you," said Jones.

"Good to see you, too, Joe" said the caffeinator with a wide grin as if the two were old friends. To the caffeinator, everyone was "Joe."

Jones put a hand in his pocket and palmed a twenty dollar coin, then reached out and shook the caffeinator's sweaty hand vigorously. As Jones pulled his hand away, the coin stuck in the caffeinator's damp palm. The caffeinator smiled, reached into his left pocket with his dry left hand, pulled out a packet, and handed it to Jones. "Some sugar?" he asked.

Jones took the packet of caffeinated sugar silently, sat at a nearby table, and poured it in. No one took any notice. Sugar, of course, was restricted too for its hyperactivity effect on kids, its contribution to the obesity epidemic, and its addictiveness. But sugar was far less restricted than caffeine, which required a prescription. So the caffeinators pretended they were offering sugar and the police looked the other way.

Jones sipped the caffeinated coffee, enjoying the slight rush. He moved to a table in the back where it was quieter and he wasn't disturbed by the marijuana smoke in the front.

"Come here often?"

Jones looked up to see Alisa Rosenbaum looking down with her lovely heterochromia eyes. The corners of her lips turned upwards in what he took to be a smile. She rarely smiled. Actually he'd never seen her smile. She reminded him of a granite sculpture. Perfect but cold. And beautiful.

"No, no," he said a little nervously. She made him nervous. Also he was afraid of getting caught playing hooky. And maybe she spotted the caffeine, though most people didn't object to caffeine.

"I come here sometimes," she said and sat down. Jones watched her hands sweep down her sides, straightening her navy blue blazer to keep it from wrinkling. Her back was straight as she sat down. She had none of the sloppy informality that most people had. "When I need to think. When I can't face another day at the office. A little jolt usually helps." She nodded at his steaming coffee cup.

There was an awkward silence for a moment, broken by Jones. "I feel a little lost these days. Things beyond my control. Beyond even government control. Or maybe part of government control. I don't know. My life was so… stable… and now things are happening. Weird things. I mean I'm happy just doing my job. Well, maybe not happy, but satisfied. Or… well… I don't want to run the entire country. I mean, that's not the way it's supposed to work, right? But I don't think I really know how things work. I don't think I ever really did." It surprised him how this all flowed out of him at once—a word gusher. It embarrassed him and he looked away. A young man at a corner table was looking at him, then turned back to the newspaper in front of him. A heavyset woman walking by glanced furtively at him, then continued on. A baby in a carriage at the next table stopped its babbling to stare at him before its mother began rocking the carriage and it turned away.

He wanted to change the subject. "Are you involved with anyone, Ms. Rosenbaum?" Where did that come from?

Before he could think of a way to change the subject yet again, she replied. "Yes. Call me Alisa. Yes, I'm involved with someone." She said it like she was giving her name, rank, and serial number. But he did notice an unfocusing of her eyes as if she were imagining the man right now. He assumed it was a man but then felt guilty for the sexualist assumption.

There was a pause. Jones wanted to change the subject but also wanted to find out more about this "someone."

"He's strong," she said after a moment, her eyes still unfocused and far away. "Strong character. Strong will. Determined to change things. For the better. To make our world better. There are few like him. There have been few like him. His name is Miles."

Jones was suddenly jealous of this Superman. Alisa's eyes regained their focus and she directed them directly at Jones. "Do you ever listen to the speakers on the streets? The ones you repudiate?" she asked.

The question caught him off guard, a non-sequitor. "Well, yes. I have to. It's my job."

"Not really. Most of the other Repudiators don't bother listening. I've asked. They say that it interferes with their jobs. That they need to keep a clear head. I call that an empty head."

"I have to listen," said Jones. "I can't do my job otherwise. How can I repudiate their arguments without knowing what those arguments are?"

"You have your PDA. It gives you the arguments. You can just read it off."

"Then I'm just a robot. They don't need me to just read off arguments. What's the point?"

Alisa smiled. This time it looked natural. "Yes, I agree."

There was another awkward pause and Jones shifted in his seat. It wasn't completely uncomfortable, actually. Jones liked watching Alisa, her straight, blonde hair framing her face. The smile really looked nice.

"Have you ever heard a street speaker making sense? Saying things that sounded right?" asked Alisa.

"Well the other day there was a speaker talking about how government works to protect the people. Protects us from ourselves. Rights wrongs. Equalizes outcomes."

Alisa's smiled dissipated and the intensity reappeared in her eyes. "And that sounded right to you?"

There was something about her that made him trust her. Maybe it was just the attraction he had for her. Or maybe this trust enhanced his attraction. He lowered his voice. It wasn't a crime, of course, to disagree with the government; it just wasn't done by civilized people. In public at least. "Not really. It bothered me."

"And you repudiated it?"

"Well that's my job."

"And how did that repudiation sound."

He lowered his voice more. "Actually good. My arguments made sense."

Alisa smiled again, just slightly. Jones got nervous. Maybe she was testing him, he thought. Had he passed or failed? Was she with the government? Or with those people in that room that want him to be president? And who are they? Are they with the government? Some rogue group? Or was Alisa just a concerned friend? He turned quickly and saw the baby in the carriage staring silently at him again. When he stared back, it started bawling.

Alisa swallowed. "Have you heard of free markets? Of private enterprise? Of personal responsibility? Of entrepreneurship?"

Now he started sweating. Of course he'd heard of these things.

Alisa leaned in toward him and in a sultry voice said "I want to show you something." Jones turned toward her. In his mind he pictured her tearing open that pressed white blouse exposing two small but perfectly round alabaster breasts. Then he could forget all this stuff swirling in his head and focus on her. Or at least on this daydream of her. He shook his head to dissolve the mental picture like windblown sand.

"I have to go," Jones said. Before she could reply he stood up and walked out of the coffee shop. It seemed to him that everyone in the shop had turned to look at him as he left, a burst of cold wind entering through the doors and rustling the young man's newspaper, the elderly woman's dress, and the baby's fine red hair. Only Alisa seemed undisturbed at his exit.

GovMintBucks

Kidnapped

There was a knock at the door. Well, not really a knock, but an amplified electronic signal from the wall speakers that sounded like an old fashioned knuckles-on-wood knock. Jones had set his doorbell to sound like that. He liked the irony.

He didn't know how long someone had been knocking before he woke and heard it. He made some quiet, unintelligible noises that may or may not have been picked up by the home microphones and relayed to the person at the apartment door. At the apartment door? It must be one of his neighbors, he thought, because otherwise they'd be buzzing him from the main door to the building.

"Minute," he yelled groggily. The knocking stopped so obviously that one was picked up by the microphones. He glanced at the clock by the bed. Three seventeen AM! Who the...? He slid/fell out of bed. The knocking started up again.

Jones pressed the switch by the bed and even the faint light in that dark room hurt his eyes and he had to stop and close them. It had taken him a while to fall asleep and he didn't appreciate the interruption at all.

The knocking continued. It sounded louder but he knew that the system had only one volume. "Coming!" he yelled and got a little nervous that this must be some emergency. Grabbing his robe by the bathroom door, he reached the apartment door still struggling to get it on. His right sleeve got tangled in the cloth belt as he put his arm through, trapping his arm behind him. With his left hand he tapped the screen by the door and said, "Who's there?" Then he reached his left arm behind him to try to untangle his right one. The screen came to life showing a picture of an empty hallway. That's odd, he thought. No one was there. He was really tired. Did he just hallucinate the knocking? Then the knocking started up again.

Suddenly he felt very vulnerable. And paranoid again. He moved more hurriedly with his left arm to untangle his right, but they were now both caught in the robe belt, the left half of the robe hanging off his shoulder, the robe dragging on the floor.

Suddenly the door slid open with the soft whoosh of an energy efficient motor, but got stuck three-quarters of the way. On the other side of the doorway was a very large truck. A human truck, big and blocky and filling the doorway opening. From his vantage point, Jones could see only khaki pants and a blue Izod sweater, separated by a plain brown leather belt, filling the doorway. This massive human being reached one gigantic hand into the doorway and easily slid the door fully into its opening. "Come with me," Jones heard the very deep but quiet voice of this giant though his face was not visible above the doorframe.

Jones felt himself beginning to perspire. He turned to look around the room. Should he call the police? Run into the bathroom and lock it? Did this person have a weapon? He had no plan and he needed one quick. "I need to get…"

A large arm reached into the doorway and a large hand grabbed Jones' arm, wrapping around it like a grownup grabbing a child's arm. "There's no time," said the voice of the giant. "They'll be coming soon."

The giant gently tugged Jones in the direction of the doorway. The giant's grip was gentle but firm. Jones decided not to resist. He allowed the giant to guide him out the door and for the first time saw its face. It was large and round, a Pacific Islander with a mop of thick, black hair. His cheeks were puffed up from the wide smile on his face, not exactly what Jones had been picturing. But he was still not reassured. Was the smile genuine or fake? Did it represent good intentions or bad ones? Who was this person? Who had sent him? Why did they want Jones? Why were so many people suddenly interested in him?

The giant was not going to give answers it seemed. Smiling but silent, he guided Jones down the stairs of his apartment building and into the cold night. Jones wore only his bathrobe, and the perspiration left him particularly cold as it evaporated in the night air. Jones thought of breaking away and running, but the giant's hand remained curled around his arm, like a flesh handcuff. It seemed unlikely he could get away. The giant began whistling a perky tune.

At the street a large black limousine was waiting, the engine running, exhaust heating the water vapor in the air into a faint white cloud that rose under the street light. The giant opened the door. "Please," he said motioning for Jones to get in. He looked back at the house. "They'll be here soon."

Jones wanted to ask who the giant was referring to, but was nudged toward the backseat of the car. Again, looking for escape routes, but not thinking he would succeed, he slipped into the car. The giant slid in beside him and closed the door. An opaque screen hid the driver from view. As the limo drove away slowly, through the rear window Jones could see a small yellow minicar pull up to his building. A thin man in an overcoat got out and walked into the building.

Kidnapped

In the Boardroom

"It will just be a minute, Mr. Jones." The giant sat patiently on the other side of the table. "Can I get you anything?"

"No," said Jones, then added hesitantly, "thanks."

There was an uncomfortable silence. The giant kept looking at Jones. He sat low in the chair at the table, his feet on the floor, his knees near his chin. He looked like an adult at the kiddie table, and he seemed to have the demeanor of a young kid—pleasant, trying to please. "Bagel, Mr. Jones?"

"No… thanks."

"You must be hungry. The bagels are fresh."

Jones was hungry. But also nervous and he didn't think he should eat something until he knew where he was and what was wanted from him.

"Mind if I have one?"

Jones shook his head. The giant pulled himself out of the chair and walked to the spread of donuts and pastries behind him. Jones hadn't noticed the food before, hidden by the giant's huge form. He also hadn't noticed the painting on the wall. It was a silhouette of a muscular, bare-chested man from the waist up, his hands in the air, breaking a chain linking his wrists. The background was a fluttering American flag. Below that were words etched in a stone block: "The Freedman Group."

At that moment, the door to the room opened. Jones immediately had a sense of who it was before anyone even entered, before he caught a glimpse. Was it clairvoyance? A special connection? A faint scent? Maybe his subconscious mind had just worked out some puzzle, put some pieces together in some background processing mode that happened to complete just as the door to the room opened. Whatever the reason, he knew it was Alisa Rosenbaum an instant before she entered.

In the Boardroom

As always, Alisa looked perfect. At this early hour in the morning she looked perfectly rested, her clothes perfectly pressed, her walk brisk and confident. She held out her hand to Jones. "Good to see you, Winston," she said. "What do you think of our place here?"

Jones took her hand absent-mindedly, mostly because despite his confusion and fear, he liked the feel of her hand in his. "Where is here?"

Alisa looked sternly at the giant who had stuffed a bagel, whole, into his mouth.

"Mack, didn't you tell Mr. Jones about this place? About us?"

Mack shrugged and swallowed. "That's your department. Everything's secret. I'm never sure what to say."

"Come on. You're a brilliant physicist. You couldn't figure out what to say?"

Mack shrugged. Alisa sighed.

"I'm sorry Winston. So you didn't see the video I assume? The promotional video?"

Jones shook his head. Alisa glanced at Mack who shrugged again.

"Okay, okay. Let me give you a quick overview before Miles gets here to talk to you. Right now you're in the boardroom for the Freedman Group."

"That seems ironic," said Jones. "I've been kidnapped by the Freedman Group."

"Kidnapped?" She turned to Mack. "Did you tell him anything at all or did you just break down a wall and carry him out over your shoulder?"

Mack again shrugged. "They were coming. I didn't have time for detailed explanations."

"Winston, I apologize. Again. This wasn't a kidnapping."

"No? I was taken out of my home in the middle of the night without an explanation and not exactly by invitation."

"We needed to talk to you. It's important. Have a little patience, please. Do you want a bagel?"

Jones looks at Alisa's face, the fine line of her jaw juxtaposed with the soft curve of her mouth. Being kidnapped by her wasn't the worst thing that could have happened. "OK. And a cup of coffee, please."

"Caffeinated?" she asked. Jones nodded. "Mack, can you bring Mr. Jones a bagel and coffee? Thanks."

Under his breath Mack uttered, "He doesn't want one when I offer it," but he brought Jones the bagel and coffee.

"The Freedman Group," Alisa began again. "We are a group of people who meet secretly to practice our ideals. These ideals will seem radical to you, but please listen with an open mind." She paused for effect. "We believe in freedom."

Jones waited. She said nothing. "Well, doesn't everyone?" he finally asked.

"I mean real freedom, not the kind that the government gives you. We believe that people have, or should have, the unalienable right to life, liberty, and the pursuit of happiness. We believe that people should make their own decisions and succeed because of those decisions or fail and suffer the consequences."

"But people could die. They could make the wrong decisions and die from it."

"Really? Do people die from bad decisions? Are people so incapable of weighing costs and benefits, risks and rewards that they would actually die if they had to make a decision on their own?"

"Well, some would. And some would hurt themselves. Some would hurt others. Society would collapse."

In the Boardroom

"Do you really believe that? Society would collapse if you made your own choices? If you ate a steak fried in trans fats? Smoked a cigarette? Had a little caffeine in your coffee?"

Jones blushed a bit.

"What if you could choose your own career?" asked Alisa. "What if you could have been an engineer?" She paused again for effect. "What if you could fall in love with, and marry the person of your choice even if the racial, religious, and socio-economic combination was deemed not ideal to assure a 'fair and diverse' makeup of our society?" Alisa's blue-green eyes stared at him, unblinking, and he wondered if she was sending him a message. She didn't seem like the kind of person to send subtle messages. She was blunt, to-the-point, outspoken. If she felt anything for him like he felt for her, she probably would just tell him, matter-of-fact. Still he hoped.

"But sometimes you have to do what's right for society, which may not be right for you personally," said Jones without a lot of conviction.

"And who decides that? Who decides what's right for society?"

"The government," responded Jones without thinking.

"And who is the government, Winston?"

Jones thought for a moment about the group of people that wanted him to be president. The Electoral Committee. They wanted him to be president or did they actually simply make him president?

"Winston, you're familiar with the Constitution, right? It's gone through a lot of changes, but it still represents government of the people, by the people, for the people. You are 'the people.' I am 'the people.'"

"Me too," said Mack who had been listening quietly.

"Yes, the government is the people," continued Alisa, "not some committee that meets in a secret room behind closed doors."

Jones recognized the irony of hearing this in a secret room behind closed doors.

"Alisa," said Mack from the corner of the room where he'd wandered. "You're not going to give one of your long winded speeches about governments and individual freedoms, and that kind of stuff are you? Maybe Mr. Jones needs a break? Maybe he needs a little time to think? Whadda you think, Mr. Jones? All of this talk gets to me after a while. And the first time I heard it, I needed some time to absorb it."

"He doesn't have time to absorb it. He's been selected by the committee already."

Jones looked at her. "Are you talking about the Electoral Committee or do you have your own committee?"

"We know about the Electoral Committee. We had to get to you before they do."

"They've already contacted me," said Jones.

"We know. That was the intro. They'll be coming back again. And again. They're relentless. They need you and the more they tell you, the more they need you."

"I think I saw one of them go into my apartment after you kidnapped… or rather, kindly escorted me here."

"We know. They're monitoring you. When Mack broke in, it set off an alarm to them."

"That's why I didn't have time for long explanations," Mack whined.

Ignoring Mack, Alisa continued. "Winston, very shortly you're going to meet a man who is setting in motion a plan to change the world. You asked me the other day about the man I'm involved with."

"Miles," said Jones. The name had stuck with him unfortunately.

"Yes," said Alisa, obviously happy to hear the name and surprised that Jones remembered it.

"He is strong willed with a brilliant mind. He is a leader of the finest caliber. He is a great man. I believe that he will change the world for the better, and I want to be there at his side when he does. It all starts when he implements his Jobs Plan. After that, there will be other plans. I'll let him talk to you himself, and I hope you will want to join him as I have."

At that time (was it staged or coincidence?) the door to the room opened. Jones could see Alisa catch her breath and knew that this was Miles entering. In walked a short, pudgy man with thick-rimmed glasses. His nearly bald head was visible under sparse strands of thin, black hair. Jones recognized him as one of the speakers in the park that Jones had repudiated.

"Hello," said Miles in a nasally voice, extending an open hand to Jones.

Jones turned to Alisa. "This is the superman who will save our world?"

Alisa was taken aback. "Mr. Jones, I'd like you to meet Miles Monroe."

"Come on," said Jones. This is the man you'll follow to the ends of the earth?"

"That's not exactly what I said, but…"

"This man? This… man?"

"Hey," said Miles. "I'm right here, you know."

"Sorry," said Jones to Miles. "You're just not exactly the person I pictured."

"Well, I…" said Miles.

"The man you love?" said Jones to Alisa. "I just figured…"

"The man I love?" asked Alisa with obvious surprise.

"The man you love?" asked Miles, looking at Alisa with perhaps a hint of hope.

The three of them paused and looked at each other. Mack started giggling, trying unsuccessfully to hide it. Alisa simply looked aghast, her mouth frozen open.

"Mr. Jones," said Miles a bit patronizingly and not by accident. "Mr. Jones, can we get to the business of your being here tonight? Can we adopt a more adult tone?" He shot a glance at Mack who immediately stopped his giggling.

"Sorry, I… I thought…" Jones hesitated. "I'm tired. I was kidnapped in the middle of the night. I don't know what's going on. All kinds of people are after me. I've been 'randomly selected' to be president of the United States." He made quotation marks in the air with his fingers. "You'll excuse me if I don't know what the hell is going on, and what I'm supposed to say or think."

Miles cleared his throat dramatically. "Mr. Jones, I am the Chairman of the Freedman Group. We are an underground group of radicals. We are attempting to change society and we want your help. We need your help.

Mr. Jones, do you know that once in our history we believed in the exceptionalism of America?"

"Of course, in the *Days of Inequality*. I must say you've picked the wrong man. Everyone has picked the wrong man. I like things the way they are. I really don't want to change anything."

"You're a tall man, Mr. Jones, are you not?"

"Well, yes…"

"Exceptionally tall, wouldn't you say?"

"I wouldn't say that because it would be unfair."

"But it would be true. You are exceptionally taller than the average person."

In the Boardroom

"Not 'exceptionally.'"

"But taller."

"Yes."

"And why was that simple truth so difficult for you to say?"

"It's not right to point out my superior… I mean different characteristics."

"And so truth takes a back seat to 'fairness'?"

Jones shrugs his shoulders. "This seems like a semantics game. How does my height matter?"

"It matters, Mr. Jones, because it is a fact. In today's society we hide facts, hide the truth, to make people feel better. To make them feel equal. But people are not equal."

Jones looked around uncomfortably.

"No one is watching us in here, Mr. Jones. No one is recording us, ready to turn us in to the Thought Police. That's the great thing about the Freedman Group. We operate in complete stealth. We need to. Why? Because we believe in the truth. We believe that each person has a potential to be great or horrible or mediocre. We believe only in the equality of opportunity not the equality of results. And that is what makes a society exceptional, that equality of opportunity not the mediocrity of sameness. Do you follow?"

Jones shrugged. He felt foggy, like looking into a muddy creek and seeing something below the surface but not sure if it's a beautiful mermaid or the Loch Ness Monster.

"Mr. Jones, your height is above average. Perhaps my singing voice is more lovely than yours. Mack here can lift a refrigerator, and I doubt any of us can do that. Alisa is a problem solver extraordinaire. Some of our talents are natural—given to us at birth by genetics or perhaps the grace of God. Other talents we have developed through years of training. At the Freedman Group we cherish the great talents and encourage people to use them for their own benefit and, in doing so, benefit all of us. And we encourage people to develop new talents and use them for their own personal benefit. And that in turn benefits all of us. You've heard that ancient expression that a rising tide lifts all boats, Mr. Jones? Well here at the Freedman Group we are raising the tide! It is not rising on its own, we are doing it ourselves."

"But raising the self-esteem of the individual…"

"… raises the self-esteem of the group. I know what you've learned by rote in school. I know the brainwashing you've undergone. Do you believe it Mr. Jones? Would you look at Mack and be jealous of his physical strength or would you appreciate his talents and partner with him to knock down walls and break free from bondage."

Mack bellowed, "Hey, I'm pretty damn good at physics, too. I'm not just a human bulldozer."

"I know Mack. But your mental ability is not as evident as your size and strength. I am just making a point here." Turning to Jones, "he is damn good at physics, too. Brilliant in fact."

"So I'm hearing all this philosophy. What exactly do you do? Is there something concrete or is it all philosophy?"

"We compete, Mr. Jones."

"Competition leads to civilization's destruction. Cooperation leads to civilization's fulfillment."

'You know your slogans well, Mr. Jones, of course. Do you know what Scottish jurist and historian Sir Alex Fraser Tyler said in the Eighteenth Century? There are nine stages of civilization. First, from bondage to spiritual faith; second from spiritual faith to great courage; third from courage to liberty; fourth from liberty to abundance; fifth from abundance to selfishness; sixth from selfishness to complacency; seventh from complacency to apathy; eight from apathy to dependence; and ninth from dependency back again into bondage."

Jones interrupted. "But we have reached the stage of abundance. We have plenty. We share; we cooperate; we survive."

"I like that in you Mr. Jones. I like that you can listen and rebut, listen and debate. It shows you are thinking about what I am saying. In fact we are in the next-to-final stage going into bondage. We are dependent on the government for our needs. Can you possess more than the government says? Can you live in a place that you've built by the sweat of your labor or by the achievements of your mind? Can you say what you feel? Marry whom you like? Can you make life better for yourself or your children? Can you achieve your dreams?"

Winston Jones began to speak, but stopped.

"We can, Mr. Jones. We all run businesses here. Independent business with no government 'assistance' or rather interference."

Jones looked stunned.

'No government investment or ownership whatsoever. All from private capital. All built by our own labors. And we keep the profits. We pay our employees according to their output. We fire whom we want. We take the risks. Some businesses fail. Others succeed. And we compete vigorously with each other. We cooperate only when it is in our best interests."

Jones was increasingly shocked with each statement. "You're running a criminal enterprise!"

"We are producing goods and services and offering only the best to our customers. We have an underground economy. We are raising the tide and everyone with it. Alisa designs computers. Mack is working on a new kind of motor capable of harnessing static electricity and transforming it into mechanical energy. And I build wooden cabinets. I use the skills of my hands to turn raw wood into useful and beautiful objects. Businesses don't need to be mammoth conglomerates. But they need to be free from constraint, free to compete, and free to succeed. Or fail."

"This all sounds good," said Jones, "but what about the failures? Are they cast away? The businesses that can't compete? The people who can't produce? Is society supposed to just toss them aside?"

"Alisa, how many businesses of yours have failed?"

"Two," said Alisa.

"And you, Mack?"

"Four, I think," responded Mack.

"I hired Mack after his last business failed. Then I invested in his latest one. If it fails, he has skills that make him a valuable employee. In our underground economy, failure is neither a scarlet 'A' burned permanently into your skin, nor is it a badge of honor. It is a sign that you work hard for what you believe in."

Jones thinks for a moment, then asked "And so you need me for something, right?"

"Yes, Mr. Jones. We want to give America faith once again. If you're going to be president, and almost certainly you will, then we need your help. It's up to you of course. Our core belief is personal freedom and we will not force you to do anything. We will try very hard to persuade you, though, and I hope we will be successful."

"And why are you so sure I'll be president?"

"The Electoral Committee does not hold our strong beliefs in personal freedom. They will make sure you take the position."

Jones thought again for a moment. "And what is it you need from me specifically?"

"We need your influence and your bully pulpit. More specifically we need you to start, when you are president, by promoting our Jobs Plan."

Jones leaned back to absorb everything he had been hearing. He gently lowered himself onto a green, grassy field. Miles Monroe floated off into the sky and Alisa Rosenbaum in a delicate, gauzy nightgown appeared next to him. She leaned closer to kiss him, then whispered in his ear, "I think we should get him home." Jones realized his eyelids had slipped shut as he listened to Miles Monroe. The words were interesting, but long. It was about time for sunrise and he had not slept much, and had not been sleeping much all week anyway.

"Yes, you're right Alisa," responded Miles. "Mack, can you drive Mr. Jones back to his apartment?" To Jones, "We'll have to drop you a couple blocks away. I apologize for the inconvenience but no doubt the Electoral Committee has you under surveillance."

"OK,' replied Jones wearily, rubbing his tongue over the overnight film that had already coated his teeth. He stood groggily and Mack steadied him.

"You'll think about what we said, I hope," said Miles. "We'll be back in touch. And please don't talk about us to anyone. It will not only hurt us, your friends—I hope you consider us your friends. But the Electoral Committee will not look upon that favorably at all."

Jones nodded and Mack escorted him out slowly and gently.

The Electoral Committee Reconvenes

Smoke filled the air and swirled around the members of the Electoral Committee of the Fairness for EveryBody Society sitting once again at the large, round oak table. They wore the same dark black trench coats. They puffed on their cigars. They sat in darkness, their voices like ethereal spirits in the shadows.

"Jones got a visit last night. Someone contacted him."

"This Freedman Group?"

"Probably."

"Why haven't we been able to find this group? How could it be that hard?"

"I don't know."

"What would they offer him? Why do they even care?"

"Not clear.'"

"We're offering him power. Everyone wants power. It's what drives the people. What the hell else is there?"

"There's community. There's society. There's equality. Isn't that what we're supporting here? Isn't that why we even have this committee?"

"Screw that."

"Look, we're bettering society, no doubt. But human nature is such that people want power. That's just the way things are. If we have to use that weakness to drive society toward an egalitarian future, what's wrong with that?"

"So the ends justify the means? Is that what you're saying?"

The Electoral Committee Reconvenes

"Let's get back to Jones."

"Yes, what's the status on him? Have we lost him?"

"Win? Lose? We don't even know what this Freedman Group is offering him. Or what they want in return."

"Or it could be another agitator group."

"No, it's Freedman. All the other groups we control."

"What?"

"Sure, we control the agitator groups. Someone wants to operate outside society's rules don't you think it's better that we control them? That we know their plans so they can't screw up everything we do?"

"Wow, I just thought..."

"You're the only one who just thought. The rest of us all knew."

"So we don't know what they want with him. Information? He doesn't have any. Influence? They don't know he's about to become president of the United States, so it can't be that. Coincidence?"

"Are you sure they don't know he's the candidate?"

"How would they?"

"A mole."

"In our group? In the Electoral Committee?"

"It's possible."

There is silence.

"Unlikely."

"Yes, very unlikely."

"But not impossible."

Silence again.

"Maybe they have surveillance."

"Tapped into the government networks. Government computers."

"We run continuous checks on the system."

"We need to look into this."

"We'll form a subcommittee."

"All in favor of a subcommittee…"

"Later. For now we need to figure out what to do about Jones."

"Talk to him again."

"Make him an offer."

"If he doesn't accept?"

"Sell it to him."

"He'll accept."

"Sell it hard."

"He'll take it. Everyone takes it. It's in their nature. Human nature."

"But if he doesn't?"

"He will."

"If he doesn't?"

"I'm sure he will."

"But if not?"

Another moment of silence.

"Excommunication."

The Electoral Committee Reconvenes

The room went silent once again and stays that way.

Encouraging the Candidate

It had been a few days since the meeting with the Electoral Committee and the abduction by the Freedman Group. Jones had come back to his house where everything seemed perfectly in place. In fact, it seemed too much in place. Shirts that he thought he'd left out were folded neatly on the shelves. Dishes that he seemed to remember in the sink were clean and stacked in the cupboard. Maybe it was his imagination. He had been very tired that night and sleeping poorly for days. Everything seemed foggy like a dream.

He had wanted to call in unwell the next day, but his spotless apartment creeped him out a bit, so he went into work and went through the motions. He felt like his life was running away without him, careening out of control. His pulse was raised and his hands shook. His eyelid twitched. His breathing was sometimes too fast. Even his head sometimes felt too heavy for his neck to hold up and it wobbled unless he concentrated on holding it still. He just felt sick. He had always appreciated control. Needed it. Now things were going off in strange directions. The worst part was he didn't understand where it was going. Or who was controlling it. Certainly not him, and that really bothered him.

In the past few days he had gone out on a few repudiation assignments, but his heart had not been into it. He just read the words he was given. He didn't hear them. Didn't understand them. Not that it mattered. It just felt wrong.

He started refusing assignments. Trading them with other Repudiators. Or just ignoring them. After a while he'd get a notice about this. About poor performance. Not that it mattered. He had always taken pride in his work, but really it didn't matter. He did the work because he had enjoyed it somewhat. And it gave his life purpose. But if he did a bad job he might be called in to see his supervisor to explain. She'd be sympathetic (it was mandatory). She might suggest training, some recuperation time, or counseling or even another line of work. It was up to him.

143

Encouraging the Candidate

Jones hadn't seen Alisa except occasionally at the end of a hallway, usually walking quickly to get somewhere. Walking away from him, or at least in a different direction, not toward him. That was fine. He didn't want to talk to her. It was just uncomfortable. He was overwhelmed. He wanted to bury himself in work—busy work—so he could avoid thinking about recent events. Avoid making a decision about anything.

Heading down a corridor he saw a glimpse of a black overcoat turn the corner toward him. He panicked. His heart raced and he struggled to breathe normally. He could hear a slight slush-slush of the blood flowing in his ears. He turned into the nearest doorway, the men's room.

Inside he paced the floor. Someone entered so he moved into a stall and latched the door. He paced around the stall, then stopped, closed his eyes, and began taking slow, deep breaths. His heart slowed a bit. He imagined cool water around his toes and rising upward, calming the nerves as it rose slowly, engulfing him. When the water got to his hands, they stopped shaking. When the water got to his neck, his head steadied. There was no threat, he thought to himself. This is all weird, but there is no threat. No physical threat. No one is going to harm him. No one had threatened harm. Everyone just talked to him, reasoned with him. He felt calm, in control again. He was just going to walk out and go about his business.

Jones opened the stall. The man at the sinks glanced up at him in the mirror. Jones ignored him, walked out of the men's room. Rom Automatic was standing outside the door and smiled. Well, almost smiled. It didn't look quite right to Jones.

"Hello Winston," said Rom.

"Hello. Fancy meeting up like this. Coincidence." Jones raised his voice at the end in a half-question.

Rom nodded at Jones' hands. "You should wash your hands. It's better that way, hygienically."

"Yeah, yeah. Wasn't thinking." said Jones and he walked back into the men's room to wash his hands.

"And required by government health standards," said Rom, his voice trailing off as the door closed.

When Jones exited the men's room again, Rom was still there. "I'd like to talk further," he said and placed an arm on Jones' shoulder.

"Sure," said Jones, "let's talk."

"This way," said Rom, and he steered Jones down a hallway, around some corners, to a conference room. He closed the door and waved Jones to the table. Jones sat. Rom sat.

"Winston, you have been chosen for a great purpose." Rom was not one for ice-breaking chit chat. "The fate of America, and of the entire free world, is up to you."

"Maybe I don't want that responsibility," said Jones.

Again, Rom flashed that insincere smile. "Ah, so that's what's bothering you. There's no responsibility. We help you. We decide for you. You are the face, the great communicator. We provide the answers. We do the hard work. It's exactly like your work here."

"I don't know. I need to think."

"All the appearances without the responsibility. What could be better?" Again that grin.

Jones was silent, looking down at the table.

"We know that you've been approached. By a radical group."

Rom examined Jones's face for signs of affirmation. Jones continued to look down at the table.

"The Freedman Group."

Jones could tell by the way Rom said it, a little too softly, a little hesitantly, that he wasn't sure. He was trying to get information from Jones. Jones remained silent.

"We don't know what they want from you, but I'm asking you to be careful. As a friend. As a mentor. As a future advisor. Please be careful. They are trying to destroy the society that we've carefully crafted. A society of equality. A society of justice. Of fairness for everybody. You don't want to destroy that, do you?"

Jones silently shook his head, still looking down.

"I know. I know that because I know you are a fair and good man." Rom got up from his seat. He walked around to Jones and squatted next to him. Jones looked into Rom's dark face and floating white eyes under the black fedora. "Mr. Jones," he continued unblinking. "If you say yes, and I know you will, you will have the things you want and be the envy of many people. There will be no responsibility, only... enjoyment and satisfaction. But if you say no, then there could be great responsibility. If you say no, we will need to start the process over again. If you say no, there could be great confusion and misdirection of the entire country. There could be chaos and a return to darker times of discrimination and competition. You don't want to be responsible for that. We don't want to be responsible for that. We—the committee—do have great responsibility and we take that responsibility very seriously. We will not let that happen. Do you understand?"

Jones was silent and still.

"We will not let that happen," Rom repeated. He stood, straightened his fedora, smoothed out his overcoat, and started to leave. Then dramatically, rehearsed, he turned to Jones, fished something out of his pocket, and tossed it onto the desk in front of Jones. The flash drive bounced once, then spun in a circle directly in front of Jones. "You'll be interested in this," said Rom.

Jones watched it spin, hardly seeming to slow down.

146

"It's your personnel files. Your government personnel files. Everything we know about you. And your family. And your friends. Essentially it's you—or more precisely a complete, solid state record of you, recorded with electrons on a crystal silicon substrate and packaged in plastic."

Rom left the room as Jones watched him stroll down a corridor, turn a corner, and vanish.

Encouraging the Candidate

Disappearing Act

Jones had waited for a while in the empty conference room. His pulse had once again climbed during the conversation. Well, not really a conversation but a monologue. A speech. A threat?

He heard a quiet tapping and looked up. Alisa was on the other side of the glass wall. She made a motion with two fingers, pointing at herself then "walking" the fingers toward the door of the conference room. Her head cocked to one side, her eyes widened, it was obviously a question. Jones nodded and she walked in and came over to him.

"I saw…"

Jones stood up suddenly, wrapped his arms around her, and gave her a full-on kiss. She did not resist. She just accepted it. After a moment he pulled away but kept her in his grasp and looked at her questioningly.

"I saw Automatic in here with you," she continued. "We know him. We follow him when we can, but we can't do it all the time. Too risky. If I'd known he was coming I would have warned you. We could have gotten you out of here. Then I saw him in here. Persuading you. Coercing you. Are you ok? What did he say? Did you commit to anything?"

He had just kissed her hadn't he, he thought? She was still in his arms, her arms at her side. His face flushed, but his dark brown skin hid most of the color except to an exceptional observer. He slowly released her, bringing his arms to his side. She did not move, still standing close to him, looking at him inquiringly.

"He asked me to be President of the United States. Well actually he told me to be President of the United States."

"Yes, these people don't ask, they demand. They just do it so politely. So fairly." She said the word "fairly" as if it were an obscenity. "Did you commit to anything?"

"Would it matter?"

149

"No, good point."

They looked at each other for a moment. Did Alisa look uncomfortable? She never looked uncomfortable. Always under control. "We need to get away," she said.

"Yes!" Jones brightened up.

"Back to the Freedman Group. Back to the Boardroom."

"No!" Jones dimmed down again.

"We need to give you more background. We need to explain our philosophy to you. We need to immerse you in it; you need to learn our methods and our reasons."

Jones stared into Alisa's heterochromia iridum. "Go away with me."

"Yes, to the Boardroom."

"No, to somewhere else. To nowhere."

"You need to learn about us. About the Freedman Group. About the Jobs Plan."

"Right now I need to be with you."

"I'm an attractive woman," said Alisa Rosenbaum, matter-of-factly. "You've been thrown into a difficult situation. Your life is changing suddenly. You are under intense pressure. It's a pure physiological reaction. Studies have shown…"

Jones pulled Alisa close once again, her face close to his, their lips only centimeters apart. "Whatever it is, it makes me feel good. You make me feel good. Right now, I need to feel good."

Alisa stopped talking, for once looking slightly uncomfortable.

"Studies must have shown," continued Jones, "that a person who feels calm, who feels relaxed, learns much better than one under stress."

"Well, yes…"

"Then run away with me. I need this right now. Run away with me and teach me about the Freedman Group and the Jobs Plan and individual rights and responsibilities."

"If we… run away… you'll listen to me?"

"Every word."

"And you'll learn from me?"

"I'll memorize it and I'll love and agree with everything you say."

"No," said Alisa, concerned. "You mustn't agree with me."

"Then I'll disagree with everything you say. Promise."

"No. You need to think about it. Absorb it. Make your own decisions. That's the whole point."

"OK, ok. I'll make my own decisions."

"And then once you've heard everything I'm sure you will agree."

Now this was getting frustrating, thought Jones. And kind of killing the mood. Then someone entered the conference room—an elderly man in a wrinkled, gray business suit. "Hey get a room!" exclaimed the man.

Alisa and Jones stepped apart. Sheepishly they looked at him. "Sorry," they said in unison.

The man looked puzzled. "We've got a meeting starting in this room in a few minutes. I have it reserved, damn it. You want to do whatever it is you're doing, get another room. You can reserve it on the company reservation system, but damn it I already reserved this one."

Alisa Rosenbaum and Winston Jones nodded and walked out of the conference room and down the hallway side-by-side, their arms and legs moving in perfect synchronization. They stepped into the elevator, in unison. There were a few people standing quietly who moved back to make room for them. The ride down was silent. At the ground floor, the elevator doors opened and everyone stepped out, replaced by another group of silent workers. Alisa and Jones continued their synchronized movements toward the lobby, out the front door, and down the street.

Jones looked at Alisa as they walked. "So where are we going?" he asked.

"I thought you knew," she replied.

Running on Empty

"In here," said Alisa and grabbed Jones' arm. She led him toward the subway entrance.

He saw where she was going and pulled back. "The subway?" he asked.

"I know a place," she said. "Trust me."

He swallowed a big blob of fear. The subway was not a place you wanted to be. Certainly not a place he wanted to be. He had pictured Alisa and himself running away to some beautiful paradise. Maybe a resort on a white Mediterranean beach where they could sip Mai Tais, read books, and stare into each others' eyes each day and make love each night. Maybe he would even find out what exactly a Mai Tai is—something you sip and they must be very good because people always seem to be fantasizing about them.

Unlike the soft, fine-grained, white of the beach in his imagination, the subway was the cold, hard, antiseptic white of cheap tile and fluorescent lights. The smell of disinfectant was strong yet hardly masked the other odors—urine, vomit, and garbage. This was the Broad Street Line that let out at the Pattison Station by the South Philly Sports Complex also known as Philly Dead.

The South Philly Sports Complex had a similar history to other sports complexes throughout the country. Originally built by wealthy businessmen to promote their sports franchises, these men came to eventually and altruistically realize that the social benefits of steroid-enhanced supermen swatting around balls of various shapes and sizes outweighed the millions of dollars they generated in profits. Stadiums were not just vast buildings to hold tens of thousands of fans paying a week's salary to watch these highly paid superstars perform their amazing feats of prowess. Stadiums were not only places to sell food and beverages and cheap souvenirs at many multiples of their cost to energized and often inebriated fans. Stadiums were more than simply large, expensive buildings that ate into the businessmen's bottom lines.

Stadiums were also great arenas of popular culture that brought together families and neighborhoods. They brought together strangers from opposite sides of town or from faraway cities who could root for their teams in a way that enabled them to forget their daily troubles, in a way that brought out the best spirit and camaraderie in people, and in a way that usually did not result in violence or at least the violence did not result in many permanent injuries. In essence, stadiums were symbols. They put entire cities "on the map" (though truthfully Philadelphia had been on the map since the founding of the country). Given the historical and social significance of a sports stadium, the businessmen recognized that the only reasonable means of paying for these expensive erections was with public funds. Governments of course agreed, and the stadiums were paid with tax dollars and eventually fully nationalized. Philadelphia, home of the Broad Street Bullies and Combat Zone Wrestling, Pro-Pain Pro Wrestling, and the Steel Cage of Death, grew to become one of the largest sports complexes in the country, and after the Riot of the Century, it also maintained one of the largest police forces and one of the largest social service provider networks too.

She pulled him through the broken turnstiles that were missing their fingers. People had long ago stopped paying fares and so there was no need to restrict access. All public transportation was now "free" anyway, meaning paid for by tax dollars.

They waited for a train to come in. You could never know when the next one would show up. The crowd grew larger in the small confined space, adding to Jones' anxiety. But it was the social workers prowling the crowd that made him the most uncomfortable. Dressed in white robes with fluorescent colored badges, they wandered through the people, announcing their services.

"Free needles," cried one social worker. "Get your free needles. Each comes with a pamphlet on the horrors of drug use—make sure you read it first." Dirty and crumpled drug pamphlets blanketed the ground.

"Condoms," yelled another. "Free condoms here. Sex is for lovers not for diseases." They seemed to be competing, each trying to drown the other out, each eyeing the other.

"Abortions this way," bellowed another. "If you love it, keep it. Otherwise nip it in the bud. And remember to take the pamphlet on sexual positions for consenting adults." The government had been catching on lately that in order to sell something you had to get the consumer's attention first. The government had taken to distributing pornography with safe sex messages throughout. Those pamphlets were very popular and the other workers had a difficult time competing.

One of the workers stepped close to Jones. "Condoms?"

"No thanks," said Jones uncomfortably.

The worker looked at Jones then at Alisa then back at Jones. "Better safe sex than no sex," he said and held out a foil package.

"No, really," said Jones. The worker continued to hold the package in Jones' face. "Really. We're just friends. Well more than friends." Jones looked at Alisa who seemed oblivious, staring down the dark tunnel for signs of the train's light. "We're not planning…"

"Doesn't hurt to take precautions," said the social worker, now swinging the packet back and forth like a hypnotists watch.

"Coming," announced Alisa.

"Huh?" said Jones.

"Train's coming, let's go."

The train pulled up to the station. The doors opened and people on board fought to get out while people on the platform fought to get on. Alisa, her hand still tightly around his arm, pulled him along. Jones watched the social worker, an unmoving pillar of white in a flowing ocean of people. "Please," pleaded the social worker as he faded out, "I have a quota."

They did not talk during the train ride, the two of them swaying back and forth with the crowd. The train made many stops, more than there were stations, but this was expected. For unknown reasons trains stopped in between stations. Some people claimed it was a government regulation to do so. Safety and security inspectors were required to inspect the train at regular intervals and there were more inspections scheduled than there were train stops. Others said the train stops were to lengthen the voyage because some workers, like the conductor and the engineer, were paid by the hour and the government required them to work a certain number of hours. Others said the trains were just in such disrepair that they could not make the entire trip without overheating. Whatever the reason, the stops were annoying but necessary and accepted by the passengers.

Alisa paid little attention to the surroundings, but seemed to be thinking, calculating. Jones liked to watch her face and this was a good time to do so because she was oblivious to his stares. The angles and tautness of her smooth skin contrasted with the flabby, wrinkled, weathered ones around her as if a spotlight shone on it. Kind of like one of those old movies where a key light would be aimed so squarely and obviously on the movie star's face in a crowd. But there was no key light here. Maybe her own intensity of thought formed an internal key light.

He watched her eyebrows arch, her jaw twitch, her lips move subtly, mouthing something he could not make out. She was so intense that it attracted him and scared him at the same time.

The train lurched to one of its in-between stops. "Here," said Alisa again grabbing his arm tightly and pulling him toward the door. She wedged her hand between the two sliding doors of the train that no longer met fully in the middle. Giving a mighty push, the one door resisted then gave way as both doors slid away from each other. She still had her arm around Jones's forearm and with the push she also squeezed his arm and it hurt. He turned the beginning of a squeal of pain into an embarrassed cough as she pulled him out the doors and onto the train tracks.

"Keep going," she told him as he stumbled and she pulled herself up onto a tiny ledge of crumbling stone and cement patches along the wall. "Keep your arms in," she said. Only a few people took notice of them, simply staring at them with blank expressions. The train slowly pulled away. She pulled him up with her.

Good Intentions

He looked at her as if to say "Now what?" But he was silent.

"This way," she said and led him along the wall in the subway tunnel. Tiny clouds of dust shot up with each footstep, and occasionally a small chunk of concrete or stone would crumble and fall off as he stepped, causing him to stumble. Alisa never stumbled.

Small, dim bulbs, lined the walls providing little light, and more than half of them were burned out anyway. The odors were unpleasant and changing every few feet. Things moved in the dark crevices—something big, probably a cat, something small, probably a rat. He could see vague shapes and movements out of the corners of his eyes, but if he turned to look directly he could not make out the shapes in the shadows. That seemed like an oddly appropriate metaphor for the events in his life these days.

At one point his foot hit a patch of something wet and sticky. He smelled something sweet, but not in a good way, and he felt that he was going to retch. He closed his eyes for a moment and took a deep breath to steady his nerves, but the breath was definitely not a good idea and the combined sweet and disgusting stench filled his lungs. His lungs started convulsing as his body tried to cough out the horrid air. A train blast suddenly filled that air loudly, startling him. He instinctively stepped back as he saw the light of the train in the distance but approaching rapidly. His backside hit the subway wall and he bounced forward toward the tracks and into the path of the coming train. He saw more nebulous shapes moving in the crevices and corners and under the tracks, and in the moment that he was falling forward onto the tracks it registered in his mind that Alisa was no longer there. She had disappeared.

As he fell, seemingly in slow motion, a slender but sinewy arm darted from the darkness. A small but powerful hand wrapped itself around his forearm and yanked him backward. He expected to hit the subway wall and braced himself for impact, but instead he found himself tripping through a doorway in the side of the tunnel as the train flew past. Alisa had turned into that doorway, nearly completely black; he had not seen her turn in and the doorway was virtually invisible.

He rubbed his forearm, increasingly quite tender from all the grabbing and tugging. Alisa looked at him. "You ok?" she asked.

"Sure," he said, feeling somewhat useless. "Thanks," he said quietly. He felt a little strange thanking her when she had gotten him into this situation in the first place—well at least this immediate situation in the subway—and he still was not sure where they were going or why. He had wanted to run away from his troubles, but this was not having the desired effect. Maybe that was the point. Maybe she wanted to show him just how bad things could get so his life would seem pleasant in contrast. That did not seem to make sense either, but not much seemed to make sense lately.

"We're almost there," she said and turned back into the darkness. At least there was some destination, he thought as he reluctantly followed her into the darkness, keeping close enough to barely see her outline and hear the clicks of her footsteps.

There were a few turns along the way and it was difficult to follow her, but he managed. He kept thinking he felt things touching him, crawling on his arm, or once even felt a warm, moist breath on his cheek. It was probably his imagination. Eventually he saw a small white light up ahead. "Move toward the light," she said to him. Why did that not make him feel better?

The light grew and made some of the shapes and shadows visible for what they were. Cockroaches scurried away from his feet—most of them did except for the few that crackled under his shoe and then scurried away when he lifted his foot. A large black cat, its hair matted and wet with something greasy and shiny, played with something in its mouth. Did he see it grin? He turned to focus on the rectangle of white light in front of them. Alisa, in her business attire seemed pristine—clean and untouched by any of the nasty things surrounding them.

The rectangle was a doorway. His eyes had trouble adjusting to the light in the middle of this darkness. He could make out figures moving quickly around the room. He could see colors and shapes but could not make out details. Alisa turned to him. "Here we are," she said as if that was all he needed to know for this journey to make sense.

Alisa stepped into the lit rectangle and turned to reach for his sore forearm. He stepped back, swinging his arm behind him and out of her reach. "Hey," he said angrily, but then immediately calmed down. She looked at him, puzzled. He smiled. "I can do it," he said, smoothed his clothes down, and walked into the light calmly.

Running on Empty

The Underground

"Welcome to the Underground." A thin Indian man in his late twenties or early thirties held out a cup of tea on a saucer. "I am Rajan. Ms. Rosenbaum tells me this is your first visit. Please have a cup of tea." The man held out the cup. The string of a teabag hung lazily over the side. Steam streamed from the top. Jones pinched the saucer between thumb and forefinger, balancing the cup on top. He had not seen a cup and saucer in a long time. Had he ever seen one? Everything was in recyclable paper cups now.

The man was dressed in a plain, dark gray suit, tattered around the edges but clean and pressed. He looked at Jones smiling, waiting. Jones was not thirsty, but courteously brought the cup to his lips and took a sip then exclaimed "Ah!" when the hot tea hit his tongue. The man continued to smile at him. "It's hot," said Jones. Much hotter than government regulation would allow, he thought. Someone could get hurt drinking such a hot beverage. This was certainly some kind of outlaw hangout.

"Yes," said Rajan proudly. "Please drink up." He continued to smile and Jones, not to disappoint his host, blew on the cup and then took a very slow and careful sip. It tasted quite good.

"It's very good," said Jones honestly to Rajan's obvious appreciation.

Finally Jones' eyes had adapted to the light. What he saw was a clean, white tile room that had hallways leading to other brightly lit, white tile rooms. It was the same kind of tile as the subway station, but spotless. And it smelled good—like roses and something. Curry? He saw other men and women hurrying through the hallways. Most were Indian but he saw other ethnicities too. The men were dressed in button-down shirts and pressed slacks, and some had jackets like Rajan. They all wore polished black or occasionally brown leather or faux leather shoes. The suits, upon close inspection, were all worn, with tattered hems. The jackets nearly all had worn elbows and the pants had worn knees. Some of the women also dressed in business suits, similarly clean and pressed but wearing thin, however many women wore brightly colored saris made of cotton and silk, though probably synthetics. Everyone seemed to have a purpose, walking briskly, but nodding and smiling at each other and voicing short greetings. There were also people busily brushing the floors and wiping down the walls. Even the cleaning people—the men in their business attire and the women in their saris—seemed to keep spotless despite the wiping, scrubbing, mopping, and brushing.

"Rajan, have you prepared a room for us?" asked Alisa.

"Yes, we have Ms. Rosenbaum."

"Rajan, please call me Alisa."

"I am sorry, but that is just not our way. I thank you for your display of friendship and familiarity but if you do not mind I will address you as Ms. Rosenbaum. Now please follow me to the room we have prepared." He swiveled and began walking.

Jones turned to Alisa. "What do they do here all day? What exactly is this? They're certainly illegals, but…"

Rajan swiveled around to face them; his face was part anger, part disappointment. "We are not illegals! We are 'The Documented.'"

"Undocumented aliens?" asked Jones.

"Documented! Documented!" Rajan seemed annoyed with Jones. "We all have our documents in order. We are all here legally." He stretched out his arms and swept the air. "We have filled out the forms, waited in the lines, gotten the appropriate stamps, taken the necessary tests!" He pulled a thick, folded set of papers from inside his jacket pocket and waved them at Jones. "We have done everything right."

Jones looked confused. Alisa spoke. "They are here legally. They have no employment…"

Jones interrupted. "But the government provides…"

162

Good Intentions

"The government does not provide! We provide!" Rajan took a deep breath and spoke again, calmly. "I apologize for my rudeness Mr. Jones. Let me explain. The government provides money for those people who come here illegally. We have all come legally. And anyway we would not take government handouts. We have come to the Land of Opportunity to work hard, raise our families, contribute to a great society. A once great society I'm afraid. We live by the law. We take pride in our work. But it turns out we are too good. According to your government we are not tired enough, we are not poor enough, we are not wretched enough to have the golden door opened to us." Rajan turned his head down and a tear fell to the floor. A nearby floor cleaner saw it, rushed over, and swabbed the floor clean with his mop before quickly walking to tackle another smudge elsewhere.

"The government has programs for those who come here illegally," explained Alisa further. "There are legal protection programs, welfare programs, and jobs programs for those illegals who want that. There are no such programs for those who enter legally. Those people suffer. Look around at people too law-abiding to jump a fence and too proud to beg."

"We came to work, Mr. Jones," said Rajan, looking up. They say there are jobs that Americans simply will not do. But we are Americans. We will do those jobs. A job provides a sense of accomplishment, not to mention a meal for us and our families. Many of us have advanced degrees. We will gladly build a next generation computer system or answer phones at a customer support center or mow a lawn or clean a toilet. There are no jobs that these Americans won't do. But we are not given the chance. Those jobs are reserved for the 'undocumented.' The illegals."

"Some of them have even attempted to 'lose' their documents." With her fingers Alisa put air quotes around the word "lose." "But the government keeps records. One thing the government is very good at—keeping records. The government databases keep track of who has entered the country legally and who has not. If you try to claim that you are undocumented when in fact you have gone through all of the legal procedures... well, the consequences can be serious."

The Underground

In the moment of silence that followed, the workers in the room quietly went about their chores. Rajan looked up and smiled politely. "I am sorry for my outburst, Mr. Jones. You did not know the situation and, more importantly, I have not been a proper host and have not properly done my job. Please accept my apology."

"There's no need…" started Jones.

"We both accept your apology Rajan."

Rajan's smile widened. "Please continue to follow me then," he said. "I believe you will find the workspace we have provided to be very adequate." He continued walking and they continued following.

They reached a closed, heavy, clean but rusted metal door. Rajan grabbed the thick metal handle and leaned his entire body backward to open it. Jones moved to help him, but Alisa waved him back. The door creaked open. "We needed a place with working circuits and enough room," said Rajan. "We have been fixing this whole area up for some time," he explained, "but electricity is still spotty. We have had to move in our own electrical generators and backup batteries and electrical wiring, including networking lines. Wireless just is not secure. Even the wired lines need to be coax cable to stop any radio frequency emissions that could escape and be read by those outside."

Rajan waved them in. Jones followed Alisa inside to see some kind of high tech mission control center. A giant high definition flat screen monitor was bolted to one wall, covering most of the wall. A small podium was situated in front of the monitors. The podium had a microphone, a small touchscreen display, and an array of buttons and switches. Several rows of folding chairs, neatly placed in parallel lines, were facing the monitor and the podium. In the back were platforms, some empty, but a few having tripods and cameras on them. There were also electrical sockets in the floors—one by each chair—and along the walls. No one would suffer for lack of electricity here. Assuming it could be supplied to everyone at once. That was a feat that was difficult even for the U.S. Electrical Company, thought Jones.

"We can supply electricity to every socket in the room pulling as much as 10 amps simultaneously and continuously for at least 1 hour," said Rajan proudly in answer to Jones' unspoken question.

Jones was impressed. He looked around, then at Rajan who looked back smiling, waiting. "Very impressive," said Jones, and Rajan bowed, pleased.

"I will leave you two alone now," said Rajan. "The phone is in the corner." He pointed at the phone. "I am extension 1776. Please call me when you are through and I will come." He swiveled to face the doorway and walked out. The door creaked closed slowly and Jones could hear Rajan's soft grunt with the effort.

"Sit down, Mr. Jones… Winston," said Alisa pointing to one of the folding chairs as she walked to the podium. "I'll show you what we're all about."

Jones sat. Alisa flipped a switch. The lights went out.

The Underground

The Jobs Plan

Alisa fiddled with the buttons on the podium in front of her in the dark. Jones waited patiently. Well, not really patiently; he fidgeted. A loud "pop" emanated from the speakers, startling him.

"Doo doo," Alisa muttered uncharacteristically under her breath. She fiddled some more.

"I can't see these labels," she whispered to herself.

The screen lit up bright white then back to black, the flash illuminating the room while blinding Jones who covered his eyes.

"Double doo doo," muttered Alisa, then to Jones, "give me a minute, I can get this working." She flipped a switch and the lights came back on.

"Can you give me a hint as to what you're doing?"

"I wanted this to be dramatic but I can't get the stupid thing to work. Especially when I can't see what I'm doing. OK I think I've got it." She flipped the switch again and the lights went out again.

"Can you tell me what to expect? I'm in the dark here."

She fiddled with a few more buttons and the old Looney Tunes Cartoon ending came on, with the short, fast musical ditty and Porky Pig stuttering "That's All Folks!" Alisa screamed a few obscenities.

"I can build this stuff and fix it, but sometimes I just can't get it to work," she said. "It's our presentation. On the Jobs Plan."

"Look. Every politician since I can remember has had a jobs plan. If that's the big secret of the Freedman Group then I have to tell you I'm not impressed. You all talked—Milo talked—about great things and changing society, but if all you've got is another plan to create jobs, I don't see how that's any different from what the government is already doing. OK, you've got your own ideas about how to do it, but so does everyone else I know."

"Shut up and listen. It's not that kind of jobs plan."

Before Jones could respond, a dot appeared in the center of the screen and grew larger until it could be made out to be letters that declared "The Jobs Plan" and then faded out. Orchestral music played in the background. Another dot grew until it read "The Freedman Group" and then that faded out. The whole thing seemed a little cheesy and over the top to Jones. Maybe the Freedman Group could use a little more attention to marketing and PR. Of course, those were dying skills in a modern noncompetitive society. The screen then listed a bunch of copyright and trademark notices, which was quaint, and meaningless, given that the government had long ago declared that intellectual property rights conflicted with First Amendment rights to free speech. They were a form of thought censorship invented by the wealthy and would no longer be protected.

A black and white image appeared on the screen of drably dressed men and a few women walking around a large room filled with ancient mainframe computers. Large tape drive reels spun jerkily to and fro on several of the refrigerator-sized gray boxes that were arranged in unimaginative rows. These serious-looking men and women examined these boxes, observed the seemingly random movements of the tape reels, squinted at the rows of lights that blinked out indiscernible patterns, pressed an occasional button on one of the boxes, and took notes on the clipboards they all carried with them.

A narrator spoke slowly with the deep voice and recognizable exaggerated emphasis of an old-time news anchor. "The beginning of the computer revolution. In the mid twentieth century, at the time of World War II, the digital computer was created. Great men like Alan Turing, Tommy Flowers, Howard Aiken, John Atanasoff, John Mauchly, J. Presper Eckert, John Von Neumann, and Claude Shannon designed and built their giant computing machines, their colossi, housed in temperature controlled rooms, accessible only by those who were trained and knowledgeable—the elite scientists and engineers, government workers, military officials, and politicians. Because these giant machines were built at great cost and required large amounts of energy to maintain, both literal and human, it made perfect sense that they would be the step children of governments and military organizations. These machines helped win wars, guided men to the moon, calculated profits and losses at the largest companies, and meticulously counted the census. They made some men very rich and put great power into the hands of those who controlled them.

"Computers came to control almost every piece of machinery that could be found from farms to factories to communication systems. Fears emerged. Would computers control man? Would a select few people be able to harness so much knowledge and intellectual power, through the use of these machines, that they could calculate and thus predict the future? Could they know the secrets of all individuals from the people on the street to the rulers of nations? Could they assemble databases of information that allowed them to coerce and control the lives of others?"

Novelists began writing of near-future dystopias where people were like machines and machines were controlled by a few. Or even where the machines were in control with no human operators. George Orwell wrote his famous novel *Nineteen Eighty-Four* about Oceana, a fictional world where the government controlled every aspect of every person's life. Orwell's book was written around the time of the development of the computer, but the computer was hardly known to him. His book was not about computers but about freedom and the government's tendency to take it away. As computers became prevalent, many saw them as the instrument of those who would take freedom away—whether by large global corporations or large centralized governments."

The pace of the pictures on the screen had picked up gradually so that it was hardly noticeable at first. Images appeared of large mainframe computers and people in rural villages and on city streets. Machinery of all kinds flashed up there including automobile assembly lines and airplane cockpits and rocket control centers, all managed by these giant mainframes with their increasing rows of blinking lights and furiously spinning tape reels. The camera moved slowly toward one of the spinning reels, the revolving Lissajous patterns working to hypnotize Jones.

The narrator continued. "Then something unexpected happened. Or perhaps a string of things that swung the pendulum backwards. Three men working at Bell Telephone Laboratories created the transistor. Ironically, Bell Telephone was one of the companies most suspected by conspiracy theorists of harboring ideas of world domination through technology. William Shockley, John Bardeen, and Walter Brattain made a breakthrough that changed not only technology but, as technology often does, it changed society. These men invented the semiconductor transistor that could shrink the great machines in physical scale and energy consumption down to a tiny fingernail-sized chip. Of course it took others to implement and productize these tiny computers, engineers and entrepreneurs like Jack Kilby and Robert Noyce, Gordon Moore and Andrew Grove. They built an industry around these tiny chips whose features grew smaller and smaller to the point where computing power many times greater than those entire rooms of machinery could fit into the palm of one's hand.

"But it wasn't these men who figured out how to use the power of the technology to burst the nightmare of possible dystopias. That took a group of counter-culturists. In the nineteen sixties, a revolution took place. In music, in dress, in hygiene, in personal responsibilities (or the lack thereof). It was a cultural revolution, a kind of testing limits. It was the adolescent years of the twentieth century, and the movement was headed by adolescents in both age and in mentality. The culture of this time celebrated the individual above all else. A culture of hedonism prevailed. Casual sex and mind-numbing drug use became an accepted norm."

The images on the screen had changed. They were now in color. Scenes showed long-haired, bell-bottomed hippies in San Francisco. Volkswagen buses plastered with "Make Love Not War" stickers on their sides paraded up Van Ness Avenue and down Lombard Street. Couples entwined in parks, their hands exploring each others' bodies, smoking, sniffing, and injecting strange things and acting in strange ways. In the background could be heard beautiful folk songs with anti-establishment and anti-war messages. There were scenes of peaceful protests that merged into scenes of armed protests. There were pictures of crowds chanting anti-war songs and other crowds burning down college buildings. A spinning computer tape reel morphed into a psychedelic spinning multicolored pattern of spirals and paisleys that similarly hypnotized Jones. And made him a little queasy.

The narrator continued. "It was a time of upheaval. Like an adolescent testing the boundaries of acceptable behavior and figuring out its place in the world, this generation was testing and figuring out. The entire world seemed to be testing and figuring out. It was a difficult time and a wonderful time, but it was a turbulent time. But it was not these people, not the people of the sixties who made the change that we at the Freedman Group celebrate. The people who changed the world were a hybrid developed in the next decade, the seventies.

"In that next decade, the world suffered a bad hangover and decided it was time to sober up. Adolescence had been fun, but adulthood was approaching. American society appreciated individual rights but many came to recognize the need for individual responsibility too. It was time to earn a living and support one's self and one's families. There were those who were just a little too young to be at the party in the sixties but who wanted to have some fun in their own way. And this fun involved technology. So people like Gordon French and Fred Moore and Lee Felsenstein created the Homebrew Computer Club in Menlo Park, California and later moved it to Cupertino, Mecca of the personal computer revolution. They probably did not start with great ideals, only with the thought of creating something cool and exciting. But creating was key. This new group of pioneers needed to engineer, to innovate, to invent. And so they began making computers that fit on a desk and were inexpensive enough that anyone could have one. These computers did not calculate missile trajectories or predict stock movements, they only played simple games like tic-tac-toe and or calculated a monthly personal budget.

The Jobs Plan

"Two of the members of the Homebrew Computer Club were Steve Wozniak and Steve Jobs. Wozniak was the shy and nerdy tinkerer who could connect together the semi conductor chips in unique ways to solve problems that others thought were unsolvable. Not being able to buy one of these cool new little computers, he decided to gather up electronic components and power supplies and discarded equipment and build one of his own. Jobs befriended Wozniak, impressed with his engineering abilities and with big dreams of the power of putting computers into the hands of the masses, in the hands of individuals. While others saw these computers as hobbyist-built and hobbyist-bought, Jobs had the ridiculous idea of putting them in every home. He recognized them as tools— powerful tools—for individuals. The two Steves founded Apple Computer and launched the personal computer revolution.

"The Apple computer became a success and spawned a new industry. But Jobs was not content just selling computers; he wanted to change the world. And so he brought together a team of brilliant and eccentric engineers to create the next generation personal computer that he called the Macintosh. It had a graphical interface so that people didn't need to memorize arcane words and abbreviations to control the computer. It used a pointing device called a mouse to allow click and point control and data entry. And it came out in 1984, the year of George Orwell's famous novel but with the opposite effect of giving power to many people rather than the few."

The famous Apple Macintosh computer commercial of 1984 came onto the screen. Jones had never seen it—it was many years ago before he was born—but he was mesmerized. Straight, uniform rows of thin, shaven-headed men marched in synchronicity to take their seats in a dim, dusty auditorium before a giant screen showing a bland bespectacled man. They marched through tubes in a large gray building. Everything was drab and gray—the concrete of the buildings, the loose fitting clothes, their complexions and their expressions. Emotionless. The scene cut to a woman, a beautiful woman with flowing blonde hair and athletic build dressed in pure white shirt and bright red shorts. She was running, a large hammer held in both her hands, her breasts swaying in rhythm with her gait. Uniformed police, armed and threatening, ran after her while the

172

crowd of drones marched unwavering, not noticing, their attention frozen to the giant face on the screen reciting platitudes, only snippets of which could be made out.

The woman stopped in front of the screen, planted her feet, and began spinning in a circle. The hammer, gripped furiously in her hands, swung outward with centrifugal force from her twirling figure, whooshing loudly with each pass. The police in the background were very near. With a short, sharp, athletic cry, she released her grip and the hammer flew end-over-end toward the screen. It hit the screen just as the talking head proclaimed "we shall prevail." The screen exploded into dust that blew across the open-mouthed drones in their seats. An announcer for the commercial proclaimed, as the words scrolled up the screen, "On January 24, Apple Computer will introduce Macintosh. And you'll see why 1984 won't be like '1984.'" And 1984 was not like the George Orwell novel, but just the opposite. Technology had empowered the individual. Put great resources and knowledge in everyone's grasp. The Macintosh was marketed as "the computer for the rest of us" and Apple's tagline was "Think Different."

The narrator continued. "Apple went on to great commercial success. It spawned an industry and changed the world as Jobs had envisioned. As the technology continued to progress, the world changed more. Personal computers led to handheld personal digital assistants and then to iPhones. The 'i' originally stood for Internet, the worldwide network that connected everyone on the planet. But now we have come to realize that the 'i' really stood for individual. It stood for all the I's in the world. Because the transformation that Steve Jobs had begun was not to build a better gizmo, but to empower each person on the planet. And it was no coincidence that in doing this, Jobs became wealthy and Apple became the most valuable company in the world. Because changing the world for the better is a good thing. And competition is a good thing. And rewarding the people and the companies that brought about this good change was considered a good thing.

"But in the early 21st century things started changing. Some say it began with the global bank crisis, but others argue that it began long before

that. Decades earlier, the government had begun regulating the banks—
how much they could spend, how much they could loan out, what kind of
risks they could take, who they could loan to, who they were required to
loan to. But banks were still businesses and businesses by their nature
take risks. Some businesses take small risks. Others take large risks.
Some banks took very large risks, encouraged by government agencies
that required them to loan money to low income people and people of
select races and those whom the government decided were
'disenfranchised.' Some banks grew large taking huge risks, foolish
risks. But when the world economy went downhill and those risks took
their toll, the government stepped in and propped them up. The
politicians' intentions were good. They wanted no one to suffer,
especially these lower income families and children and historically
discriminated minorities and others. And the bankers. Though they did
not say it, they let the bankers take their millions and billions with hardly
a punishment other than a few nasty words and more regulations. The
politicians had decided to rig the game in the name of fairness.

"Politicians believed that they could make the world 'fair.' They had
their good intentions; few of them were actually bad people. They
wanted to help the tired, enrich the poor, house the homeless. For this
they needed control. And so they took it. Gradually. It had begun many
decades earlier, but accelerated in the 21st century. Politicians began
regulating businesses. Limiting their income, and their goods. To
accomplish this they needed to discourage competition and fund those
companies that they decided, in their 'great wisdom' were the 'right'
companies. They did not understand free markets. They did not
understand capitalism. They did not understand the economic miracle
that had been the United States of America for over 200 years.

"And the politicians began to spread the wealth. They distributed it from
those with the greatest ability to those with the greatest need. While
America had all but wiped Communism from the face of the earth in the
20th century, America's own leaders brought it back in the 21st. Karl
Marx, would have been proud. And Vladimir Lenin. And Joseph Stalin.
American politicians were not violent. They were not murderers. They

were not evil. They just knew that they knew best what was best for American business and for the American public.

"Movements sprung up. The Tea Party was formed and spread throughout the country to fight for individual rights and 'conservative financial principles,' though really they were not 'conservative' principles as much as they were American principles. The Tea Party movement was attacked and vilified. A counter movement sprung up, much smaller than the Tea Party, called the Occupy Movement. This began as groups of well-intentioned people who put individual rights above community rights or individual responsibility. Not unlike the Hippies of decades earlier. This movement also spread nationally, with politicians supporting them as they supported entitlements. Not all politicians—there was a great struggle between political ideologies at that time.

"As the Occupy Movement grew, it became infiltrated by anarchists, the mentally ill, extremists and zealots. It became violent. The tent cities erected in major cities became disease ridden encampments and places for crimes like rape and even murder. The protesters, wanting something they could not describe but were mostly just unhappy with their situations and believed that the government and those who had struggled to produce goods and supply jobs should give them more than just a salary for a day's work. 'We are human beings,' they would shout, 'and we deserve…' Well, you name it and they felt they deserved it, from a college education to a high-paying job, to medical care, to their video games and their MTV.

"The violence of the Occupy Movement—the burning of flags to the burning and looting of buildings—made them a force to be reckoned with. And the entitlement and regulation politicians kept the Occupy Movement going because it fit with their agenda of making our civilization a better, fairer place by any means necessary. The counterbalance to the Occupy Movement, the Tea Party Movement, was mostly a bunch of angry people who had worked very hard most of their lives only to see much of their wealth taxed and distributed to others. But they were older and for the most part objected to the violence and terror of the Occupy Movement. Eventually a smaller, more violent wing of the Tea Party, called the Koffee Klatch, sprang up. This new group was also violent and spread terror, and the entitlement/regulatory politicians fed the flames because it allowed them to grow stronger. These politicians began ever so subtly, and later very transparently, to start a class war between those with wealth and those with less wealth. We must not forget that America had the highest standard of living in the world and even those with very little were better off than nobility in many countries and the majority of the population in most countries.

"There were still many Americans—hard working people having a difficult time finding work in a terrible economy—who still believed that their hard work would pay off. They were embarrassed by the aid they received by the government, considering it a necessary evil. Yes, 'evil.' They looked to the day when they could earn their worth and support their family and make their children's lives better not by handouts but by the labors of their bodies or the ingenuity of their minds. They saw the rich not as the enemy, but as the goal. They saw themselves in that position one day, if things went well. They saw the rich not as better than themselves, but not worse either.

"But there was also a growing group of people who lived off of government assistance. Children who grew up not knowing or understanding the American ideal that each individual, with equal opportunity, had the ability to be as successful as he or she could, working as hard as he or she wanted to reach that goal. Also understanding that success was not always measured in dollars, and that one person's wealth gained legally, ethically, and morally, was a reason for admiration not jealousy. These children grew up learning that others owed them. That they deserved not to pursue happiness, but to be happy. And these children grew up to demand from others, to demand from the government. The 'E/R politicians' supported these people and these people in turn voted in the E/R politicians. A dangerous cycle had begun.

"Before long, the government's primary job was to make people happy and to make sure that no one person was happier than any other. The government created more regulations on business until it discovered that it was more efficient to simply run the businesses themselves. That way they could ensure fairness. And the government could distribute the wealth among all people. And all of those iPhones that gave individuals so much power, had to be replaced. In their stead the government issued personal digital assistants, PDAs, so that no one person had a better, faster, fancier device than another. These PDAs were connected to GovNet a network controlled by the government to ensure 'equal access,' and 'net neutrality.' The government could make sure that everything that was fed to each individual was 'fair and balanced' and inoffensive.

"Everything had started with good intentions."

Jones took a deep breath. So much of this he knew, but it had sounded different when he had learned it in school. Alisa walked over to him, putting her hand on his shoulder. "Interesting, isn't it?" she asked rhetorically. Her hand felt good on his shoulder that he had been tensing without realizing it.

The Freedman Group Logo appeared on the screen, the silhouette of a muscular man, his hands held high, breaking a chain between his wrists. Behind him was a freely flowing American Flag. Underneath the logo appeared the words, "The Jobs Plan."

The narrator continued. "The Freedman Group formed to protect individual rights, restore the freedom to compete, and make the government once again serve the people not the other way around. We have instituted The Jobs Plan as our first step."

With each point in the plan, the words exploded onto the screen as the narrator announced them:

"One. Disconnect from the GovNet. Replace it with a free network of individuals, corporations, nonprofits, and interest groups that all compete for the attention of the people.

"Two. Remove government controlled currency. Replace it with electronic currency that can be used for transactions and lent by private institutions.

"Three. Allow risk. Allow reward. Allow failure. Encourage success. Allow businesses, including banks, to take risks. Allow individuals to take risks. Require only that businesses be transparent about the risks they take. Provide education for the individuals who invest in the businesses. And provide only the most meager of safety nets that allow people to survive downturns long enough to become productive members of society but no longer than that."

The Freedman Group logo appeared on the screen again as the narrator went silent. The screen faded to black. Jones continued to stare at the screen, absorbing the message. He felt calm, relaxed as if something had connected with him deep inside. Or it may have been the fact that Alisa's hand still rested on his shoulder. In the darkness, the smell of her hair wafted into his consciousness. It was nice.

An alarm signal suddenly blasted from the walls, echoing around the complex, and breaking his reverie. "We need to go," said Alisa authoritatively, clasping his shoulder and pulling him up to attention in one quick motion.

Rain of Terror

"This way," said Alisa, moving toward the back of the room.

Jones followed her. Between blasts of the screaming siren he could hear sounds outside the room. People shouting. Hurried, frightened footsteps on the clean and smooth tile. Somewhere nearby, uniformed police, armed and threatening, ran toward this facility.

At the back of the room Alisa threw her arms around a large filing cabinet and with a loud groan, slid it away from the wall. Her strength was always surprising to Jones. She seemed so thin yet had amazing strength and endurance when she needed it.

Behind the filing cabinet was a roughly cut plate with an indented handle so that it would not obstruct the cabinet when the cabinet was pushed against the wall. Alisa reached her thin hand into the handle, and wrapped her long, delicate fingers around it. She braced one heeled shoe against the wall, coiled her leg, and then leaned back, pushing with her feet. The plate swung open, revealing a dark, narrow opening behind it.

"I'm sorry about this, but we have to get out of here. These escape hatches are placed throughout the facility. This won't be pleasant." Then somewhat quietly she added, "I'm afraid this facility is useless now that it's been discovered." At that she plunged into the narrow cavity.

Jones knew when Alisa opened the hatch that things were going to get worse. The alarm bells had already put him on edge, though he hadn't really known what the alarms meant. The odor that emanated from the hatch was horrendous. And it was dark in that hatch. He had no idea what was inside. It seemed even more frightening when Alisa launched herself into it. He watched her body disappear slowly as if being consumed by a giant python.

"Come on!" he heard her say from the other side of oblivion. "There's no time."

Rain of Terror

The alarm siren was still squealing and in addition to panicked footsteps he could hear pairs of feet jogging in unison. Those were the police no doubt. He wasn't sure which he had to fear most, the police or the Freedman Group or the Electoral Committee or that beckoning hole in front of him. On the other side of that hole was Alisa Rosenbaum and that tipped the scales. Jones took a deep breath and plunged his head through the opening.

"Are you through?" he heard Alisa say somewhere in front of him. Jones couldn't bear to open his mouth for fear of breathing in the malodorous fumes. He went to stand and slammed his head into a very low ceiling, letting out a harsh groan.

"Winston?" asked Alisa. "Are you with me? Are you ok?"

Jones forced out air: "Yes." He was on his hands and knees and the surface was slimy and slippery.

"You're going to have to breathe if you intend to get through this," said Alisa. "And we have to move fast! But stay low. Crawl."

Jones let out the rest of the air in his lungs and took a quick, sharp breath through clenched teeth, hoping that somehow he could filter out the noxious element. He couldn't. He vomited loudly.

"Good, that's out of the way," said Alisa. "Now move!" It was a command.

Her voice receded and he followed her. Behind him there were sounds coming from the room they'd just left. Between the blaring siren, the panicked footsteps, and the synchronized jogging he thought he heard screaming. He couldn't be sure. He wondered if they would be followed, but he didn't want to ask. He didn't want to talk. He wanted to focus on moving and he wanted to ignore his surroundings so that he would not form a mental picture of what he could only feel and smell.

Alisa barked short orders at him. "Turn left… bear right… keep straight."

Good Intentions

Jones thought he felt things move beneath him. His knees kept slipping out from under him, and one time his face landed in a gooey puddle. He vomited again. In front of him he heard a sharp gagging noise. "Alisa?" he asked partly out of concern and partly out of fear.

"Keep going!" she responded. He realized that she was not immune from all this. She had also vomited. In a way it endeared her to him—she was human after all. It also made him sick and he too vomited again.

After about 20 minutes of winding through narrow, unseen pathways, Alisa stopped. "Catch up to me because the next part is tricky."

"Tricky?" thought Jones. What was the part we just experienced? Does she mean the next part is worse or more dangerous or just different? His eyelid began twitching violently. He kept crawling forward until he ran into what he assumed were her legs.

"Stand up," she commanded. He did so hesitantly, expecting to bump his head again. He didn't. He couldn't see her—it was still pitch black in whatever place they were in—but he could sense her face in front of his. Even here the thought of her face so close to his, her lips so near to his, gave him a slight thrill. Then his mind pictured how she was probably covered in the same substance that he was, the same substance that smelled so putrid, and he was only able to stop himself from retching with the knowledge that doing so at this moment would definitely not impress her or improve his chances with her. Then he heard a sharp noise and felt a warmth moving down his arm.

"I… I'm really sorry," he heard her say.

"Oh… Yeah… That's ok," he replied. He really was not prepared for a situation like this and was at a loss for words. There was silence that took him by surprise. "What next?" he asked gently.

"You need to climb," responded Alisa. "There are rungs on the sides. Grab them and move up. When you get to the top, push against the cover to move it out of the way. I'll be behind you."

Jones felt the walls, nicked his hand on a sharp object that no doubt drew blood, but he ignored it, eager to get out. It seemed like he was close to the end of this escape route. Close to escaping.

Jones felt one of the rungs and grabbed onto it hard. It was wet and slippery, so he had to grasp tightly. He maneuvered in front of it and was able to put his other hand on it too. Lifting his foot he swung it around until it made contact with a lower rung. He placed his foot onto it and then stepped up. Rung by rung he climbed, not knowing where it would lead. His foot slipped from the rung a few times, but he caught himself from falling. Once or twice he thought his foot kicked something soft, but he wasn't sure and could only think of the freedom toward which he climbed.

Every few minutes Jones and Alisa acknowledged each other, checked on each other.

"You ok?"

"Yeah."

"Still with me?"

"Yeah."

"Hanging in?"

"Hanging in."

Jones' arms were tiring. He held on with one hand and shook out the other, then switched hands and repeated. He frequently swept a hand above him, feeling nothing. Until after a few minutes it brushed against something solid. "I feel it," said Jones. "The cover."

"Push it up and slide it over." said Alisa. "Can you do that? I'm exhausted, but if you need me…"

"Got it," said Jones. He pushed but it was heavy. He had to hold on to the rungs with one arm and push the cover with only one arm. He moved up a rung for better leverage, took a deep breath, and pushed hard while exhaling slowly and steadily. The cover moved a bit. Daylight started streaming in on top of them through the sliver the he had created. And water. They had reached the surface and it was raining.

Jones breathed in again deeply and slid the cover over. Water showered upon them. Jones climbed up and out onto the street. He had pushed over a manhole cover on a sidewalk. It seemed so cliché, like something out of a movie or a cartoon. He had expected something else—not sure what—but here he was.

Jones saw Alisa's hand reach out of the manhole. It was dirty and bloody. He shuddered at the site, or maybe it was just something that had been building in him for a while. Then he grabbed her hand in his and assisted her up and out of the hole.

They were on a sidewalk in a dark alley. There were people walking by, but they paid little attention, choosing instead to avoid the couple that had emerged from the sewers and to avert their eyes. That was not unusual. People tended to avoid getting themselves into undesirable situations and from the looks of the couple, this was definitely an undesirable situation.

Jones looked at Alisa and saw her covered in filth, her nice clothes ripped and stained. A millipede circled her collar. Jones reached over and flicked it off with his finger. He knew he was in similar condition but preferred not to think about it.

The rain was coming down fierce but it felt good. Jones and Alisa looked skyward, held their arms out wide, and let the rain wash them.

After a moment Jones turned to Alisa. "What happens to them? To Rajan? To those documented aliens?"

"They'll be taken to the Psychic Cleaners."

Jones stared at her without comprehending.

"It's a place," explained Alisa. "The government runs it. Brainwashing. Reeducation. Psychic cleaning. It's all the same thing. Those people in the Underground will be changed. Their citizenship may be taken away. Then they'll be illegals... excuse me, undocumented. At that point the government may give them jobs or put them on welfare. It will destroy their morale, hurt their pride. They'll be very unhappy. It's very sad. And out of our hands. Unless we change the system. We must change the system!"

At that moment, a clean white sedan came screeching to a halt at the end of the alley. A window unrolled and someone poked her head out. "Come with me," she yelled at them.

Jones looked at Alisa. "One of your comrades?" he asked.

"No," she replied.

"The police are coming. The psychic cleaners are coming. They've tracked you. There's little time," exclaimed the woman in the car. "Come with me if you want to live!"

"She's probably right," said Alisa. "I don't know who this is, but the government will find us pretty soon." She nodded at the cameras on the buildings. "I say we accept her offer and figure things out later."

Jones shrugged. This was all very new for him and he was having a hard time keeping the players straight anyway. "OK. I'm trusting you," he said.

They ran toward the car at the end of the alley. They opened the door and slid in, drenched but not quite as foul smelling as they had been only a few minutes earlier. The car sped off in dramatic fashion.

Game Change

The large, round oak table had a presence that could be felt if not seen in the dark, smoke filled chamber of the Electoral Committee of the Fairness for EveryBody Society. The members of the committee, as always dressed in dark suits and dark overcoats, puffed away at their cigarettes and cigars, their voices floating around the room, disembodied.

"I heard we found him."

"Almost found him."

"He got out?"

"What's the story?"

Rom Automatic stood. Though no one could see him, they somehow knew he was standing. It was a feeling. Not always a good one. "We were able to track him into an underground control center of the Freedman Group."

A visible hush filled the room as each member exhaled a burst of smoke.

"So we shut them down? The Freedman Group?"

"No."

"We found their center and we didn't shut them down?"

"And we didn't catch them?"

"They have many centers; they're decentralized. We shut down this center. There are many more."

"What was it like?"

"Very clean. Very tidy. They had a sophisticated IT operation. Very sophisticated."

"How?"

"It was being run by 'legals.'"

Another visible hush.

"We believe they were tapping into GovNet."

"Tapping into?"

"At least we think that. We don't know if they were successful."

"You don't know?"

"We don't know, but we put a stop to whatever they were doing. We're examining their source code, their databases. Unfortunately they used encryption."

"But we can crack encryption, right?"

"We can if they used legal encryption. Turns out they used illegal encryption. We're not sure we know how to crack it."

"Wow. Here we work so hard to create an open society and these people go and…"

"What about the legals?"

"Yeah, what happened to the legals?"

"Psychic cleaning."

A few mumbled words and low utterances could be heard throughout the room, causing streams of smoke to add to the cloud already settled there.

"Where is he now?"

"Yes, where is Jones?"

"He got away."

"He got away?"

"Escaped?"

"I thought you were following him?"

"How did you let him…?"

"We know where he is," said Rom.

There was a moment of silence.

"How do you know?"

"He's with one of our agents. That's how we tracked him in the first place. We've been tracking him for a while."

"The Iowa Caucus is coming up."

"Yes, the Iowa Caucus. And we don't have a candidate."

"Without a candidate, the caucus will be thrown into confusion."

"Yes, confusion."

"The whole country will be thrown into confusion."

"Pandemonium."

"Chaos."

"We will have a candidate. Winston Jones will be the candidate and he will agree to be the candidate before the caucus. And we will have a big announcement, a big reassuring press conference."

"How can you be sure?"

"Our agent assures me. She has rarely been wrong before. She is very capable. And as smart as she is beautiful."

"That's sexist," was uttered by someone softly. It was followed by silence.

"He'll need a running mate."

"A vice president."

"Yes, we need to choose a vice president, too."

"She'll be his vice president," said Rom.

"Who?"

"The agent," replied Rom. "Alisa Rosenbaum."

There was silence as the group contemplated one of their own as vice president. They had usually distanced themselves from the candidates, picked outsiders who were simply figureheads but who couldn't be traced back to them.

"You sure that's a good idea."

"It's a good idea," said Rom.

The group thought about this and seemed to approve.

"And you know where they are?"

"Yes, I just said…"

"So where are they?"

"They're heading west."

"To California?"

"To Lancaster."

Again a moment of silence.

"Eden?"

"Yes."

"But that's…"

"I know. We're being very careful."

"Yes."

"Be careful."

"Eden, huh?"

The people in the room thought about that without saying anything. The room remained silent, everyone puffing away for minutes, before they began leaving. There was no formal adjournment as there typically would be. Instead people just started getting up and going out. Only Rom remained.

"Eden," he muttered, shaking his head. He squashed his cigar forcefully into the ash try on the table and glided out of the room.

Game Change

Strange Bedfellows

The white sedan sped through the mostly empty streets, speeding around corners, brakes screeching, swerving to avoid unseen obstacles, running red lights, throwing its passengers from one side to the other. The woman driving was small with a pasty white complexion and stringy black hair down just past her shoulders. Her features were pointed and her painted eyebrows formed a V of concentration as she maneuvered the streets like a race car driver, which seemed particularly odd since the streets were completely empty. She wore a dark business suit, not unlike the ones that Alisa favored, but it was just a size too big for her small frame.

"My name is Marla McGivers," she said glancing briefly in the rear view mirror before bringing her eyes back to the road. "I'm going to take you to a safe place. You'll find friends there. People with common goals, common structure. We know about you."

Jones was confused. "You know about me?"

He was greeted with silence. Suddenly Jones became nervous that he had so easily fallen into a trap. Who was this woman? Who was the group she talked about? He turned to Alisa. She appeared a little stiff but otherwise calm.

"It's an honor to meet you," said McGivers. "We know what you're trying to accomplish. We want to help. We can achieve more in combination than competition. But the structure matters. The physical structure."

"I've heard some things," said Alisa. "I'm flattered that you know about me. I'm looking forward to finding out more. I understand the structure."

Jones contorted his face in confusion. "I don't know what the f…" Alisa reached over and pinched his hand. He turned to her as she lifted a finger to her lips as a sign of silence.

"I understand the structure," repeated Alisa.

191

Strange Bedfellows

Marla McGivers smiled briefly before resuming her intense concentration on the road. The next hour and a half were driven in silence, with Jones both very confused and very nervous. Alisa squeezed his hand a few times for comfort.

Their trip took them out past the Philadelphia city limits into the rural areas of Lancaster County that had long ago been Indian Territory, home of the Shawnee, Susquehannock, Gawanese, Lenape, and Nanticoke tribes. Later the Amish settled there. They called themselves "The Plain People" but were known by outsiders as "Pennsylvania Dutch" because of the German language they spoke from their home country. "Deutsch" is the German word for German.

The Amish were Christians who traced their roots to the Protestant Reformation of the 16th century in Europe, where there was an emphasis on purity and simplicity. One group of reformers, the Anabaptists, rejected the popular concept of infant baptism. These Anabaptists believed that baptism was for adults, and only those who confessed their faith. These faithful must remain physically and spiritually separate from the immorality of the rest of society. These Anabaptists were united in 1536 by a young Catholic priest from Holland named Menno Simons, and they became known as "Mennonites."

One Mennonite, Jacob Amman, felt that the Mennonites had become too lax. The Mennonites had a practice of banning or shunning a church member who did not repent, as a way of "encouraging repentance," but this practice had been eased by the time of Amman. In 1693, Amman split from the Mennonites, forming his own sect called "Amish."

These Anabaptist groups were strongly persecuted throughout Europe; thousands were put to death as heretics by Catholics and Protestants. Many of them fled to the mountains of Switzerland and southern Germany where they took up farming and holding worship services in their homes rather than churches. William Penn, founder of Pennsylvania, was a member of the Religious Society of Friends, or "Quakers," and thus also familiar with religious persecution in Europe. He offered land to the Amish as part of his "holy experiment" of religious tolerance. The Amish settled in Lancaster County in the 1720's and 1730's.

By the twentieth century, Amish Country had become a tourist destination. The Amish eschewed modern technology. They rejected the combustion engine, farming their land with only human and animal effort. They rode in buggies drawn by horses. They restricted all use of electricity and forbade the watching of television or the listening to radio. They read, mostly the Bible and little else. They had strong family lives centered on farming and worship.

By the twenty-first century, the definition of "modern technology" had begun to change. Some Amish groups allowed the use of transistor radios—AM frequencies only however. Television was allowed but with rabbit ear antennas—no cables or satellite dishes—and only receiving the three broadcast networks. And of course, only small black and white screens not color. Internet access became acceptable at dial-up modem speeds of 56 kilobits per second maximum. A market sprung up for computers with Intel 386 processors running DOS or Windows 3.1 and the Spynet Mosaic Internet browser but definitely not Microsoft Internet Explorer of any version. The Amish became good at repairing and restoring old computers.

The Amish tourist industry grew, bringing in good money as those in the modern world came to marvel at the simple lifestyle of the Plain People. Eventually some cash-rich Amish realized that hiring workers to farm their fields would give them more time for religious learning. The Great Patent Wars of the twenty-first century brought a huge demand for restoring, repairing, and reverse engineering older technologies, and the Amish were naturally set up to reap the rewards. Eventually the wealthy Amish community moved elsewhere (no one is certain exactly where they moved), and their communities were replaced with Amish World, a combination Disneyworld and Las Vegas that surpassed both locations as the world's most visited, and profitable, vacation getaway.

But the car in which Jones was riding did not stop at Amish World, instead skirting it and continuing a short ways beyond it. Jones saw a small dome in the distance. As they approached, the dome grew and

Jones realized that its immense size had been disguised by their distance from it. It took a while to reach it, and when they did, it loomed over them about five stories tall and about a city block in diameter. It was simple, round, smooth. There were windows, but no spires or towers, only a gently sloped point at the top. It was white, almost pure, unblemished white, with gold trim. The car pulled into a driveway in the front. The tiles of the driveway formed an intricate abstract mosaic. A few women mulled about outside. This was a mosque, he realized, because the women all wore white head-to-toe burkas that completely covered them. Their hoods left only slits for their eyes. They milled about aimlessly until the car pulled up, then one walked over and opened the door for McGivers to exit, bowing to her. She must be important, thought Jones. Then the woman opened the back door and bowed as Alisa exited. No one came to open his door, so Jones slid across the seat. The burka clad woman straightened, and Jones could make out her eyes widening. Even that small movement and the quick expression gave Jones the notion that he was not appreciated here.

McGivers entered the mosque and Alisa followed. Jones felt the stares of these covered women. As he passed, he noticed that several were larger than him, and he was a pretty tall guy. Those that were not taller were beefier. These were big women.

In a large entryway McGivers stopped and turned to face them. "I think you'll want to take showers before entering. We have those here." She pointed to a fancy one to her left labeled "women" and then a simpler, plainer one to her right labeled "men." Alisa looked at Jones and nodded. Jones shrugged. They each went their ways.

Jones entered a locker room like any other men's locker room. The freshener only just covered the odor of sweat that seemed to bring back a primal memory in Jones of hard labor, though he had never done hard labor or really any labor of any kind that he could remember. American citizens did not perform physical labor except for exercise or in one of those popular reality television shows. All other forms of physical labor were declared unhealthy by the Attorney General and outlawed for the most part. But Jones breathed it into his lungs deeply, embracing it. He laid his clothes as neatly as he could in a pile on a bench, but they were soggy and torn and ragged no matter how well he folded them. He stepped into the showers and enjoyed the hot water, ignoring the few large, hairy men that were also in the locker room but who said little.

Alisa stepped into the women's locker room and found a giant perfumed spa. She followed a maze that amazed her and seemed to go on and on. She saw whirlpools and massage stations and hair stylists and manicure stations and pedicure stations. She saw makeup counters and little jewelry bazaars. Rooms led to other rooms that led to still other rooms. There were clothes racks of fabulous, fine women's wear. And throughout, women strolled and talked and laughed. Some were clothed in clingy silk dresses, others in only a few well-placed towels, and others in nothing at all. Alisa actually felt uncomfortable. This was not her world.

"Please find a shower," said McGivers who had been following Alisa as she had meandered around the spa. McGivers pointed toward a room from which steam was drifting out. "I'll take your clothes and destroy them," she continued, "and I'll find you something nicer."

Alisa undressed uncomfortably. She handed her clothes to McGivers in a nice folded stack and walked toward the steamy room. Though Alisa had a very attractive, thin, athletic build, she preferred the formality and the distinction that a nice business suit provided. Picking her head up she strode confidently if stiffly toward the showers and the steam room beside it while the other women chatted and mostly did not take notice of her. The warm shower felt very good on her cold skin and she let herself relax for a few moments to enjoy it.

Alisa stepped out of the shower and McGivers was waiting with a towel and a robe. Alisa was now clean and more relaxed and began to ask a question, but McGivers quieted her with a short, subtle motion of her hand. She led Alisa to another room, talking about mundane things like the weather and fashion and movie stars and other things in which Alisa had little or no concern, but in which she feigned interest. In this next room, filled with racks of designer clothes, women milled around gossiping and laughing. McGivers reached into a closet and took a hanger holding fine silk underwear and brassiere and a slinky dress of fine blue and white material.

"I know it's not what you prefer," said McGivers blushing slightly, "but I think you'll enjoy it."

Alisa knew better than to object. She was still not certain where she was, who these people were, or what they wanted from her. Or for her. She had an inkling, but needed to find out more. She felt she needed to cooperate, and so she slipped on the dress. It felt soft, smooth, and comfortable, which made her uncomfortable.

In the men's locker room, Jones finished his shower and found a towel hanging outside his shower stall. He dried himself off then looked around for clothes. He wandered around the locker room and the few men inside ignored him in silence. One door was labeled "exit" and so he opened it slightly to see rows and rows of women on their knees, bowing and chanting. Suddenly a burka-covered woman put her face in the door opening and said "back" to him in a deep growl. Jones backed up and the woman entered the locker room. The other men seemed not to notice but Jones' hands quickly shot downward to cover himself up. The large woman pushed past him, to two large closet doors and opened one to reveal a long row of white burkas similar to the one she wore. The woman pointed to the burkas and said, "Here!" Jones stood frozen, still covering himself with his hands and afraid to move. The woman reached a large hairy hand upward and tore off her head covering and veil to reveal… a man! These were not women in burkas, these were men. "Here," repeated the man. "Put this on. You can't leave this area without one of these."

Jones sidled over to the closet of burkas, still cupping himself with his hands, still confused. The man put his head covering back on, grunted in annoyance, and went back out the exit door. Jones picked one of the white burkas that seemed to be his size and put it on.

McGivers led Alisa out of the spa complex and into a very large tiled room filled with rows of fabulously dressed and bejeweled women all bowing down on multicolored mats, facing the same direction. They were all chanting quietly, together producing a loud hum.

"Can I get you a mat? Perhaps a nice dark green to complement your skin tones?"

"No thank you," said Alisa hesitantly. She did not want to offend these people—there were a heck of a lot of them, hundreds she estimated—but she was still uncertain about what was going on.

McGivers gave Alisa a stone cold stare for just an instant before sighing. "Of course," she said, shrugging. "I'll take my position right here," she said pointing downward to the small patch of open floor space in front of them. "You should listen to what Imam Gina has to say. It will open your eyes, and you're mine."

Alisa shivered. Did she hear McGivers right? Certainly she said "and your mind" not "and you're mine." McGivers fetched a stunning red and black mat with gold trim from a rack on the wall, placed it on the floor, kneeled down, and began chanting. Every so often she looked up at Alisa and smiled. The phrase "and you're mine" kept going through Alisa's head.

Jones exited the locker room into a large, spotlessly clean room. Rows and rows of women were kneeling and chanting, creating an annoying, loud buzz that echoed throughout the chamber. The women all looked nice, though, dressed in slinky, colorful outfits, and most of them were fairly attractive. Across the chamber he saw Alisa exit from a fancy wooden door framed in intricate carvings of what appeared to be ivory but was no doubt a synthetic. Still it looked impressive. She was talking to the woman Marla who had driven them here. Jones instinctively waved at Alisa, trying to catch her attention. She glanced in his direction then back to Marla. Did she see him? He began to wave again but saw a large gray burka heading his way.

"This way," said the burka. Jones followed him along a narrow pathway past the kneeling, chanting women who paid no attention to them. He was led into a side room of plain folding chairs. Hundreds of men in burkas sat in the chairs. This room had its own hum, which almost certainly was that of soft snoring, and occasionally loud snoring, coming from beneath the burkas. "Sit," said the large burka and pointed to a chair. Jones sat. A loudspeaker at the front of the room carried the sounds of the chamber into this smaller room for the men to hear.

The chanting of the women became softer and softer as the women began finishing and fewer and fewer were contributing to the overall sound. Eventually silence befell the chamber. The women were all facing forward with looks of anticipation.

After a few minutes of absolute silence broken only by an occasional cough or throat clearing, a tall, lithe blonde in stiletto heels strolled onto a platform above the crowd. She was wearing a tight-fitting, sheer red skirt. Her hair was full and bleached pure blonde. She wore seductive, wet red lipstick. Her skirt reached just below her knees and closely fit every curve of her body. Every curve. She looked over the mass of women in front of her, all facing her with looks of awe. "Allah Akbar," she said quietly.

"Allahu akbar," replied the crowd softly in unison.

"Allah akbar," said the blonde woman a bit louder.

"Allahu akbar," replied the crowd a little louder. This continued for several iterations, each iteration louder than the one before it.

"Allah akbar!" shouted the blonde woman.

"Allahu akbar!" shouted the crowd back at her.

The blonde said nothing, staring out at the crowd, smiling. The crowd's murmurs dissipated into total silence.

"Welcome to Eden, ladies. I am Gina Inviere."

The murmurs grew. A few people applauded hesitantly and then quieted when the rest did not join in.

"You have made the pilgrimage and you have been washed of sin."

Again more murmurs and a few hands clapping in the stillness.

"Except for those of you who could not get appointments at the spa, and for that I apologize, but turnout has been greater than expected. For those who could not get appointments, please stop by the front desk for a rain check and a twenty percent discount on any secular goods at the gift store."

This time there was great applause that died down quickly.

"Today's lecture is on the Nine Jewels of Femlamism," said Gina Inviere as she held up a necklace of nine large, different colored jewels. "These are the principles upon which Femlamism is built. Many of you know them, but you must keep them in your heart and you must teach them to your daughters. You must talk of them when you sit at home or in coffee shops, and when you walk along the malls and the markets. When you lie down, and when you get up. And you shall decorate your house with these jewels, wear them on your hands and around your necks, and we even have some nice hats.

"Always remember that while these jewels are beautiful, and a bargain, they represent more than just pretty stones that can be used to accessorize just about any outfit. They represent the nine principles of Femlamism.

"One. There is no god but Allah and Mohammed is the Profit of Allah.

"Two. Say your prayers daily.

"Three. Be charitable to women. Women are all allies; men must not be trusted.

"Four. Allah does not forbid you to be kind to men who are not unkind to you.

"Five. Diet to keep your body fit and trim. Your power over men has its roots in your beauty and sexuality.

"Six. Jihad is the struggle against patriarchy, and it is the most important struggle.

"Seven. Allah divided society into sex-classes. The male class has fallen from grace. The female class is ready to take its position of power.

"Eight. Make pilgrimage to Eden at least once a lifetime, but preferably much more often.

"Nine. At the end of days, Mohammed will return as a woman and the sexes will be separated into two societies—women and men."

As each principle was recited, oohs and ahs could be heard throughout the mosque chamber. These noises grew louder with each principle until the last when there were grunts of approval, a few scattered fists pumped into the air, and a number of high-fives.

"Now go forth! And remember to stop in at the gift store on your way out. There are many bargains right now as we prepare to clean house in preparation for Ramadan. You can get the Nine Jewels in a beautiful necklace or bracelet to impress your friends and to proudly display your faith. And unlike other religious symbols, this one goes well with almost any ensemble for all occasions, formal or casual." Gina Inviere paused to allow a sternness to return to her face. "Allah Akbar!"

"Allahu akbar," replied the women as they rose and stretched and began meandering throughout the chamber smiling and nodding and talking amongst themselves. Gina Inviere looked over the crowd, pleased, before quietly retreating from her platform above the chamber.

Alisa had listened to the speech alternating between admiration and disgust. She had heard about radical Femlamists, but never had she believed that there was actually an organized movement. And such a large organized movement that obviously had significant resources. This leader, Gina Inviere, was a very attractive woman, which made her message dangerously easy to absorb—even Alisa found herself wanting to believe despite the disturbing content of the message itself. It seemed empowering on its surface. And Gina Inviere had a way of talking and moving a crowd; she was very inspiring. Alisa shivered at the thought.

Good Intentions

"Are you ready to meet Gina Inviere?" Alisa had not noticed McGivers once again next to her, a bit too close.

"Okay," said Alisa noncommittally. McGivers motioned for Alisa to follow her as she led her along a walkway into the back of the chamber and through a large, bejeweled door.

Jones had been impatient listening to Gina Inviere's speech. Fortunately he could not see her, and how beautiful she was, or he might have fallen under her spell, though certainly her message would not have appealed to him in any case. The hypnotic inflexions of her voice were lost through the tinny speakers in the side room. Anyway, the speech was not intended for him nor for any of the men in the building.

Jones began to fidget and noticed that no one was paying much attention to him. Maybe they wanted to, but it was too difficult for them to see out of the eye slits of the burkas. The men mostly sat, with their heads down. Jones got up slowly, looking around to see if anyone was noticing him or coming after him. No one was. He began walking around the room, looking at the walls that were all bare. He was nervous that without any side vision, due to the burka, he was vulnerable from all sides. His heart rate began increasing. He wanted to get out of this place. Wandering along the wall he came across a nondescript closet door at the opposite end from where he had entered. He turned around very slowly to see if anyone was watching him. No one was. He slowly grasped the door handle and turned it. It turned. He slowly pulled the door opened and heard sounds of machinery and the groans and grumbles of human labor. He opened the door more and put his head in to see a very large room and an assembly line manufacturing things. He squinted and could see the products of this labor—rockets, guns, bombs.

Suddenly a nicely dressed woman stepped in front of him and opened her mouth to make a cackling, shrill scream as she pointed at him. The men in burkas stopped their work and turned to look at Jones. In an instant the woman leaned over slightly. Jones leaned over to see what she was doing, in time to observe her foot swinging upward rapidly and planting itself into his groin. Jones keeled over and passed out.

Strange Bedfellows

Exposing Herself

McGivers had led Alisa to a large room and left her there alone. The room looked like the pictures she had seen as a young girl in textbooks of the luxurious, expensive apartments in city high rises that were owned by the robber barons of decades gone by. In those days if you had enough wealth you could buy yourself a grand room in a tall skyscraper, filled with beautiful upholstered furniture, crystal chandeliers, plush carpets, graceful sculptures, and walls decorated with colorful paintings in gilded frames. In those days the wealthy could entertain guests with fancy meals of exotic meats and rare spices that were as delicious as they were unhealthy. Of course those days were gone because unhealthy foods have been mostly outlawed, large apartment buildings have been turned into low-income housing, and accumulation of wealth was a criminal offense. Children had been taught about those days to understand the evils of unrestrained capitalism, but as a child Alisa had secretly yearned for those times and envied those apartments. So did most of the children in her class. They lived in a small town in West Virginia in the Appalachian Mountains, where most families were white and thus their poverty was rarely noticed by the government and where most families did not trust the government anyway and would have refused any housing or aid had it been offered to them.

A door opened and Gina Inviere walked in. Or rather slithered. She moved in a sensual undulating way that seemed instinctive rather than deliberate. She was tall, lean, and confident. Her skin was alabaster, giving her the appearance of an ancient Greek statue of the goddess Athena in a slinky red dress. Her blonde hair flowed around her head like a flaming corona. When she spoke, her ruby red lips perfectly formed each syllable. Alisa found herself mesmerized.

"Greetings," said Inviere.

Alisa nodded.

"I am honored to have you here."

"Honored?" asked Alisa.

"Alisa Rosenbaum, I know who you are. I know what you have been through. I know what you are capable of. And I know you will want to join us, because through us you can achieve greatness."

"You know me?" asked Alisa.

"Yes," said Inviere. "Our resources extend far and wide. Our network is very large. Our knowledge base is extensive. We know something about every woman on the planet and much about some women. You fall into that latter category. And we know even more about the men on this planet because as the great Chinese military strategist Sun-Tzu said, 'Keep your friends close and your enemies closer.' You are a friend, Alisa Rosenbaum."

"A friend of whom?"

"A friend of Gina Inviere. And a friend of Femlamism. We are important friends to have in these times."

"Then I'm flattered," said Alisa. She was still uncertain what they wanted of her. Or why they wanted her at all. She had heard rumors about a group of radicalized women. Religious fanatics. There had been some attacks in recent years that the government had simply labeled "human directed incidents" or HDIs—explosions at baseball stadiums, beer breweries, NASCAR races, and novelty gift manufacturing plants. There were rumors of a radical feminist group being responsible, but the government only used the term HDI to avoid blaming non-Judeo-Christian religious groups like Muslims, Hindus, and Buddhists. Some thought that these attacks were simply mislabeled by negligent government clerks, but others conjectured about Islamist Feminists, though few could describe what such a group would look like. Now here she was in the midst of it.

"You have no doubt heard of us," said Inviere.

"No I haven't."

"Damn," said Inviere, "our public relations department is not at all what I need it to be. This is a complex game we play. We need to fly under the radar, yet we need women to know about us. It is a difficult balance. It is a metastable state, like a rigid pendulum balanced precisely upside-down. It is perfectly stable until some perturbation, no matter how small, causes it to swing down." Inviere illustrated the pendulum with her forearm. "We must keep that balance between our philosophy and the rest of the world until we are the stable state. We need smart women to work with us to keep that precarious balance until then. You understand what I'm talking about, don't you?"

Alisa was shocked but tried not to show it. Back in college her secret engineering thesis had been on solutions to the metastability problem of asynchronous inputs to field programmable gate arrays. Did Inviere know this or was it a coincidence? Alisa stared into Inviere's emerald green eyes and Inviere stared back unblinking. Inviere knew.

"Then let me explain about Femlamism. It dates back to the Biblical days of Sarah. It was passed down through generations of women who kept it secret for fear of being killed by the men who had usurped the true religion of the one true Goddess. These brave prophets taught the knowledge and the customs of Femlamism to their daughters who passed them to their daughters. All in secret. All verbal. Nothing in writing. Over the millennia these women prophets waited patiently, knowing that men would screw things up good; knowing that their time would come to reveal the truth to the world. Can you imagine such patience? Such perseverance? For millennia! Of course you can. You know such patience yourself. You know how patient women can be."

Alisa listened patiently. How much did they know about her?

"The great prophet Khadija al-Kubra heard the word of the Goddess Allah from the Archangel Gabriel and wrote secretly of Femlamism. She recognized that women were the future. She also recognized that the world was not ready for this plan and so she hid the great book of the Hadith of Khadija and gave the Koran instead to her husband Mohammed who set about to spread Islam. But she knew that he was setting the stage for something greater in the future.

Exposing Herself

"Several decades ago I was infected with a sudden desire to travel. I had lived all my life here in Eden and had never thought to leave. But one day I awoke with a fever and an unknown mission. I stole money from my father and bought a one-way ticket to Israel. I wanted to travel to Mecca but Saudi Arabia's restrictions on women, particularly non-Muslim women, made that trip difficult. So I went to Jerusalem. I went to the Al-Aqsa mosque and was able to sneak into a small closet. Allah was with me because how else could I have gone unnoticed? Having no money for a hotel room, I slept in the small closet and for seven days I wandered out unnoticed to tour the Holy City and returned each night. On the seventh night I had difficulty falling asleep but when I did, I dreamt of Mecca. But it was not a dream; I had somehow been transported to Mecca.

"I was angry to find that many of the old, historic buildings had been destroyed in modern times for the construction of hotels, apartments, parking lots, and other facilities for the Hajj pilgrims that visit every year. I tried to get through the massive crowd that surrounded Al-Masjid al-Ḥarām, the Sacred Mosque, but I could not get through. I worked my way for what seemed like several hours to get into the mosque, but could just see the top of the holy, adorned black cube in the middle, the Kaaba. After a while in that hot sun, I felt the urgent need—well I had to leave to find a restroom. I struggled back through the crowd and was fearful that my self control was not great enough. Eventually I found my way to a public restroom and entered the stall and… well… what happened next was unbelievable.

"A woman entered the stall. She was a beautiful woman with fair, smooth skin and long, dark hair in thick braids covered with a modest shawl. She appeared to be in her early forties, but there was a wisdom in her face that said she must have been in her sixties or more. I said to her 'Hey, I'm in here!' but she just smiled. I was quite embarrassed but she seemed not even to notice the odor. She replied to me, 'I am Khadija and this is my house.' 'Could you wait outside for a minute?' I asked. 'I'd like to…' 'Yes, of course,' she replied and exited the stall.

"I cleaned and washed and turned to her. I knew right away that it was in fact Khadija the Great, wife of Mohammed. 'Your house?' I asked. She replied sadly that the Saudi Arabian government had torn down the old buildings so as not to allow them to be worshipped, a form of idol worship disallowed by Islam. In their places the Saudis then built money-making facilities for pilgrims and tourists. 'This place,' she said sadly, opening her arms to envelop the public bathrooms, 'was my house many centuries ago.'

"Khadija took me around Mecca and showed me many historical sites that are long gone. She led me to Al-Masjid al-Ḥarām and the crowd magically parted for the two of us, though they seemed not to notice either of us. We walked straight up to the Kaaba and she hoisted me up and through the gold doors that were raised about 6 feet off the ground. We went inside, an honor reserved only for religious dignitaries and even then only on rare occasions. The Kaaba was empty. Khadija placed a mat on the beautiful marble and limestone floor for me and her, and we prayed together. A strong, powerful, inspiring scent of fancy oils filled my nostrils. The Arabic inscriptions on the walls made perfect sense to me though I had never studied Arabic. After prayers, Khadija placed a small object in my hands and gently clasped them together.

"When I awoke I found a flash drive in my hands. I knew there was something important on the drive. I kept it close. I protected it dearly. In my pocket I found exactly enough cash for an airplane ticket back home. Exactly enough! I knew what I had to do. I bought that ticket and flew home that day. Arriving home I inserted the flash drive into my computer and found the previously unknown Hadith of Khadija. The books held all the knowledge, all the stories, all the traditions of Femlamism that had been passed down verbally for millennia. And the books had been translated from their original Arameian into English! This came to be known as the Miracle of the Translation. I began my mission as Sarah had told me before I woke, to awaken the women of the world to their true destiny. To save civilization. By whatever means necessary."

Alisa had sat stoically throughout the narrative until that last part. Her eyebrows arched slightly.

Exposing Herself

Inviere leaned in toward Alisa. "People understand religion more than reason. Reason is difficult. Religion is easy when it doesn't ask you to think. And while the government subverts mainstream religions, there are some religions it won't dare touch. That gives us freedom."

Alisa was quiet, in thought. She didn't fully understand why she was getting this lecture. Inviere seemed to read her puzzlement and continued. "You have been subjugated, repressed by men all your life. As I said, we know about you. You were born dirt poor in the city of Hebron in West Virginia. In the Appalachian Mountains. In a shack with three brothers. Your grandfather had an attraction to young girls—very young girls—and you were always there."

Alisa hung her head. Memories came back to her. Unwanted memories.

Inviere continued. "Once in a while your father caught your grandfather and made a show of it. Yelled at him. Threatened him occasionally. Hit him a few times. But your father still left you alone with him time and time again. Your mother knew but pretended not to. She looked the other way as a good wife was supposed to do. She claimed years later to have protested in private. In private! Some women are as bad as the men!"

Alisa started for a moment, about to respond, but stopped herself.

"When your parents divorced you were left to take care of your three brothers. You cooked and cleaned and were all but ignored. Except when you did something wrong. When you failed to get your brothers fed and to the school bus in time. When you forgot to clean the house. When you showed disrespect for your grandfather. When you did nothing at all.

"To escape from this you ran. The dirt paths and the mountain trails allowed you to take refuge. You burned off your rage on these twisting, turning paths. You found you could run for minutes, then hours. Your feet blistered and your ankles swollen, the pain distracted you from your miserable life, from the men who made your life miserable. This is all accurate: am I right?"

Alisa nodded silently, her head still hung low.

"These were in the days when athletic scholarships were still awarded for ability, and you had the ability to run. You applied to college without your father's knowledge and were accepted on an athletic scholarship to Stanford University, the Palo Alto campus, I believe."

Alisa, still looking downward, nodded again.

"In addition to your studies you kept running. You ran so well that you qualified for the Olympics. And in those days, that meant something. Nowadays everyone qualifies for the Olympics, but in those days it meant you were among the best. And you were. You were a fantastic runner. You could have beaten the other women. You could have beaten the men. But there was the crash."

Alisa nodded again.

"The plane was flying to Argentina when the engine failed and the plane came crashing down into the jungles of Peru. You and your teammates were stranded. You were miles from civilization. Your teammates argued. Was it best to stay and wait for help or venture out? You ventured out. You led your teammates through the jungles. You found paths through the thick foliage and just kept running. Those who stayed behind died one by one, serving only as nourishment for the survivors who in turn died one by one. Those who went with you could not survive. Their feet bled, their ankles swelled, and they eventually could not continue. But you could. You ran to the nearest village and collapsed. The people of the village proclaimed it a miracle. And it was!"

Alisa sat motionless. Inviere could not read her, so she leaned in and continued quietly, staring at Alisa's downturned head for signs of comprehension. "You are a miracle. You could be a prophet of Allah. If I look into your face, I will know if you are a prophet of Allah. If I say you are a prophet—if I recognize that divinity in you—then you will be one. You can join me and together we can keep the metastable pendulum in place until it is ready to swing down upon the patriarchy that has enslaved you, enslaved all of us for so long."

Exposing Herself

Alisa looked up slowly. Inviere had assumed she had been crying. That was a sign of disappointing weakness, but it was also a sign that she was getting through. But when Alisa looked up, her face was defiant and her cheeks were dry.

"I was not the best runner," said Alisa looking directly into Inviere's eyes. "I would not have won my race; I would not have won a medal. I am often very good at what I do but I don't fool myself into thinking I'm better than I am. I don't think about that plane crash because I find it a weakness that I could not help those other people. I could not convince them to follow me and I could not carry those who followed me but who could not continue. I survived for one reason. I survived because I had learned to run on an 'unlevel playing field.' Those majestic Appalachian mountain trails with its rocks and dirt and twigs had calloused my feet. Those unlevel hills and valleys had strengthened my calves and hardened my thighs. It was the obstacles that made me a great runner and it was the obstacles that saved my life in the Peruvian jungle.

"I would never wish my life on any young girl. Or young boy. And if I saw it happening I would do all in my power to stop it. But I do not want to find my 'rightful place' in society. I just want to find a place. I don't want to live in a man's world. I don't want to live in a woman's world. I want to live in a free world where I only expect the opportunity to excel or fail based on my actions and accomplishments, not whether I do or don't have an appendage between my legs or a Y chromosome."

Both women were silent and stared defiantly at each other. After a moment, Inviere sighed loudly and looked away. "I'm sorry to hear that. After all these years of human history of men being at the top, I was hoping you'd see the justice of women taking their place."

A door opened quietly in the back of the room and Marla McGivers stepped in looking hopeful.

"She has decided not to join us," said Inviere and McGivers' hopeful smile drooped and her hopeful eyes narrowed. "At least for now," said Inviere and McGivers perked up slightly. "Please take her back to her quarters here, and we will talk again."

McGivers stepped up to Alisa and gently took her elbow, guiding her out of the room.

"We are a religion of peace," said Inviere quietly as they were leaving, but loud enough to be heard. "Often violence is required to show people the alternative to peace."

Exposing Herself

The Good Escape

Jones awoke in a small, white room with a few furnishings—a couch, a couple chairs, a bookshelf—all white. His vision was blurry. He was lying in the couch. He felt groggy and dizzy. He reached up to his forehead, found it beaded with sweat, and wiped his hand across it to dry it, then on his pants to dry his hand. He began to swing his legs off the couch when an intense burning pain returned to his crotch. His forehead dampened again. He lay back down. How could he have possibly forgotten about that, he thought as he visualized that woman's stiletto heel planting itself into his groin as he watched and then collapsed.

"Good. You're awake."

Jones craned his neck to see who was talking. A figure walked into his side vision but he couldn't make it out at first. Then she walked in front of him. Alisa. She squatted down so that her face was level with his. She leaned in close, her lips were about to touch his. He felt the excitement in his groin, which in turn brought back the intense pain, but he used all his willpower to ignore it and stare into Alisa's beautiful bichromal eyes, awaiting her kiss. He pursed his lips and closed his eyes.

"They probably have the room bugged," she said.

He opened his eyes.

"We need to keep close and talk very softly," she continued.

"Of course," he replied, a little too loud. "Of course," he said more softly.

"They have some strange cult here. Femlamism. I'd heard about it but never experienced it. It's a female dominated form of radical Islam."

"Of course," he replied. He hadn't meant it to come out so sarcastic, but he didn't really follow what she was saying. She stopped talking. Her lips were so close to his. So perfectly smooth and deliciously red. He should kiss her. He should just move his lips that quarter inch onto hers. He really should.

The door burst open.

"OK ladies, time to go!"

Alisa stood up suddenly.

Jones strained to look up, His vision was clearing, but it was still painful to move. Two figures came to stand in front of him, one small and one very large. The small one came up to him, leaned close like Alisa had done, and said, "We're getting you out of here." All Jones could think about was how unattractive this little sliver of a woman was. Most of the women here seemed concerned with their appearance—dressed well, nice makeup. This one was… well when she got close… something seemed disturbing.

The little woman stood up. "Get his hood on him," he said to the large woman who was, very large. Very, very large. Someone put the burka back over his head and it was abrasive as it rubbed against his damp forehead. He felt a little nauseous.

Then the large woman bent down and picked him up like a little girl picking up her ragdoll. She wore a shapeless Hawaiian flowered muumuu. She cradled Jones in both arms, held him up to her face, and whispered, "Glad to see you again." The woman had a large, round, Asian face with a mop of straight black hair that covered most of her features. That face was comforting somehow, with a big smile. Also very unattractive, though, and he felt bad for even thinking that. The giant woman swiveled and Jones could see Alisa and the other women hugging. Tightly, joyfully, obviously pleased to see each other. Jones' heart sank. Did they kiss or were they just whispering—he was not sure and did not want to think about it further.

The giant woman stepped easily over the couch and the three headed for the door. They went through corridors where a few women lingered, talking, but all of them stopped to watch this strange sight as it went by.

They finally came to the large chamber that was now much less crowded since prayer time was over. It seemed like a long way to the door, even with the giant footsteps taken by the giant woman who still cradled Jones in her arms. And then again, he still did not know who they were except that Alisa seemed to trust them, so he figured it was best to do the same.

As they approached the door, their pace quickening, an official-looking woman stepped in front of the door. "What's going on?" she inquired. "Where are you going?" "Who is this? And who are you?" Her questions came out fast and intimidating.

The small woman and Alisa were standing behind them. The small woman stepped around the large one to say something, but the official at the door stared her down. "I want to hear from this one, not you," she said, and turned her face upward and into the eyes of the giant woman.

The giant woman seemed hesitant. "We're taking him... You know he's sick and so... We were told to take him outside. To that place where... you know. What's her name told us to... take him... and... Oh hell." At that point the giant woman slung Jones over her left shoulder and wrapped her large, thick left arm around him, freeing her powerful right arm to whip around and slam into the official, throwing her against the wall.

At that, some of the women in the chamber rushed toward the back, out of the way, but a few women rushed toward the door and toward the large woman who had spun around, Jones flopping around like a small sack of potatoes on her shoulder. The women coming at her were fast and one reached her quickly, planting a solid kick to the giant's calf.

The giant spun around to confront the woman who had kicked her. With each movement, Jones' groin ached and his stomach twisted. In front of them was a wall of well-dressed, large women assuming martial arts poses. The giant woman sighed loudly. "Come on, let's do this!" she shouted. The woman ran at her. What followed looked like something out of an old Japanese karate movie. The large women each attacked the much larger woman with complex, precise martial arts moves that the giant woman easily deflected with her own surprisingly precise and even

215

elegant moves. Jones got only glimpses of this action as he was whipped up and down and side to side. He was concentrating very hard on not vomiting, so he missed some of the better action.

After several minutes—or was it longer—the fighting stopped. Around the walls were horrified women cringing. In front of the giant was a pile of beaten martial arts experts. The giant turned to go. Jones, facing backwards, saw a sight and tried to warn his carrier, but he couldn't get the words out quick enough. Gina Inviere had appeared from somewhere, was running toward them, and launched herself through the air landing a heel squarely into the giant's back. Jones and the giant fell toward the floor. Quickly the giant got up and was able to gently place Jones on his feet. Alisa and the small woman were waiting at the door, virtually unnoticed, and waved for him to move toward them. The giant got up and faced Inviere. "That hurt," she said in a surprisingly deep voice.

"I don't know who you are," said Inviere looking intensely into the giant's eyes and maybe even into her soul, "but this is my place and these are my women, and those are my guests, and you have been very rude."

"Can we get over the clever talk and just get to the fighting?" asked the giant. "My back hurts and I just want to get home."

Inviere leaped at the giant before she could finish speaking, but the giant blocked and pivoted. Inviere threw a roundhouse kick followed by a flurry of elbows and fists. They were all blocked except for the last, a palm smash to the chest that knocked the wind out of the giant. As she struggled to breathe, Inviere executed another spinning roundhouse kick that caught the giant in the ribs, knocked her down. Her wig went flying off. In the chamber was a series of loud gasps. Jones felt stupid for not realizing it earlier—the giant woman was Mack. He turned to the small woman with Alisa. Of course. That was Miles.

Mack stood up quickly for someone his size. "Are you kidding?" he bellowed to everyone in the chamber. "You actually couldn't figure out that I'm a man?"

Inviere said something under her breath then again launched herself at him. He blocked another fast bout of chops and punches and then smacked her in the chest, sending her to the floor. She quickly sprang up and grabbed each of his arms in her hands and held tight. He looked at her and should have seen it coming, but did not. Her foot swung up with great speed and great force, right into his groin. Mack went down screaming. It was a scream that echoed in the large chamber. Some of the women cupped their hands over their ears. Inviere walked over to Mack and looked down triumphantly. Mack lay on the ground, moaning, rocking slightly, his hands over his groin. His face was a mask of pain.

"Men," said Inviere disparagingly, shaking her head.

Mack quickly brought a massive leg up in the air, placed his huge foot against Inviere's chest, and catapulted her toward the other side of the room. "Women," he said disparagingly, shaking his head as he leapt to his feet.

"Let's go!" shouted Mack to the three at the door. They all ran outside into the parking lot and got into a car near the front. Miles started the engine and they sped off out of the parking lot and onto a narrow, winding dirt road that led out of the complex. Alisa sat up front in the middle; Jones sat up front on the passenger side. Mack took up the whole back seat.

"You ok?" asked Jones.

"Yeah, fine."

Jones looked at Mack in puzzlement. And amazement.

"You think I'd go into a place like that and not wear a cup?" said Mack. "I keep telling everyone I'm a pretty smart guy, not just a big bag of muscles."

"So for a rocket scientist," said Miles pulling off his own wig, "how come you froze when that guard confronted you?"

"I didn't expect that. I was under pressure, you know."

The Good Escape

"And the best you can manage is 'that place… you know… what's-her-name.'?" asked Miles jokingly.

"Give me a break," said Mack. I got us in there and I got us out. How about a thank-you?"

"Don't pout, Mack," said Alisa. "He's just ribbing you. We all appreciate every aspect of you, brains and brawn. Thank you."

"Yeah, thank you." said Jones.

Just then there was a loud explosion and the rear window shattered.

"They're after us," said Miles as he started swerving the car to avoid being an easy target.

"They're shooting," said Mack. No one thought it was a good time to give Mack a hard time for stating the obvious.

Alisa reached into the glove compartment and pulled out a gun. "I've got it," she said. "Duck Mack," she ordered.

"This is the best I can do," came back Mack.

"Then cover your ears," said Alisa as she pointed the gun out the back and near Mack's head. He leaned his head away as far as possible and put his large ham hands over his ears. Alisa began firing at several cars behind them. The cars seemed to be catching up and they obviously had better firepower as multiple shots seemed to whistle by them, occasionally hitting a metal side panel or piercing a plastic bumper.

As the cars got closer, the gunshots got closer. A side view mirror was shot out. One shot cracked the bumper in half, one half falling to the ground and bouncing behind them. That slowed the cars behind them a bit. Jones could make out three cars. Maybe there were more behind those.

Suddenly the cars behind them slowed, then stopped. Jones could see them in the distance. The women were getting out, placing mats on the ground, and kneeling. "They stopped," said Jones in disbelief and relief. "What's happening?"

"Daily prayers," said Mack. "They have to stop for daily prayers."

"Really?" said Jones. "Wow, lucky break."

"Not lucky," said Miles. "We planned it that way of course. How could we expect to escape otherwise?"

Jones thought about that for a moment. "Where are we going now?" he asked.

"To safety," said Alisa.

They travelled along dirt roads for a while, mostly in silence, Jones nursing his wounds—at least as much as was decent—and Mack nursing his. After about an hour and a half, they arrived back in Philly at the building where the Freedman Group was located. They exited the car.

"I want to go home first and freshen up. I should be about an hour," said Alisa and walked off without waiting for a response from anyone.

The others went inside, took the elevator to the twelfth floor, got out, and then walked up one more floor to the hidden thirteenth floor.

Alisa walked along the streets of Philadelphia toward her apartment. As she passed one alleyway, a tall, dark figure in a black trench coat appeared next to her, walking in synchronization.

"Well?" asked Rom Automatic.

"We have him," she replied flatly.

Rom nodded, then turned into another alleyway as Alisa continued to her apartment.

The Good Escape

Execution

Jones wandered around Alisa's apartment. It was all whites and blacks. Smooth walls and floors of glass and Formica. He wandered through a maze of small rooms, each one opening to another and none having four walls. Very open yet confusing, like a maze. The black walls were opaque; the white walls were translucent, and the glass walls were frosted so that though the rooms were open it was difficult, if not impossible to see from room to room or even get one's bearings. It was a maze—confusing, misleading, mysterious.

"Are you awake?" Alisa whispered from somewhere nearby, but Jones couldn't tell where. Sounds bounced easily from wall to wall, disguising the location of their source.

"Yes," said Jones, looking around for her. "Where are you?"

Out of the corner of his eye Jones saw a shadow pass by and turned toward it. A figure swept fleetingly behind a frosted glass pane. He couldn't make it out though he was sure it was Alisa. He couldn't see where she went, but he tried to follow, exiting the room in the direction of the shadow. Looking around, he could not see her—it was just more black and white walls and floors. "Where are you?" he said softly.

"Over here," she replied. "Where are you?"

Jones looked around. "I'm here. I don't know. I'm … here."

"But I'm not there," she replied cryptically. "I'm here."

Jones again saw a shadow through the corner of his eye and turned to see a trail of chiffon blowing past a doorway, trailing a thin silhouette against a white translucent wall. He walked after it, not rushing, not wanting to seem anxious or confused though he was both.

In the hallway he saw only more rooms, more hallways, more pitch black, translucent white, and frosted glass walls. A maze. "Alisa?" he called out. Silence.

Execution

Jones walked quickly through the maze, peeking around corners. Occasionally he saw movement out of the corner of his eye but when he turned there was nothing there. "Alisa?" he called out a little louder. Still no reply.

His hands left streaks on the glass walls from perspiration. His heart rate rose and he could hear the blood rushing in his ears, the beat echoing in his head. After twists and turns he came to a room that seemed to be at the center of everything. Unlike the rest of the apartment it had plaster walls painted in soft, comforting pastels. He moved into the room cautiously because it seemed so out of place that at first he was disoriented, mistrusting. This room looked more like that of a little girl. More feminine. More fanciful. There was a cushiony beige couch against the far wall facing shelves of knick-knacks and stuffed animals. There were colorful paintings on the walls, some looking childish and others very sophisticated. In one corner stood a stuffed unicorn about 4 feet from its toes to its horn.

Jones moved to the center of the room, taking in this out-of-place scene. His heart slowed—this place was nice and comforting. His palms dried. He felt relaxed.

"Hi." Alisa walked in, covered only in a flowing chiffon nightgown that swirled around her, hiding nothing of her lithe figure. Her small breasts poked up against the material. She walked toward him smiling. She came up to him, her mouth centimeters from his, then put her arms around him and pulled him close in a tight hug, his head on her shoulder. Jones noticed that the unicorn's eyes were bichromatic like Alisa's. That seemed odd. They tumbled onto the soft couch.

He held Alisa close but stared more closely at the unicorn. "I'm dreaming aren't I?" he asked.

The unicorn shrugged.

Jones held Alisa away from him and looked into her smiling eyes. "Are you awake?" she asked, but the voice was high and nasal and annoying.

"Are you awake?" asked Miles Monroe.

Jones shuddered then opened his eyes slowly. He was on a cushiony chair with a covering that was soft and comfortable but worn. He was in a small room—an office with a big mahogany desk in front of him. The desk was also worn and scratched in places. Miles Monroe sat at the desk looking at him. Mack stood in the corner looking around, bored. Behind Miles was that painting he had seen before: the muscular, bare-chested silhouette breaking a chain connecting his wrists, the American flag fluttering in the background, the words "The Freedman Group" etched in stone at the bottom.

"Hello again, Mr. Jones."

Jones wiped the drool from his mouth.

"You've been asleep and we figured you needed the rest."

Jones nodded, still a bit groggy.

"You're back at the Freedman Group headquarters, Mr. Jones. I know you've been through some pretty rough experiences. There's a lot of *mishigas* in the world these days. We're not the solution to that. We're just the path to the solution. I hope you'll see us as your friend. And as a way to return self-respect and self-determination. To freedom."

"And what if I refuse?" asked Jones.

"Please, Mr. Jones. It's not a question of acceptance or refusal. Either you see the nobility of our cause or you don't. Either you decide to help us of your own accord or you don't. We definitely need your help, and society needs your help. But there are no consequences that we enforce. There are only the consequences of inaction. "

"Well, first I'm not going to be President of the United States despite what you want or what you think."

"Unfortunately that's not the case, Mr. Jones. That's not our decision, and sadly that's not your decision. You've been chosen by the Electoral

Committee and they don't believe in freedom like we do. They believe that they above all others know what's best for society. They have decided that you are best to lead this country, or rather to represent their leadership of this country, and they will not stop until you agree to do so. The ends justify the means in their minds, and now that you know of the fraud that is the presidential election, it will be difficult for them to let you have this knowledge that could undermine their operations."

"They'll kill me?" asked Jones.

Monroe hesitated, thinking for a moment. "No, probably not. They're not violent people. But they do know what they want and they will do what's necessary to get their way." He added "For the benefit of mankind," using air quotes. "Violence is a very last resort for them. But they will make things miserable for you until you relent."

"I want to think it over," said Jones. "Whether I'll help you, I mean."

"That's reasonable," replied Miles. "You know about the Jobs Plan, but you also need to understand how we plan to execute it. And how you can help. Then you'll have, I believe, all the facts to consider when you make your decision."

"OK," said Jones.

Miles continued. "You recall the three parts of the Jobs Plan:

"One. Disconnect everyone from the GovNet and replace it with an open network of individuals, corporations, nonprofits, and interest groups that all compete for the attention of the people. The government won't notice the disconnects at first. It will be attributed to normal system failures that are pretty common occurrences. Or the government will assume the disruption is due to the Chinese cyberattacks that occur regularly and are considered to be as unavoidable as natural disasters like hurricanes and earthquakes.

"Two. Remove government controlled currency and replace it with a floating electronic currency that can be used for transactions and lent by private institutions.

"Three. Encourage risk. Allow reward. Tolerate failure. Celebrate success. Permit businesses, including banks, to take risks. Permit individuals to take risks. Require only that businesses be transparent about the risks they take. Offer education for the individuals who invest in the businesses. And provide only the thinnest of safety nets that allow people to survive downturns long enough to become productive members of society but no longer than that.

"To do all this we need someone on the inside, in a position of power. Someone who does not need to take action, but needs to ensure government inaction. Government inaction—that seems like a truism. But when government's power is in question, it will react quickly—probably the only time government reacts quickly. And so will the extremists who believe in the power of the group over the individual. The Fairness for EveryBody Society. Others too. All those people with good intentions that are paving our way to hell. They will come together to repair GovNet and take control of currency and regulate risk and reward out of business and, in fact, out of all human endeavor."

"And so where would I fit in?" asked Jones. "You said yourself that the President of the United States is a figurehead. How could I possibly help, against the direction of the Electoral Committee or the FEB or whatever they call themselves?"

"You're an orator, Mr. Jones. Surely you understand the power of words."

"I say what I'm told to say."

"Do you? When your PDA malfunctioned, did you know what to say?"

"Yes, but. How did you know that my PDA malfunctioned?"

"We have a plan to take down the entire GovNet. We can obviously take down a single PDA."

At that moment Alisa entered the room. Miles nodded in her direction. "And we have plenty of technical know-how." Alisa seemed a little confused, not knowing the context, then smiled and nodded back at

Miles before going over to him and planting a kiss on his cheek. Miles blushed. It annoyed him a bit because she was usually so professional and he was trying to create a certain kind of atmosphere of historical consequence, impressing on Jones the significance of this mission that he could choose to go on. The kiss did not really fit into that kind of presentation and it made Miles kind of pissed off, but he knew from experience that if he said something he would sound whiny and she might get indignant and then the message would be lost for good. He sighed while his carefully planned staging went down the toilet. Damn it!

The kiss didn't really help Jones' state of mind either. "Look, I wish you good luck with all this nonsense, but I'm not your man. I live my life according to the rules set for me. I just want my liberty. I just want to be happy or at least die trying. I don't want to be part of a revolution as much as I don't want to be part of the status quo. I just want to be. It's unfathomable to me that for some reason the future of mankind seems to rest on my shoulders!" Jones shrugged and turned toward the door. "I just want to go home."

Miles looked at Mack, still hiding in the corner, as much as a man of his proportions can hide in such a small room. Miles nodded at Mack who turned to follow Jones out of the room. "I'll take you home," he said quietly and with obvious disappointment.

Revelations

Jones, back in his apartment, watched the sun rise over the cityscape. He lay across a vinyl sofa, legs draped over one armrest, his neck resting on the other, his butt pressed into the cushion. His long, lanky arms were splayed above his head. He looked like a long, skinny scarecrow that had been tossed hurriedly onto the sofa. A chocolate covered scarecrow. He tapped his forehead repeatedly. He was exhausted and it felt like a background task in his mind was trying to work through all the recent events, but he was consciously unaware of the details. Only that some process was hogging his mind's CPU time, leaving little left over for other mental tasks like feeding himself or even breathing. Sometimes he would realize that he had stopped breathing and then, scared because he could not remember how long he had stopped, began breathing heavily making himself even more light-headed.

Jones twisted over to face the back of the couch, further withdrawing into his own seemingly blank thoughts, and something stuck him in the hip. He reached into his pocket and pulled out the flash drive that Rom Automatic had left with him. "It's everything we know about you" he could hear Rom say. "And your family. And your friends."

Those words snuck into his conscious thoughts and stole some mental CPU time from that unknown, subconscious task that was consuming mental resources. He slowly unfolded off of the couch, slinked to the computer in the corner, and inserted the flash drive. A window popped up with all kinds of subfolders and files. His whole life was displayed on the screen in front of him, recorded in electronic documents, spreadsheets, pictures, audio recordings, and video recordings. He was both amazed at the amount of information about him and yet also nonplussed. Everyone knew that the government kept voluminous records on people in order to classify them, guide them, categorize them, and generally help them out in all sorts of ways. Still it made him a bit uncomfortable to actually see the files. These comprised private information that really only the government should know and even he himself was better off not knowing. It was like the old question, if you could see into the future and learn the circumstances of your death, should you do so? Could you change it? If so, then you had not really seen the future in the first place. That led to all kinds of paradoxes. If you could not change it, would you spend the rest of your life preparing for your death at every moment? Not a useful, or pleasant, way to live. Suddenly Jones had the strange idea that maybe his death was already recorded in the government files and though he knew it was crazy, began searching for the file. After some time, he convinced himself it was not there. He did find all kinds of records such as birth certificate, school transcripts, residences, and job history, but also more personal things like information about hobbies, friends, girlfriends, and personal habits like weekday routines, weekend routines, and vacations. It felt more and more creepy. Had Rom given him this to show what kind of information he would have access to as president or to intimidate Jones by demonstrating how much the government knew about him?

Fishing around the drive Jones came across files on his parents. His mother's file was small. She had lived a simple life. He did find a few things he had not known. She had had a miscarriage only a year before he was born. She had never told him about that. It was not his business and would not have changed anything anyway, but it was strange to learn a secret, however small, in this government file. It also made him think about his fortune that the first pregnancy had ended badly. He immediately felt bad about that thought, though he realized that his parents would almost certainly have not had a second child and he would not have been born.

His father's file was fairly large. That surprised him a bit. He wondered why the government kept such a large file on him. He poked around and clicked on various files and found many documents about his father's business. His father ran a small business and after a few initial successes it had failed pretty badly—why was there so much information in the file? He began opening documents including newspaper articles. Most of them were about his father's business contract to install the HVAC system at the Chicago Mercantile. Pictures in the paper showed a trim, grinning, self confident man. Many of the article headlines proclaimed this "African American" success story. He remembered that his dad hated that label. "I am an American!" he dad would rail. "And anyway, doesn't everyone trace their roots back to Africa eventually?"

Still his dad looked proud and Winston remembered just how proud the whole family had been. And how the future had looked so bright. So much anticipation. So much naiveté. So much disappointment.

Jones began going further through the files and found some puzzling documents. Government inspection forms showed safety hazards on the job. There were claims of discrimination against his father by a group of employees. There were complaints about corners cut, shoddy workmanship, inferior parts, and eventually a lack of funds to complete the project. Winston had a strong picture of his dad during those days. Overly optimistic. Overworked. Highly stressed. But always a perfectionist. His father expected near-perfection from those who worked for him and complete perfection from himself. He was not mean about it, just insistent. His father's stories and lectures to Winston often were lessons in always doing the best possible job. Always reaching higher than others thought possible. Always creating something not just useful, but of the highest achievable quality. How is it possible that his dad would hold these strong values out to his son but not practice them himself? No, Winston had been on the job with his father when his father would have his workers tear apart ductwork, at his own expense, to replace it with a more efficient size or layout. He had seen his dad lecture his men on safety and fire those who cut corners or did not get the appropriate inspection sign-offs. This just didn't sound like his dad.

In the file were also video recordings and audio recordings. Winston listened to them and watched them and a picture grew in his mind. The events surrounding these government documents started to mean something different than his first impression. The trajectory of his father's business was not the one he had thought for all of these years. And his father's death… his father's death… This really changed everything. He read and listened and watched and the picture of his father's last years suddenly was clear and not at all what he had believed and… and he felt ashamed.

C:\Jones, Winston\family\father\Jones, Morris\GE\application\

Revelations

Morrie Jones walked proudly with a jaunty gait and a wide smile. He felt good and he figured he might as well let everyone know it. His suit was neatly pressed and his shoes polished to a shine. Looking closely, one could see the frays on the edges of the lapels, shirt cuffs, and collars. Underneath the bright shine of the shoes, the soles were worn through with penny-sized holes. Inside his chest his heart beat a little too fast, and his stomach growled just a bit, but for all appearances he looked like success. His reservations and doubts were buried deep while his confidence bubbled to the top. That's the way Morrie Jones was—had always been—and it served him well. His appearance of confidence led people to trust him which in turn led to success. People on the street took notice and glanced at him as he passed. His self-assurance was contagious and people just started feeling good as he passed, many not sure why.

In his hand Morrie Jones gripped a spiral bound set of papers that comprised his business plan. He had done the research, ran the numbers, calculated costs, figured out the market—total available market, serviceable available market, and share of market. TAM, SAM, SOM. It was a mantra that he said to himself each word echoing in his head with each step on the pavement. He found it comforting.

Morrie Jones turned right into the double glass doors of the bank. He had an appointment with the branch manager. He paused in the lobby and looked around. Tellers sat behind a long, plain beige counter that stretched from one wall to the other with a thick Plexiglas wall between them and the customers. A long line of customers snaked across the black-and-white tile floor. The walls were white but in need of paint, with a few posters advertising bank products and services. And of course the required regulatory notices. The bank looked pretty plain, he thought, for a branch of one of the world's largest banks. Well then again, the way to make money is to save money and spend it judiciously he thought and patted the business plan in his hands. That's his philosophy and it's recorded right here in his plan.

Behind Morrie Jones was a row of cubicles and a small waiting area consisting of a couple of worn brown couches and a table covered with sports magazines. A short, heavyset man in a plain, grey suit approached him. "Can I help you?" he asked.

"I have an appointment with Mr. Bailey."

"And you are?"

"Morris Jones," he said proudly, almost childishly, and immediately felt silly. He forced his mouth to undo the excited smile and adopt a contemplative look. Morrie Jones knew that he needed to appear professional and serious. It should not show that this was his very first business loan, even though it was. He needed to come across as sophisticated and experienced and knowledgeable about his business. He did know his business inside out, and he knew all the numbers cold. He also had recommendations from his supervisor at the HVAC repair company where he worked and from local business people he knew. Most importantly he had orders for jobs. Not big jobs, but a lot of them. Enough to get started. He was a real entrepreneur, and today was the beginning of a new exciting life. The smile crept back onto his mouth and into his eyes.

The short man in the grey suit walked through a door to one side that Jones had not noticed before and disappeared inside. Other than a plain silver doorknob, the door looked like the wall—white, scuffed, unnoticeable. The short man in the plain grey suit reemerged shortly followed by a tall, thin man in a similar plain, grey suit. The short man motioned toward Jones then walked back to his cubicle. The tall man approached Jones and extended his hand.

"Mr. Jones?" asked the man then continued without waiting for an answer. "Right this way."

Morrie Jones shook his hand and followed him through the nondescript door on the nondescript wall to a similarly nondescript office. The man sat at a black metal desk overwhelmed by a large computer screen in the corner. He motioned Jones to a brown vinyl chair on the other side.

Revelations

"So I understand you want a business loan," said Mr. Bailey. He examined the details of Jones' application on the computer screen without actually making eye contact with Jones.

"Yes," said Morrie Jones smiling, then putting on his serious, business-like face. He slapped the business plan on the table. Mr. Bailey jumped slightly but continued to look only at the screen. "Here's the business plan. You'll see that I already have customers lined up. I have extensive experience in refrigeration engineering. I have a great reputation. And I'm ready to take the bank's money, build my business, and return a nice profit to you on the interest on the loan. And of course a nicer profit for myself."

Morrie Jones fidgeted a bit as Mr. Bailey continued to review the application on the computer.

"Just checking the application, Mr. Jones. I want to make sure everything is in order." Mr. Bailey continued examining the computer screen, squinting at several things on the screen that Morrie Jones could not see. Morrie Jones' confidence was waning, but only slightly. His stomach let out a loud growl that embarrassed him, but Mr. Bailey seemed not to notice.

"Everything's in the business plan right here. You'll see that I've been conservative, but the numbers look good. In four years…"

"I see that you missed the section of the form that asks about your college degree Mr. Jones," said Mr. Bailey. "I just need to get that from you to continue processing the application. Mr. Bailey placed his fingers just above the keyboard, ready to type.

"I don't have a college degree," replied Morrie Jones.

Mr. Bailey turned to look at him for the first time. "Pardon?" he asked.

"I don't have a college degree," repeated Morrie Jones. Mr. Bailey stared at him silently, and he felt like he needed to say something to fill the silence. "I went to the School of Hard Knocks," said Jones smiling uncomfortably.

Mr. Bailey looked puzzled. "Just give me the name of the college, please, and we can proceed."

"If you'll look at the business plan, you'll see that I reach break-even in two years worst case. In year three we make a big publicity push, which bumps up expenses, but also projected revenues though profits remain flat. In year four, profits start to track revenue as the return on investment…"

"Mr. Jones, this is just a formality. I need the name of the college you attended."

"I didn't attend college," replied Morrie Jones.

Mr. Bailey looked shocked, his eyebrows arched severely.

"I went off to war. Fought for our country."

"The government provided full paid scholarships for veterans, Mr. Jones. Surely you took advantage of that."

"No. I… I wanted to go into business. Make a living. Do something useful."

"College is very useful. And a man of your… complexion… could get into any Harvard or Stanford campus across the nation. I believe the Stanford Chicago campus is very nice, but the Harvard Chicago campus is also fairly prestigious and not quite so demanding."

"Yes, I know. But I wanted to do something different. I already knew a lot about business and such. I wanted to apply it. I wanted to work."

Mr Bailey glanced down at the business plan then up to Morrie Jones. "I'm sorry Mr. Jones, I can't approve this loan."

"Why?"

"Because you have no college degree."

Morrie Jones just stared at Mr. Bailey, dumbfounded.

Revelations

Mr. Bailey saw Morrie Jones' confusion and continued, though he thought the explanation should have been obvious. It only confirmed his opinion that Morrie Jones was not sophisticated or reliable enough to give a loan for a business. "Mr. Jones, a college education makes you competitive in the job market. It teaches you all the things that you need to be successful in life. If nothing else it's a test of your ability to study and research topics that you find uninteresting and persevere and graduate. A great deal of business is simply persevering. If you can graduate college, you can succeed at just about anything. And certainly at business. Just look at me, for example."

Morrie Jones simply continued staring, a feeling of anger coming over him that he controlled by simply saying nothing.

"Anyway," continued Mr. Bailey, "it's required on the application. I can't submit an incomplete application. You understand that, don't you?" He said this as if Morrie Jones were an idiot. An idiot because he did not go to college.

Morrie Jones was still silently staring and Mr. Bailey grew uncomfortable. He contemplated pressing the button under his desk for the security guards, but decided instead to simply show Morrie Jones the door and keep an eye on him while maintaining a safe distance. Out the door into the lobby he guided Morrie Jones, where he nodded and smiled to him, then quickly retreated to his office.

Morrie Jones still had the dumb smile on his face, but only because he was unaware of, and not completely in control of his facial expression at all. He could not understand. He rolled his business plan tightly in his hand—the plan with all of the numbers and projections that he had worked so hard on.

As Morrie Jones walked down the street, the people who passed had a different reaction this time. They saw the wild, smiling expression on his face. The frays and loose threads of his jacket seemed more apparent than before. The shine seemed gone from his shoes and the scuff marks stood out instead. People on the street moved out of his way, or crossed to the other side, as each footstep planted solidly on the pavement while in his mind he repeated the mantra of TAM, SAM, SOM… TAM, SAM, SOM… TAM, SAM, SOM.

C:\Jones, Winston\family\father\Jones, Morris\GE\seed round\

"Thank you Mr. Automatic. Thank you very much." Morrie Jones held out his hand but immediately regretted it.

Wesley Automatic struggled to lift his huge bulk out of his gilded leather chair, but the leather seemed to stick to him and suck him back downward. Wesley Automatic continued to wriggle and push upward, somehow just barely able to keep his air of dignity while doing so. But just barely. Finally shooting upward to his feet, the chair releasing him with a soft *shplupp* sound, he extended his chubby hand forward to Morrie Jones. "It's a pleasure doing business with you Mr. Jones. I believe we're going to make a lot of money together."

Morrie Jones smiled wide. He grasped Automatic's hand and squeezed to keep it from slipping out of his grip like a watermelon seed. For some reason, Wesley Automatic always seemed greasy. His skin seemed to have an ultrathin coating. They shook. "I really appreciate your confidence, Mr. Automatic. I appreciate your investment in my new company. I do believe we're both going to be rich," said Morrie Jones. Automatic smiled ironically and Morrie Jones blushed. Jones looked around at Automatic's office filled with posh leather, thick velvet, plush carpet, mahogany, gold foil, silver objects, and jewels. It was opulent. Famous paintings crowded the walls and renowned sculptures were clustered in the corners. Wesley Automatic was already one of the richest men in the city of Chicago. One of the richest in the country.

"I'm looking forward to it," said Automatic. "I've always wanted to be rich," he said, and they both laughed.

Morrie Jones pulled his now-greasy hand back and fought hard against the temptation to wipe it on his pants. "Thanks," he said softly.

Morrie Jones began to turn to leave, but a picture of a young boy on Automatic's desk caught his attention for some reason. "Your son?" he asked.

"Yes," said Automatic. "Eight years old. Fine boy. Has a promising future."

"I know what you mean," said Morrie Jones. "I have a son about the same age. I'm very proud of him. He's a smart kid. And a good kid. I want to give him a good future. Better than mine."

"Your future looks pretty bright, Mr. Jones. It had better be; we both have a lot invested in it."

"That's true," said Morrie Jones still staring at the boy in the picture but thinking of his own son.

"Bring your son over some time," said Automatic. "I'm sure my Rommy would enjoy your boy's company. His friendship."

"Sure," said Morrie Jones absent-mindedly. "I'll do that."

"OK. Time for both of us to get back to work. Make some money." Automatic nodded and waved Morrie Jones toward the door. Jones came out of his trance and nodded back, smiled, and walked out of Wesley Automatic's office. He felt good—he had just done a business deal with Wesley Automatic. He had to control himself to stop himself from skipping. Oh what the hell, he thought, and skipped into the elevator, out of the building, and down the street as the people passing by tried not to notice or rather tried not to appear to notice as they couldn't help but notice. A few of them crossed to the other side of the street while appearing not to notice. Morrie Jones noticed, but he didn't care.

C:\Jones, Winston\family\father\Jones, Morris\GE\growth\

In a private, dark, isolated back room of the famous La Tomate Rouge restaurant, sat Morrie Jones and Wesley Automatic, facing each other in a booth behind a thick, dark, velvet curtain. A small candle in the center of the table threw eerie and wavering shadows across their faces, distorting their features. The grins on their faces could be clearly seen, though, as if they radiated their own light.

"Forty-six percent growth this quarter," said Morrie Jones proudly.

"Great," said Wesley Automatic. "Great job," he added.

"Yes, I'm really happy about it," said Morrie Jones, beaming. "I expect to hire 3 more engineers, a sales person, and possibly an office manager-slash-executive assistant." He felt a little uncomfortable talking about an executive assistant. He had never had an assistant. He felt a little guilty about it. He had always handled his own paperwork, done his own chores, made his own phone calls. It felt wrong to have someone else do these things for him. It felt lazy. But he knew that he no longer had time to do all those things and also run the business. He was more valuable managing people and projects, reviewing drawings, guiding the marketing and sales efforts, making financial decisions. It just made sense to hire an assistant. And it meant one more person on the payroll. It felt good to have people on the payroll. It felt good to know that his company—because of his hard work—was providing regular, decent wages to people in the neighborhood, allowing them to put meals on the table every day. He saw the pride in the people working for him. Working for Galt Enterprises was considered a prestigious honor in his neighborhood and in all of Chicago. To work at GE you had to be the best. You did not cut corners. You did not slack off. And when you made mistakes, you did not make excuses. Those who did not meet GE's high standards did not remain long at GE. Those who did, found a good salary, good benefits, and a good job for a good long time.

"You should definitely hire the assistant," said Automatic. "You need to be efficient. And I need to protect my investment. I need you doing important stuff. I need you running and growing the business, not taking in your dry cleaning or running checks to the bank."

"OK," said Morrie Jones quietly. It still somehow felt strange or elitist, but he knew Wesley was right.

Revelations

"A toast to our success!" said Wesley. He lifted his wine glass a little too quickly and a few burgundy drops leaped out and onto his finely tailored suit. The suit was hand-made by a renowned Indian tailor from Bombay. The materials were hand-woven on wooden looms and each seam was hand-sown with needle and thread—no machines of any kind were involved. The material was the finest pure cotton, not a cotton blend, and no synthetics were used at all. The dyes were imported from farms in China that grew genetically engineered, patented shrubs whose berries had colors, the subtle spectrums of which were duplicated nowhere on the planet. The tailor was flown to Chicago for multiple custom fittings so that the suit accentuated certain aspects of Automatic's large physique and deemphasized others.

And yet, Automatic's suits always seemed a bit frumpy. Or maybe it was Automatic who seemed frumpy, but wrapped in exquisite clothing. His continually increasing girth meant that no suit, no matter how well-tailored, ever fit perfectly for very long. And the suits always had a growing number of small stains here and there, in clusters around his chest, his stomach, and the ends of his sleeves.

Morrie Jones' suit was off-the-shelf and not particularly expensive. It was machine made from inexpensive, synthetic materials. It was black and fairly plain but it nonetheless fit well and emphasized his impressive physique. The sleeve edges were slightly worn, with a few threads hanging off here and there. Holes had been worn into the pockets, but they had been replaced at least twice. Jones admired the expense of Automatic's suit, but could not imagine spending so much on any single piece of clothing. He had no desire to impress anyone and he preferred utilitarian goods. In fact, while he was fascinated by rare and expensive things, he shunned them himself. He wondered if great wealth would change his attitude, and he felt sure that if things continued the way they were going, he would learn the answer to that question rather soon.

"Yes, a toast to our success," responded Jones, lifting his glass. They both drank. The wine was expensive. And very good.

Automatic leaned in. "I have a surprise," he said, then faced the curtain and called out "we're ready." Then turning again to Jones, "I hope you're hungry."

A hand reached between the curtains of the booth and pulled them back suddenly. A tall, thin, young man walked in carrying a covered plate and ceremoniously placed it on the table in front of them. He reached for the cover's handle but Automatic stopped him.

"Just a minute," Automatic said, and started thumping his hand against the wall next to him. After a few thumps there was a click and a bright overhead light went on, blinding them all for a moment before their eyes adjusted. It was a single incandescent light. "I want to see this in all its glory," said Automatic.

Automatic noticed Morrie Jones squinting a little anxiously at the incandescent bulb. "Don't worry," said Automatic, "I've got a special permit for that." Then to the waiter he said, "Now you can show us."

The waiter slowly uncovered the plate as if to an unheard drum roll. On the plate, steaming slightly and set in small puddles of diluted blood, were two large, thick slices of filet mignon. Yes, real beef. Slightly marbled. Medium well. Jones' eyes widened at the sight of them.

"Got a permit for these too," said Automatic. "Have you ever seen anything like these babies? Have you ever seen anything that looks so lovely? So delicious?"

In fact, Morrie Jones had not. Steak required permits that took a long time to get. And the taxes on beef made it so expensive that only the very wealthy could afford it. Large, wealthy men were often called "Beefeaters," sometimes as a measure of success but sometimes as an insult. It was used to mean snob or elitist. Morrie Jones had only eaten steak on a few special occasions, but never a cut as fine as the two in front of him. Again he felt a bit uncomfortable. Where he grew up, beef was shunned as "rich men's food," but he had often thought about it. This was a pleasure that he definitely wanted to experience and felt that he had earned it through his hard work.

Revelations

Automatic slammed a big fork into one of the steaks. "This one's mine," he proclaimed, and plopped it down onto his plate. A few drops of blood splattered onto his shirt. He sliced off a small corner with his knife and slid the piece into his mouth. Still chewing, he proclaimed, "Beautiful. Just beautiful," then added "You want to get it while it's hot."

Morrie Jones put his own fork into the remaining steak and placed it gently onto his plate, treating it more like delicate blown glass. He too sliced off a corner and slid it into his mouth. Chewing softly, the meat virtually disintegrated on his tongue leaving only the fine taste. It was beautiful. It tasted like paradise. No it tasted like success. He savored the flavor and more importantly savored the moment. He did not know if it would ever be this good again. It wouldn't.

C:\Jones, Winston\family\father\Jones, Morris\GE\dissolution\

"Is he still out there?" asked Wesley Automatic into the intercom.

"Yes, Mr. Automatic. He's waiting patiently."

Automatic sighed heavily. It was getting late and Automatic could find nothing else to keep himself occupied. He wanted to get home. He lifted himself up slowly from his chair, took his overcoat from the stand by the door and exited his office into the waiting room. Morrie Jones sat on the couch dressed in a shabby, worn suit that was just a little too tight on him. His physique had softened and wrinkled a bit. Around his eyes the flesh was dark and puffy. Automatic looked at his receptionist who shrugged and smiled nervously. Automatic sighed deeply again.

Morrie Jones did not seem to notice Automatic until he heard the sigh. Then he stood. "Wesley, we need to talk. The business is growing. I need capital. I don't understand why you don't return my calls."

Automatic hurriedly threw on his overcoat. "I need to get to a meeting, Jones," he said. "Arrange a time with Sally here and we'll talk." Then turning to Sally he quickly added, "I think I'm booked for a couple months, though. The strategy meetings." Turning back to Morrie Jones, "You heard I'm considering a run for governor didn't you?"

"Wesley, this will just take a minute. I'm trying to protect your investment."

Again Automatic sighed loudly, then turned back into his office. "Just a minute, then. I'm very busy."

Morrie Jones followed him in and he shut the door. Once inside, Automatic turned to him. "I can't do it. You need my help but I can't do it."

"Why not? Business is good. We're growing. I need money. We've got jobs lined up. I've got people ready to be hired. Our growth is still well into double digits."

"Then go to the banks."

"They won't talk to me. I don't know why. We're a good investment. Our accounts receivable is terrific but no one is paying. I don't know why. People have been saying I should talk to you, but I haven't been able to reach you."

"I'm running for governor. I'm going to be announcing my candidacy in about 6 weeks."

"So? I don't get how…"

"Damn it, Jones. You're a problem. You're a big problem for me."

Morrie Jones stared at him, dumbstruck.

"You're a successful business here in the blighted district 12. You're rebuilding the district. You're providing employment. You're creating jobs and creating wealth."

"Yes," said Morrie Jones weakly, still confused. "Yes, we are both doing this together. Your investment, my commitment." He paused a moment, then continued more strongly. "This will be great for your campaign. You're building up the poorest district in Chicago. Think about what you could do for the entire state. Give me another round of funding and we'll make this district a model of success. That will cinch your election. There's no downside."

"The whole plan is a downside," screamed Automatic. "Didn't you hear me? I'm running for government office. I need to use government money—taxpayer dollars—to remake Chicago. I need to show that the government has everything under control, but only if I'm in control of government. That's how government works."

"But what about your investment? You'll be destroying your own investment."

Automatic shook his head. "That's the cost of my election. My investment in your business is peanuts compared to what I'm going to spend to get elected."

"What about the people? My employees? Their families? Think of what's going to happen to this district if my business collapses. The other businesses will go one by one. The dominoes will fall."

"Jones, I'm going to propose that District 12 be a model Development Zone. After I'm elected there will be a flood of money into this district like it's never seen before."

"And you really think that government money will make a difference?"

"It will get me elected and keep me in office." Then as an afterthought, "And it will help a lot of people who simply cannot otherwise help themselves. Minorities. The disenfranchised. " Automatic opened the door again and motioned Morrie Jones toward it. "Please leave now," was all he said.

Morrie Jones hesitated, then slinked out the door. Automatic followed. As Morrie Jones walked out of the waiting room office, Automatic leaned in and spoke softly to the receptionist. "No meeting with him. Cancel that. And if he comes back, now or anytime, just call security."

C:\Jones, Winston\family\father\Jones, Morris\GE\report\

Good Intentions

Several months later, Morrie Jones was found dead of a self-inflicted gunshot.

* * * * *

Winston looked up from his computer. The information in the files had allowed him to piece together parts of his father's life that he had never known, never understood. A tear fell onto his desk in front of him. From the back of his mind, Winston Jones heard the tune that he remembered his father sadly singing in the last year or so of his life. This time, the words were clear:

Yesterday when I was young

The taste of life was sweet as rain upon my tongue.

I teased at life as if it were a foolish game,

The way the evening breeze may tease a candle flame.

The thousand dreams I dreamed, the splendid things I planned.

I'd always built to last on weak and shifting sand.

I lived by night and shunned the naked light of the day

And only now see how the years ran away.

Yesterday when I was young.

So many happy songs were waiting to be sung,

So many wayward pleasures lay in store for me

And so much pain my dazzled eyes refused to see.

I ran so fast that time and youth at last ran out,

I never stopped to think what life was all about

Revelations

And every conversation I can now recall

Concerned itself with me and nothing else at all.

Yesterday the moon was blue

And every crazy day brought something new to do.

I used my magic age as if it were a wand

And never saw the waste and emptiness beyond.

The game of love I played with arrogance and pride

And every flame I lit too quickly, quickly died.

The friends I made all seemed somehow to drift away

And only I am left on stage to end the play.

There are so many songs in me that won't be sung,

I feel the bitter taste of tears upon my tongue.

The time has come for me to pay for

Yesterday when I was young...[2]

---

[2] lyrics by Charles Aznavour and Georges Garvarentz. English-language lyrics by Herbert Kretzmer.

Making an Offer He Can't Refuse

It had been several weeks since everything that had happened to him had happened. Weeks since he examined the flash drive containing his life. Weeks since he discovered the real history of his father's business and why his father had done what he did. These weeks allowed the memories to fade just a bit, and the emotions to fade a lot so that he could think somewhat rationally about everything.

Alisa had avoided him at work. He went looking for her, but she was never around somehow. After a couple weeks he stopped trying and went back to focusing on his job, though it had become increasingly difficult. He no longer believed in the messages he was giving. He did not believe that life needed to be "fair and balanced." He began to believe that the government, in its current form, was wrong, was controlling, was intrusive. He saw the rightness of free markets, of competition, of struggle, of failure and of success. He understood his father's dream to provide services, to train and employ people, to build up a company and in doing so, rebuild a neighborhood. And he realized that his father knew that the only way to give his family a better life was to work hard and reap the benefits. Government regulation and government handouts had brought down that old neighborhood and only if the government got out of the way would it ever improve. But government was a juggernaut that his father could not stop. His father's final solution was wrong, but Winston Jones finally understood it.

The presidential elections were approaching and he had assumed that he was no longer the candidate of choice for some reason. Probably all the trouble he had caused them. Whatever the reason, he was happy about it. Kind of.

Jones watched the sun setting over the cityscape from the window of his apartment. There was an electronic knocking at the door. He walked over to the door. The screen showed Alisa. "I'd like to talk," she said. Jones brightened and pressed the switch. The door swooshed open. Alisa

Making an Offer He Can't Refuse

Rosenbaum stood there. Rom Automatic stood next to her. Jones' heart sank.

"Mr. Jones," said Rom Automatic, eking out a smile. "Our offer is still on the table. We need your acceptance."

The two walked into the apartment.

Jones looked at Alisa. "What are you doing?" he asked. "With him" he added.

"Alisa Rosenbaum is one of the leading members of the Fairness for EveryBody Society," responded Rom. Alisa nodded slowly, looking down. Jones had never seen her so solemn. He had seen her serious. But not solemn.

"Mr. Jones," continued Rom, "Ms. Rosenbaum keeps tabs on the Freedman Group. They are a dangerous group that is attempting to subvert the government of the United States. I think you've seen that. They kidnapped you; they involved you with several underground and illegal groups and activities. They risked your life. We were in touch with Ms. Rosenbaum the entire time, ensuring your safety. If it had not been for the U.S. government, and the FEB Society in particular, you might not have survived your ordeal. You owe Ms. Rosenbaum and us a great deal of thanks for protecting you. But that's our responsibility and we take it very, very, very seriously." The repetition of the word "very" sounded ominous to Jones. "The government protects you and in return simply asks for loyalty. A smart man like you sees the logic of that."

Jones looked at Alisa whose head was still bowed. He had never seen her cowed before. Was she frightened of Automatic? Ashamed of misleading Jones? He could not tell.

"Mr. Jones," Automatic continued. "It is time to begin introducing you to the public as the next President of the United States. The American public needs to see you. They need to know you. They need you to make them feel safe and secure. Your face will be the face of America."

"And if I say no?"

246

Alisa looked up at him. Her eyes were just a bit wet. "Winston, this is really important. What you are about to become, what you are about to do, as Rom says, is important for America. Perhaps the most important thing you'll ever do."

"Remember, Mr. Jones," said Rom, "that the Fairness for EveryBody Committee will be guiding you. There's no need to be nervous. There's no reason to be scared. We will be guiding everything you do and keeping America on track throughout your presidency."

"It's very important," repeated Alisa.

"And I don't have a choice, do I?" asked Jones.

Rom said nothing. Alisa looked down again.

"Good," said Rom after a silent moment, effecting a veneer of cheerfulness. "Your job will be terminated tomorrow, and we'll begin working on your presentations. You will begin memorizing key phrases that we've prepared for you. We'll also begin the training on your first speech in which you announce your candidacy. I think you'll like it. We have some great speech writers working on it. It will touch on the great principles of our society—fairness, security, safety, cooperation, multiculturalism, diversity, equal opportunity. The speech will be broadcast into an earpiece for you, but we'd like you to try to memorize it anyway. You never know when technology can go bust, leaving you with a blank slate. We don't want that. It's our job to write on your blank slate, and even you will be impressed with the brilliant and inspiring words that emanate from you."

Rom did not wait for a response from Jones—it was no longer necessary—and turned to leave, obviously pleased.

Jones looked into Alisa's eyes, her blue and green eyes, her glistening eyes. He tried to look deep to understand. She had really sold him on that Freedman group stuff. Her speeches had seemed heartfelt, genuine. She had actually gotten him to digest it all and you know what, he believed it now too. But it was all a show? Was she that good an actor? He squinted, trying to see beyond the eyes into her mind. What was inside that mysterious soul? Alisa's lips twitched, as if she was about to form a word with her mouth, but stopped. An apology? She hung her head and walked out.

Reaching Out

It was dusk. Jones was walking down the street toward his apartment after another long day of memorizing phrases and speeches. Being President of the United States involved a lot of memorization. He was getting used to the idea, eventually accepting it, and maybe even enjoying it a little. He would be the most powerful person on the planet. Well, at least it would appear that way. He would be treated differently. He would have perks, advantages, privileges. Rom and the others drilled that part into him and it started to sound pretty good. Given the stress of the last months, this all sounded good.

He walked alone down the street. He had not yet been officially announced to the voting public, so he did not yet need a security detail to follow him. As far as most people knew, he was just an ordinary guy. Soon his face would be plastered on buildings and bumpers throughout the country. He enjoyed strolling alone down the street knowing that in a couple of days his life would change for good and such privacy and solitude would never again be an option.

Jones passed an alleyway and a long, slender arm reached out. A delicate but strong hand wrapped itself around his forearm, pulled him sharply into the alleyway, and spun him around so that his back smacked into the wall.

Alisa stood in front of him, close. "Please don't say anything. You need to hear me out first. Then say what you want."

Jones looked at her, stared into her beautiful eyes. She looked strong again. Calm and confident. He nodded agreement.

"Becoming President is the most important thing you'll ever do in your life. Rom and the others at FEB will lead you to believe you're a figurehead. You will be, but figureheads can do a lot. You can use your bully pulpit to spread the word on freedom and liberty. You can spread the philosophy of the Freedman Group. You can even change laws. You have that power in the constitution. We'll show you how. We'll work with you. You'll have to start slowly so that they don't put a stop to it. It could be dangerous. Your life could be threatened. But if you believe, like I do, in personal freedom and personal responsibility, then it's worth it. Together we can take power away from government for the elite and return it to one of the people, by the people, for the people. Are you in with us?"

Jones looked at her. "With whom?"

"With the Freedman Group. Standing for freedom. I hope you never doubted that?"

"You were with Automatic. You're with the FEB. You brought him to me, gave me up. I'm a little confused. I'd think you'd understand that. Where do you stand on all this?"

"Winston. How could you doubt what I've been saying to you for so long? I'm for freedom. I'm for liberty, for free markets and competition. I'm for capitalism and industry. I'm for doing good by building good products and delivering good services. I'm for all the things we discussed when we were together." She stopped and looked deep into his eyes. "The FEB is powerful. We needed to survive. The Freedman Group needed to survive. The FEB runs the government, which in turn can shut down any organization for subversive activity. They could monitor our racial makeup and decide we were violating the diversity laws. They could find out that we were running private enterprises that were outside the reach and control of the government. There were a whole lot of things they could have done to us. We needed a mole. So I became that mole."

"A mole? But for which group?"

"A mole inside FEB for the Freedman Group. That's how I could steer them away from our real activities. I fed them enough to keep them hungry. Threw a little light but kept them in the dark. Of course they thought I was their mole. That's how we kept them in the dark."

"But you tracked me. You betrayed me!"

Alisa moved closer and held his hands in hers. "They already knew about you. They had already selected you. If one of them had tracked you, reported on you, we would have no control. I could give them the information we wanted them to have. I was hoping you'd figured that out."

Jones liked the feel of her hands in his. "I guess I'm not as smart as you thought."

She smiled. "You are. We're going to do great things. We're going to bring America back to greatness."

"You really think so?"

"Well, we're sure as hell going to try. And we'll be working together very closely."

"Oh?"

"I convinced the FEB that they needed a loyalist to keep tabs on you. There were still some doubters, but they knew you'd been 'contaminated' by subversive ideas. I convinced them that we needed someone deeply connected to the FEB to be on the ticket as Vice President. The choice became clear to them without me needing to state it outright. Who better to be at your side than me?"

"And they agreed?"

"They agreed."

Jones felt good. He had not really felt good in a long while.

"I need to go now," she said, squeezing his hands. "We'll be seeing a lot of each other." Then she let his hands fall and walked nonchalantly out of the alley.

Jones looked after her and smiled. "I'm looking forward to that," he said, but she was out of earshot.

Reaching Out

It's Morning Again in America

Washington, DC was windy and cold that January 20, but the sun shone brightly. A large crowd had gathered on the Capitol West Front lawn, talking and laughing and enjoying the variety of refreshments including the alcoholic ones that were permitted, unregulated, for this very special occasion. The loud murmur of the crowd faded in and out as the wind redirected the sounds in different directions. The Chief Justice of the Supreme Court was bundled in a thick, black, wool overcoat. He hunched slightly against the wind blowing at him. Winston Jones stood tall and seemingly unaffected by the wind at his back. Alisa Rosenbaum stood at his side, close to him. Rom Automatic stood behind a line of dignitaries separating him from Jones, but arranged so that Jones was still in Rom's line of sight. Jones raised his right hand and repeated after the Chief Justice, "I do solemnly affirm that I will faithfully execute the office of President of the United States, and will to the best of my ability, preserve, protect, and defend the Constitution of the United States."

Some in the crowd let out a cheer that got mostly swallowed in the wind. Most were not paying attention. The murmur of the crowd got a little louder as the alcohol took effect. The previous president, a short young woman with big green eyes and pretty blue hair looked around at the crowd, impatient to go back to her regular life now that her term had ended. The teleprompter buzzed softly and sparked occasionally as the prepared words of President Jones' speech plodded slowly across it. Winston Jones read and spoke the words:

"Senator McCoy, Mr. Chief Justice, President Muffley, Vice President Hoynes, Vice President Rosenbaum, Senator Butcher, Speaker Ryan, and my fellow citizens: To a few of us here today, this is a solemn and most momentous occasion, but to the rest of us this is a time to celebrate and express our hope for the future. This orderly transfer of authority routinely takes place as it has for centuries and I for one…" Jones squinted at the teleprompter and continued hesitantly, "think this is really cool.

It's Morning Again in America

"The fairness and goodness of our nation keeps us moving forward. These United States are confronted with challenges of great proportions. We suffer from the longest and one of the worst sustained periods of inequality and unfairness in our national history. It distorts our thinking, penalizes those who should not be penalized, and crushes the hope of the young and the elderly alike. It threatens to shatter the lives of millions of our people."

The teleprompter sparked a bit and the rolling word froze before a large spark, followed by a loud pop, killed the lettering altogether. A repairman in jeans and t-shirt ran to the teleprompter with some tools and, of course, a large roll of duct tape for just such an emergency. He leaned over the base of the teleprompter, applying his tools in an attempt to find the correct location to apply a capacitor and some tape. His butt crack slid out from behind his belt as he leaned over, and the television stations cut to a commercial that was due pretty soon anyway. Jones looked at the black screen then back at Automatic, who simply nodded.

The crowd noticed the loud popping noise and became suddenly silent, but only for an instant before resuming their partying. Jones looked at the crowd then at the blank screen, and finally at Alisa beside him. The edges of her mouth rose almost imperceptibly and she nodded just a little.

Jones cleared his throat and continued on his own, without the Teleprompters. "Our society is broken," he said. "There is much suffering. Our machines break and we are not prepared to fix them. We have lost the knowledge, the ability, even the desire." He pointed at the teleprompter with the open palm of his hand. The repairman stopped and looked up at him quizzically.

"We have lost the spirit we once had."

People in the crowd began to notice the new president. A few stopped their talking and looked up at him.

"Idle industries have cast away workers, leaving government to supply do-nothing jobs. People want a purpose to their lives. They want to contribute to something greater than themselves. They want to create something from their minds and their hearts that they can look upon proudly. Without that kind of accomplishment people feel only misery and indignity. And those who do work hard and do create and do produce are denied a fair return for their labor by a system that penalizes success, penalizes achievement, and keeps all of us from reaching our full potential.

"In this present crisis, we must ask ourselves difficult questions. We must ask ourselves if government is the solution to our problem. We must ask ourselves if government should right all wrongs—actual and perceived—and if it in fact can right all wrongs."

More of the crowd stopped what they were doing to listen. Something was different. Something sounded interesting. Something resonated with a nearly extinct human instinct within them.

Rom Automatic was not used to listening to the presidential address. He had more pressing concerns and it was all ceremonial anyway. He did notice a few phrases and words here and there that caused concern, but he also saw the crowd paying attention. He knew that Jones' oratorical skills would be particularly useful in these trying times. So in balance, he was happy as he strategized in his mind about laws that needed to be passed and which legislators needed to be convinced and which measures needed to be pushed through Congress.

Jones continued. "For a long time we have come to believe that society is too complex to be managed by self-rule, that government by an elite minority is superior to the government envisioned by our founders—for, by, and of the people. But if no one among us is capable of governing himself, then who among us has the capacity to govern someone else? All of us together must bear the burden. The solutions we seek must be equitable, with no one group singled out to pay a higher price and no one group favored for any reason whatsoever.

"And with the understanding that while our laws must treat each person equal to each other person, the results will not be equal. Because the laws of nature, and the laws of civilization, require this inequality. Requires inequality because some people prefer to practice medicine while others prefer to fix machinery. Because some desire to build skyscrapers while others desire to build a table or a desk. Because some seek the thrill of driving a race car while others seek the security of driving a truck. Because some people are graceful and some people are musical and some people are artistic and some people are none of these things. True tolerance means understanding these different goals and desires and not minimizing any of them. True diversity means accepting these differences and giving people the opportunity to excel according to their talents and their desires. True equality means that each person is given an equal opportunity to succeed or fail according to their own standards, not those determined for them by others. And each is rewarded according to their ability and determined only by supply and demand. When the government gives each person the opportunities and then stands out of the way, then each person succeeds or fails, but society as a whole progresses."

By now the large crowd had become silent and was listening intently. President Jones' words were clear to only some in the audience, but they felt inspiring to all of them. Something sounded different than previous inaugurations. Something made them feel good about themselves. About America. Maybe it was just temporary. Or maybe it was the beginning of a resurgence of something long forgotten. It felt that way, but it was hard to be sure. In any case, the words comforted even more than the free snacks and free booze.

"My administration's objective," continued President Jones, "will be a healthy, vigorous, growing economy that provides equal opportunity for all Americans, with no guarantees of equal outcomes but also no barriers born of bigotry or discrimination. All must share in the productive work and all must share in the bounty of a revived economy. With the idealism and fair play that comprise the foundation of our society and our strength, we can once again have a strong and prosperous America.

"If we look for the answer as to why, for so many years in the not-too-distant past, we achieved so much, prospered as no other people on Earth, it was because here, in this great land, we unleashed the energy and individual genius of people to a greater extent than has ever been done before. Freedom and the dignity of the individual have been more available and assured here than in any other place on Earth. The price for this freedom at times has been high, but we have never been unwilling to pay that price.

"Can we solve the problems confronting us? I say, yes we can. I want you to see change and hope for the future. Together we will change the scope of government and together we will work hard to give hope to our children and to all future generations. Together we will restore the principles declared in the Declaration of Independence and enshrined in the principles of our Constitution by our Founding Fathers. 'We hold these truths to be self-evident, that all men are created equal, that they are endowed by their Creator with certain unalienable Rights, that among these are Life, Liberty and the pursuit of Happiness.' My job will be to make sure that the government does not take away your liberty. Your job is to live and to pursue happiness."

Jones looked around at the crowd, silently looking at him. Each person—and there were thousands on the Capitol West Front lawn—was silently staring, waiting. They were hearing words like they had never heard before, or at least not heard in a very long time. "Are you with me on this?" he asked, shouting.

"Yes," came the booming response from the crowd.

President Jones looked at them and smiled. The crowd burst into applause.

Rom was pulled abruptly from his reverie by the shout and the applause. He looked up and saw the audience applauding and heard the cacophony of noise from thousands of hands slapping together amid shouts and whistles. He saw the respect and admiration these people had for the candidate that he and the FEB had chosen and he felt good. Very good. He walked over to Jones who was standing humbly, facing the crowd.

"Great job," said Rom to Jones. "Really great job. I knew we picked the right man. I knew it."

Jones simply nodded at Rom Automatic.

"You did a great job of improvising when the teleprompter failed. Just look at the crowd. Look at their reaction."

Jones simply nodded at Rom Automatic again.

Rom put his hand on Jones' shoulder. "Do watch the ad-libbing, though," he said. "You don't want to get off message."

Jones nodded once more, smiled at Alisa, and turned to fully face the crowd as their appreciation continued.

* * * * *

Jones walked slowly around the Oval Office, taking it all in. First he walked in a circle, keeping close to the wall and examining the paintings on it that he had selected. All were American painters. All were from the eighteenth century.

In accordance with the tradition, he had designed an oval carpet for the room. He had designed something simple, a light blue with two thick white stripes and two thin red stripes forming concentric ovals.

Jones brought back the "Resolute desk," a large, nineteenth-century ornately carved desk that had been a gift from Queen Victoria to President Rutherford B. Hayes in 1880. Built from the timbers of the British Arctic Exploration ship Resolute, the front had a worn carving of the Great Seal of this great nation—the American eagle holding arrows in its left talon and olive branches in its right one. Jones walked over to the desk and ran his fingers lightly over the carvings. "I can almost feel that I can divine the wisdom of the many great men who had preceded me here," he said. "Especially those who had actually been elected by the people."

Alisa stood near the windows looking out, looking into the future. She turned to him, smiling. "You were great out there," she said and walked over to him. "You were really great."

She reached her arms around him and kissed him on the lips. A big, wet, thrilling, exceptional kiss.

He pulled away. "What should we work on first?" he asked. "How about bringing the tax rate down?"

"OK, what's the target?" she asked.

"We should start small. We can't raise suspicions too soon. We need to move slowly."

"Agreed," she said.

"How about 80% to start?" he asked. "Bring the tax rate down to only 80%?"

"OK. That sounds like a good start." She kissed him again passionately.

Jones pulled back again. He stared into her beautiful, mysterious, bichromal eyes. His eyes glanced downward to her smile, a smile he had not often seen before.

"You think anyone has ever made love in the Oval Office?" he asked her.

She laughed. "Are you kidding?" she replied. "This is where John Kennedy and Bill Clinton worked."

"OK," he replied, "then there's another American tradition we need to revive," as he pulled her tight and they slid to the floor and onto that plush, soft, comfortable new carpet that he had designed.